Linc

COUNTY COUNCIL

Working for a better future

discover libraries
**This book should be returned on or before
the due date.**

NAT 1/20

To renew or order library books please telephone 01522 782010
or visit https://lincolnshirespydus.co.uk
You will require a Personal Identification Number
Ask any member of staff for this.
The above does not apply to Reader's Group Collection Stock.

EC. 199 (LIBS): RS/L5/19

05112204

The Shrine Virgin

An Akitada Novel

I. J. Parker

I · J · P
2015

Copyright © 2015 by I. J. Parker.

Published 2015 by I.J.Parker and I·J·P Books
428 Cedar Lane, Virginia Beach VA 23452
http://www.ijparker.com
Cover design by I. J. Parker.
Cover image by Ogata Gekko
Back cover image: Kasamatsu Shiro
Publisher's Note: This is a work of fiction. Names, characters, places, and
incidents are a product of the author's imagination.

The Shrine Virgin, 1ˢᵗ edition, 2015
ISBN-13: 978-1505990157

Praise for I. J. Parker and the Akitada Series

"Elegant and entertaining . . . Parker has created a wonderful protagonist in Akitada. She puts us at ease in a Japan of one thousand years ago." *The Boston Globe*

"You couldn't ask for a more gracious introduction to the exotic world of Imperial Japan than the stately historical novels of I. J. Parker." *The New York Times*

"Akitada is as rich a character as Robert Van Gulik's intriguing detective, Judge Dee." *The Dallas Morning News*

"Readers will be enchanted by Akitada." *Publishers Weekly* Starred Review

"Terrifically imaginative" The *Wall Street Journal*

"A brisk and well-plotted mystery with a cast of regulars who become more fully developed with every episode." *Kirkus*

"More than just a mystery novel, (*THE CONVICT'S SWORD*) is a superb piece of literature set against the backdrop of 11th-cntury Kyoto." *The Japan Times*

"Parker's research is extensive and she makes great use of the complex manners and relationships of feudal Japan." *Globe and Mail*

"The fast-moving, surprising plot and colorful writing will enthrall even those unfamiliar with the exotic setting." *Publishers Weekly, Starred* Review

". . . the author possesses both intimate knowledge of the time period and a fertile imagination as well. Combine that with an intriguing mystery and a fast-moving plot, and you've got a historical crime novel that anyone can love." *Chicago Sun-Times*

"Parker's series deserves a wide readership." *Historical Novel Society*

"The historical research is impressive, the prose crisp, and Parker's ability to universalize the human condition makes for a satisfying tale." *Booklist*

"Parker masterfully blends action and detection while making the attitudes and customs of the period accessible." *Publishers Weekly* (starred review)

"Readers looking for historical mystery with a twist will find what they're after in Parker's latest Sugawara Akitada mystery . . . An intriguing glimpse into an ancient culture." *Booklist*

Characters

Characters in Mikawa:

Sugawara Akitada	new provincial governor
Yukiko	his young wife
Yasuko & Yoshitada	his children
Tora	Commander of the guard
Saburo	Tribunal Secretary, a former spy
Lieutenant Mori	provincial police chief
Kitagawa	manager of a private estate
Hozo	a former warrior monk

A merchant from Owari Province

Characters in Ise:

Junichiro	a dwarf
Mrs. Akechi	owner of a silk shop
Michiko	her shop assistant
Mrs. Inabe	owner of the River Palace
Inabe Seijiro	her husband
Keiko	her daughter
Nakatomi	High Priest of Ise shrine
Princess Takahime	the shrine virgin
Minamoto Sadamu	her cousin
Tamba Shikibu	her senior lady-in-waiting

Lady Tachibana   Lady Tamba's mother
Lady Ayako   young lady-in-waiting
Murata   ship owner
Lieutenant Matsuura   local police officer
Sukemichi Yasunori   provincial high constable
Precious Butterfly   courtesan

Gangsters known as "prowlers"

Since our love was no deeper
Than a stream too shallow
To wet the hem of your robe. . .

Farewell note by an Ise Virgin to her lover.
Tales of Ise, 10[h] century

1

The Messenger

The messenger arrived on a beautiful day in the early autumn.

Akitada listened as the last sounds of his flute faded and sighed with pleasure. Gradually the real world invaded this dreamlike existence again. Somewhere a horse neighed, and a guard shouted an order. A clatter came from the kitchen area, and the loud laughter of boys floated over the garden fence.

They sat on the veranda overlooking the garden. Akitada looked with pleasure at his companions in their pretty summer robes. "Well done!" he said. "Well done indeed! Yasuko, you've made great progress. I know I have to thank my lady wife for it. Yukiko, your pupil does you proud."

1

Their small orchestra consisted of a zither, played by Yasuko, a lute played by his wife, and his flute.

His daughter blushed and shot a glance at her companion. "Thank you, Father. I worked very hard," she said pointedly.

Akitada, newly married and even more newly governor of Mikawa province, winked at Yukiko, his young wife. Life was good again. He had money, a promotion and this very good appointment, and one of the loveliest women in the land for his wife.

Beyond the garden lay the many halls, galleries, stables, and outbuildings of the Mikawa tribunal and government headquarters. And beyond all of that was Komachi, the capital of Mikawa Province.

He still could barely believe it.

Yukiko, not much older than Yasuku, smiled at him. "It's true. Yasuko works very hard. Much harder than I ever did. Isn't it pleasant to make music together on a beautiful autumn morning? I could wish her brother took an interest in music."

Akitada glanced toward the fence when someone shouted "Gotcha!" and burst into boyish laughter. "Yoshi is still all boy," he said defensively. "He prefers the manly arts of practicing with swords and shooting arrows. Tora and Yuki are better company for him."

"Oh, do you rate womanly pursuits over martial ones, Akitada?"

She was teasing. Yukiko claimed to have fallen in love with him because of the heroic adventures of his youth. He smiled. "Not at all, my love. But I do prefer

2

to gaze at my two favorite ladies to watching Tora and a couple of grimy boys."

His daughter giggled. Yukiko gave her husband a melting glance and said, "Thank you. Well, shall we play another one?"

Akitada was about to suggest "Deer in the Autumn Mountains" when Saburo came striding down the gravel path in the garden and bowed to his master and his family.

"Sorry, sir, ladies. An important messenger has arrived from the capital."

A little regretfully, Akitada slipped the flute back into its brocade pouch. "I'd better see what it is. Thank you, my dears, for giving me such pleasure."

He and Saburo walked back to the main hall of the tribunal. Saburo had come to him some seven years ago in Naniwa. He had been horribly disfigured and out of work. His background—he was a renegade monk and former spy—made him a useful addition to Akitada's staff. He had a good education, used his brush with considerable skill, and knew a thousand ways of entering a building to find out what the people inside were up to. Most of his time he now spent as senior secretary of the Mikawa tribunal.

Akitada asked, "Do you know what it's about?"

"The officer wouldn't say, but he's a very superior sort of messenger, sir. My guess is that he's a member of the palace guard."

And that made him a ranking nobleman. Akitada raised his brows. "You don't say? He rode all this way to bring me some communication? From the palace?"

3

Saburo raised his shoulders. "I couldn't say, sir. He glared at me when I asked what it was about."

"Very strange." Akitada hurried a little more, partially out of curiosity and partially in recognition of the effort made by his visitor.

The young man waited in Akitada's private study. He had not bothered to sit down and seemed to have spent his time pacing.

Akitada closed the door behind him and said, "I'm Sugawara. And you?"

The young man came to attention. He was in uniform, though he did not wear any of the insignia of the various guard companies. Still, Saburo had recognized the cut of his coat and trousers, and the fine boots, now somewhat dusty. He also wore a very handsome sword.

Not an ordinary soldier by any means.

He did not answer Akitada's question but studied him with a frown. "How do I know you are who you say you are?" he asked coldly.

Akitada smiled. "We're at an impasse." Walking to his desk, he sat down. "I don't receive people who refuse to identify themselves. My secretary should not have admitted you. You'd better leave."

The officer glared. Akitada, not as easily impressed by the manner of high-ranking persons as Saburo had been, merely stared back.

The messenger cleared his throat. "I carry an important message for governor Sugawara. It is personal and I have been charged to deliver it to no one but him."

4

Akitada cocked his head. "But how do I know this is the case? Who is the message from and, I repeat, who are you?"

The young man suddenly looked pale and swayed on his feet. He took a gasping breath.

Akitada half rose. "Oh, for heavens' sake, man, sit down. You look exhausted. And let's stop this nonsense. I'm Sugawara."

His visitor took a few steps to a cushion, where he knelt and sat back. "It was a long journey," he muttered, brushing perspiration from his forehead.

Akitada got up. On an ornate lacquer stand stood cups and a flask of wine. He filled two cups and handed one to the young man, taking the other back to his seat. "Drink it all down. There's more if you want it."

The officer looked at the cup and set it down. "Thank you, sir, but my duty doesn't permit it."

"And your duty won't get done, if you don't put some color back in your face and some strength in your belly. Drink. That's an order."

The young man blinked, then emptied the cup. He sighed. "Are you really Sugawara? I'd expected a younger man."

Akitada winced. "I'm Sugawara. Now what is this all about?"

"I am Kiyowara Yasunori, lieutenant in the left Palace Guard. I'm to give you a letter of instructions from His Majesty's private secretary, Tachibana Nakahira."

Akitada stared at him. Not only was Lieutenant Kiyowara a member of an important noble family and a most unlikely messenger on a long-distance journey between the capital and Mikawa province, but Tachiba-na Nakahira was one of only a handful of men permitted to attend His Majesty.

"Dear me," Akitada said after a moment. "You came all this way by yourself?"

"No. Not by myself. I have attendants. But we did not dawdle. The message is urgent, you see."

"Yes. I can understand that. Well, may I see the letter?"

The lieutenant hesitated only a moment, then drew a flat package from inside his coat of armor and handed it to Akitada.

Akitada verified that the seal was that of the imperial secretariat and unwrapped the purple silk cover. Inside was another, thinner package, this one with spidery writing addressed to him and another seal, the seal of Tachibana Nakahira. He undid this also and found a short letter inside in the same crabby hand as the address. This he scanned rapidly, then reread more slowly.

Refolding the letter, he looked at Lieutenant Kiyowara. "Do you know what is in this letter?"

"No, sir."

"Very well. You'll be my guest here until you're rested enough for the return journey. There is no answer except that I accept the charge and will leave immediately. Under the circumstances, I regret not being able to entertain you myself, but my people will offer any assistance you may require." Akitada rose.

The lieutenant, looking slightly better already, also got to his feet and saluted. He even managed a smile as he said, "Then I must wish you good success wherever you go, sir."

When he was alone again, Akitada sat back down. He was not sure if he looked forward to this assignment or resented it. It would take him away from his family, and he was still so newly a husband that he hated leaving. Besides, there was the matter of Yukiko's feelings. She would resent being left behind with only the children and servants for company. He almost wished his sister were here. In the capital, Akiko had taken his young wife in hand with an enthusiasm that had kept both entertained and him free to work. He had never wholly approved of the social lives of the "good people" but Akiko enjoyed them. Here in Komachi, life was quieter, though being governor of a comfortable province like Mikawa was not as time-consuming as his past provincial assignments had been or, for that matter the daily grind in the Ministry of Justice.

On the other hand, he looked forward to a brief journey, and the problem intrigued him.

He sighed and clapped his hands for Saburo, who appeared on silent feet. The man's quietness was often disconcerting. No doubt his past as a spy had taught him to creep up on people.

"Saburo," Akitada said, "I must go on a short journey across the bay. I'll be gone only a few days, but I have to leave tomorrow. Inform Tora and send him to the harbor to arrange for ferry transport. Don't use my name or title. Say the reservation is for . . . hmm . . .Yoshimine Takatsuna." He smiled a little, remembering Yukiko's admiration for his mission on Sado Island. "I'm an archivist in Mikawa. Best write it down."

Saburo's eyes lit up. "Immediately, sir. Shall I pack to accompany you or will you take Tora?"

"Neither. I'm going alone."

2

The Goblin

Akitada stepped ashore from the ferry in Oyodo, a coastal hamlet in Ise province. He had enjoyed crossing Ise Bay. The weather was calm and sunny, and the scenery of blue sea and green islands had been beautiful.

Oyodo bay had a busy harbor. Not only ferry boats landed here, bringing and taking away steady streams of pilgrims visiting the shrine, but goods travelled more cheaply and quickly by water than by the Tokaido highway. Besides Ise province produced much timber for building. He reflected briefly that his own province also enjoyed prosperity from the water trade, though this brought its own worries for its governor. Well-equipped pirate ships plied the coasts along the eastern seaboard.

The harbor scene was familiar to him. He had seen much the same in Hakata and Otsu and now in his own provincial capital, Komachi. He paused to watch the activities. The shipping seemed to involve mostly lumber here and, of course, a large number of shrine visitors.

As he watched the bustle of pilgrims and watermen, he noticed a well-dressed man. He was tall and heavy-set and looked like a wealthy businessman in his expensive silk gown. After all the travelers had left the ferry, the wealthy man walked along the waterfront to a place where he met with three rough-looking characters. To Akitada's surprise, a long conversation ensued between them. Perhaps they were just porters or fishermen, but Akitada had seen enough gangsters to wonder what the merchant was up to.

Reminding himself that his own assignment lay farther inland and he had no time for idle curiosity, he turned away from the harbor. Like any other pilgrim taking advantage of a brief vacation to pay his respects to the gods in this sacred place, he followed the other passengers into the hamlet Oyodo. At an ordinary noodle shop, he stopped for a bowl of soup. The shop was small and crowded as other pilgrims were also refreshing themselves before continuing their journey inland. The soup, when he could get served, was barely edible, the broth thin and flavorless, the noodles overcooked, and the vegetables sparse. He said nothing, however, and thanked the woman. Eating slowly, he watched the other pilgrims gobble their soup and set out on the road to the shrines. They were a boisterous bunch for pilgrims to a holy place, but he knew well enough that pilgrimages were often an excuse for some fun and entertainment.

When he was the only one left, he complimented the woman on her hard work—there was nothing good he could honestly say about her soup—and was rewarded with a long recitation of her burdens in life. These included a drunken husband and lazy children. He asked, if there was not plenty of work for men in such a harbor town.

"Oh, there's work, but then there's also many that rob a man of his earnings," she said, frowning in the direction of the shrines. It's evil and shames the gods, but nobody cares."

"You surprise me. Are there highwaymen on the road?"

She scowled. "Them, too, but I meant the harlots and gamblers. They don't fleece just the visitors. It's our men they rob of their hard-earned coppers, leaving their women and children to starve."

Akitada glanced around at the town. What he could see seemed to consist primarily of warehouses and fishermen's shacks. "Where are they?" he asked.

"Not here. In Uji-tachi. Right between the two shrines. But don't you worry, sir. Stay away from the loose women and gaming, and you should be fine."

Akitada laughed. "No fear. Is it far to Uji-tachi?" He cast an anxious eye at the declining sun.

11

She eyed him and said dubiously, "Seven miles by the road. You could walk it. But there's a shortcut about half a mile along the road where two pines grow side by side. That'll get you there in four miles."

"Well," Akitada said with a smile, "I'd better get started."

∞

An hour later, Akitada was following a narrow track through a dense forest of cryptomeria trees. Very little light was coming through the thick branches overhead. It was already dusk here, and he was convinced that he had become lost. He had found the turn-off with the two pines easily enough, but after that, other tracks had branched off here and there and it was not always easy to tell which was the main path. If this was a shortcut, he should have been in Uji-tachi before now. In fact, he would have been there, if he had followed the main road.

The forest was quite silent. He had encountered no one else since he had left the main road. With so many unwary visitors carrying ample sums to pay for their stay, the area must be crawling with robbers. Thus, when he heard the sound of a child singing up ahead—a sure sign that he must be close to a house—he felt distinctly relieved.

Up ahead was a bend in the path, and after a moment, the child, about five or six years old, appeared. But there was something peculiar about this boy, and Akitada stopped. He was dressed in the most brilliant colors of blue, red, and green and had a very large head with spiky orange hair.

A small goblin!

A veritable goblin, if one was of a superstitious nature. Akitada was not. There were no goblins, though this creature coming closer was ugly enough. And then the goblin grinned at him and, with a pang of pity, Akitada realized that this was neither a child nor a goblin, but a young man who had stopped growing at three feet. His head had kept going a bit longer so that it was almost normal size, though with oddly sharp and mature features.

The goblin youth came to a halt before him and chuckled. He seemed to enjoy the moment. "You're lost," he announced with great satisfaction in a high voice. "For a piece of silver, I'll show you the way."

Akitada shook his head. The boy's pleasure in his dilemma and his greed irritated him. "I'm not lost," he said firmly. " I'm going to Uji-tachi."

The youngster chortled. "No, you're not, but suit yourself." He skipped aside and walked past him.

Akitada capitulated. "Wait! I'll give you ten coppers."

The little man stopped and turned. "For a piece of silver, I'll take you *and* answer all your questions," he offered. "It's a bargain, seeing it's getting dark, and the prowlers will be out."

"The prowlers?"

"Robbers. They're always looking for lost tourists." He grinned.

It was a good deal of money just to be shown the way, but Akitada felt sorry for the dwarf. His odd assortment of multi-colored clothes consisted no doubt of

13

cast-offs from some well-to-do child and he probably had a hard time making a living. People were not kind to the deformed, as he knew well enough from Saburo who had been rejected for his disfigured face. Besides, with his short stature, the boy was not likely to find work as a laborer. He said, "Very well. A piece of silver it is." He added rather rashly, "And if you're useful to me later on, I'll pay you for your services. What's your name?"

"Junichiro." The youth made Akitada a bow, grinned widely, and asked, "And yours, master?"

"Yoshimine. I'm from Owari." Akitada enjoyed his alias. This time he need not fear the terrible events that had befallen him last time he used it.

"And what's your business here?"

"I'm just a visitor."

The youngster cocked his head and looked Akitada over. The spiky reddish hair and colored clothing gave him a raffish air, reminding Akitada of some of the acrobats he had seen at country fairs. After a thorough evaluation, the dwarf said, "You're some kind of official on a jaunt, I think. Do you like pretty girls? Kinky sex? Perhaps some nice boys? Or a good party with lots of partners? I know all the best places in Uji-tachi."

Slightly affronted by this misreading of his character, Akitada snapped, "I bet you do—and get paid for bringing in customers to be fleeced. No, I definitely don't want any of that. But you can tell me a little about Uji-tachi. I take it it's full of brothels. Anything else of interest?"

Not at all embarrassed, Junichiro gave a shout of laughter. "You're right about the town and me getting paid. See, if I don't hustle, I don't eat, and I'm a growing boy." He laughed again. "But I know everything there's to know about the shrines and the town. Go ahead, ask me anything."

"Later. You'd better take me there first."

"Well, follow me!" The dwarf started walking again, and Akitada followed. He had indeed taken a wrong turn because Junichiro soon took him down another track. It was not very long before the woods thinned and they came out into a wide valley between two mountains. To both sides of the track stretched rice paddies, now close to harvest, and ahead stretched the roofs of the town along a river.

Akitada thought it likely that he would have found his way out of the forest eventually since he had been this close, but he said nothing.

The valley was bisected by the Isuzu River. A wide road followed the river, and the town lined the road. He recognized Uji-tachi from his earlier visit, though the place had grown amazingly over the span of twenty years or more. The sun was low already, but there was still a great deal of traffic on the road.

His companion gave a sudden shout. "Look over there," he cried. "By the river. Something's happened." He started into a sort of waddling run on his short, bent legs toward a place on the river bank where a crowd had gathered.

Akitada followed. People made room reluctantly, but Junichiro passed through between people's legs. His

15

short legs slowed his pace, but he used his arms and elbows to good effect and soon disappeared from sight.

Akitada could not see over people's heads but guessed they had found a body in the river. Reeds grew thickly along the bank, but he caught glimpses of the red tunics of policemen.

He did not want to attract undue attention but, given his assignment, he was curious to know who had been killed or why. With some maneuvering, he managed to get closer to the scene where he found Junichiro already in position. The body in the reeds was that of a young woman. Young women drowning in towns with a lively sex trade was nothing new. In Eguchi, prostitutes had killed themselves on an almost daily basis. And this particular girl had whitened her face, though her clothing was proper enough.

"Who is she?" he asked the dwarf.

To his surprise, Junichiro raised a stricken face and, after a moment, turned away and left.

A tall police officer arrived belatedly, and the crowd parted to make room for him. The three constables with the body snapped to attention and saluted. "A drowning, Lieutenant," one of them informed his superior. "Suicide, most likely."

The officer grunted and bent over the body.

"Not a mark on her," the constable prompted.

The lieutenant turned the woman's head, and Akitada saw that she was younger than he had thought. But there was something else wrong. He stepped closer.

The constable snapped, "Stay back, sir. This is police business," and the lieutenant looked up for a moment.

Akitada retreated.

The lieutenant straightened up. "You're an idiot, Hiroshi," he said. "This one had her throat cut. It's murder. Take her back to the station and fetch the coroner." Glancing at the crowd, he asked, "Anyone know who she is?"

There was some silence and some foot shuffling, then a woman said, "She worked in Mrs. Akechi's shop." The lieutenant said to his constables, "Send for her employer." With that he turned and walked away briskly. The dead girl was unceremoniously shouldered by one of the constables and carried away.

Akitada had noticed the pale gash on the girl's neck and had been tempted to correct the constable himself, but it was just as well that he had not meddled. The dead had a way of finding him and claiming his attention, but he had no time for Mrs. Akechi's maid. He turned away from the scene and called out, "Hey, Junichiro!"

The dwarf appeared by his side, still looking rather pale. He clearly had no stomach for corpses.

"Did you know her?" Akitada asked.

"I knew her. She was nice to me," Junichiro said. He added, "And they don't know the half of it."

"Oh?"

"She went to work in a brothel. That's what killed her. I told her not to, but she liked the money. Those girls never know who they are with."

"Shouldn't you tell the police?"

Junichiro shook his head. "Let them find out for themselves."

"Very well. I need a place to stay. What do you recommend?"

Junichiro gave Akitada's plain black ramie robe a glance and sighed. "Best stay at the River Palace. The Golden Dragon and Jade Pavilion will rob you."

Such advice was dubious. Akitada assumed that Junichiro had an agreement with the River Palace's owner. But he said nothing and agreed.

The inn was close to the river, but it was hardly palatial. It was small, elderly, and somewhat run down.

The innkeeper was a muscular, brutish-looking man in his thirties. Akitada asked for a room and a bath, signed the register as Yoshimine Takatsuna, tax official from Mikawa, and parted from Junichiro, who hopefully suggested a tour of the town. But Akitada was tired from his long trek through the woods and said good bye.

3

Lieutenant Matsuura

Somewhat later, greatly refreshed after a nice soak in the inn's bath tub, Akitada decided to go out again after all. He would walk the length of Uji-tachi first to get an impression of the town and then have a bite to eat before going to bed. The town was perhaps irrelevant to his special assignment but he liked to be informed about his surroundings.

To his surprise, the dwarf was still in the reception room of the inn, squatting in a corner and watching some new arrivals making arrangements for their lodging. When he saw Akitada, he bounced up and waddled over.

19

I. J. PARKER

"There you are, master, and looking rested for a night on the town."

Akitada had recognized one of the new guests. He was the merchant from the harbor at Oyodo, and again he wondered about his behavior. Given the man's obvious wealth, he would have expected him to stay at one of the better inns. And what was more, the surly innkeeper greeted him like a long lost friend.

Junichiro plucked his sleeve. "Let's go! You must be starving."

Akitada chuckled. "If you do a good job showing me around, I'll buy you dinner."

Junichiro practically danced out the door, followed by a laughing Akitada.

The sun had set, and all up and down the single main street lanterns and torches glowed. It was a pretty sight. The lights made the colors brighter, while the night softened their garishness. The shrine visitors were enjoying themselves among the fleshpots of Uji-tachi, walking up and down the street in groups or singly, disappearing into wine shops or eyeing the pretty girls who stood outside the shops and eating places, inviting the customers in. Several of the young men wore the uniform of the imperial guard, reminding Akitada that, whatever low pursuits took place in Uji-tachi, an important member of His Majesty's family resided here. Several of the businesses were brothels, their staff dressed elaborately and their faces painted. The dead girl had worked in one of these at night but was said to have been a shop girl during the day.

Junichiro was waddling and hopping beside him, pointing and explaining the varied delights of the town. Akitada interrupted him, "Junichiro, you knew the dead girl quite well, didn't you?"

Junichiro shot him a glance and nodded. "She was kind. Not like the rest. They make fun of me and laugh. She never did that."

"All the more reason why you should tell the police what you know. Don't you want her killer found?"

"What good would it do her? Besides, those constables just give me a hard time. Why should I help them?"

They walked along in silence for a while. It was none of Akitada's business, and the dwarf must have his reasons for staying away from the police. But still, something about the murder nagged at him.

"They say she worked in a shop," he said.

The boy brightened. "A very fine shop," he said. "Mrs. Akechi sells only the best silks! The High Constable himself is a customer. I saw him there just the other day. You need a present for your wife or girl-friend?" He waggled his eyebrows. "Think how pleased your lady will be. She won't ask about your pleasures here."

"Enough, imp. There won't be any pleasures, and you know nothing about my ladies."

Junichiro giggled and hopped ahead. "There's the shop," he cried, pointing to a sign.

In spite of the death of one of the employees, the shop was open for business. Three women, all dressed in black or gray cotton robes, waited on several male customers who seemed to have had the same idea as Junichiro. Business was good, for one of them rose from his place and directed a boy to carry his purchase of several lengths of figured silk. Akitada eyed these as the boy passed him and decided that they were quite handsome. He went inside the shop and took the place vacated by the previous customer.

An older woman, very handsome in black silk, approached, bowed deeply, and asked how she might serve the gentleman.

Junichiro suddenly appeared beside Akitada. "This is my gentleman, Auntie Akechi," he said.

So this was the shop owner. She stiffened, though her fixed smile never left her face. "Good evening, Junichiro," she said. "Perhaps you might wait outside until the gentleman has finished his shopping."

The dwarf made a face. "Oh, all right, but don't forget. I brought him to you directly." He waddled away.

The shop owner seemed uneasy. She glanced after him and scanned the people in the street outside. Guessing at her worries, Akitada said, "I happened to arrive today just as the police found the body of your, er, maid. I was afraid you would close your shop."

The woman flushed. "Poor Michiko was my assistant," she murmured. "She was a great help in the shop. I hope the police find the animal who did this. It's getting so women aren't safe in the streets anymore." She twisted her hands together and looked toward the street again. "I cannot afford to close my shop. The employees depend on their wages, and so do I. I'm a single woman with obligations."

"Yes, I see. Well, can you show me something special for a young woman, please?"

"Is it for your own lady or someone else, sir?"

"For my wife," Akitada said firmly.

She left and a moment later a boy brought an armful of silks in sedate colors. One of the sales women followed with another stack of more brightly colored fabrics. The darker colors would have suited Tamako, his first wife, but Yukiko was only twenty. For a moment, he was at a loss. What should he aim for? Something a young girl would like, or the more elegant shades Tamako had favored. He was in his forties, and at times the discrepancy in their ages still shocked him, but he was also secretly proud that such a young and pretty woman should have chosen him.

And Yukiko *had* chosen him. In retrospect, none of his marriage had been his own doing. He had not expected that a pretty girl her age and rank would look twice at a dull, middle-aged stick like him. He smiled a little, then quickly selected a pretty sky blue silk for his daughter Yasuko. His selection for Yukiko took longer, but he finally settled on a deep rose-colored fabric that was heavy and glossy.

Mrs. Akechi returned and, recognizing weak resistance when she saw it, she complimented him on his good taste and immediately sent for several pieces of embroidered silk to demonstrate how these would improve the rose-colored silk if made into jackets or trains.

He bought two of these and had everything sent to his inn, then left much poorer but quite happy with his purchases. Both Mrs. Akechi and Junichiro, who had watched the transaction from the door, were smiling.

They continued their tour of Uji-tachi. The shops were of a bewildering variety, selling all sorts of things the jaded traveler might wish to take home with him as a memento. First and foremost, of course, were the sellers of amulets carrying blessings from the sun goddess, but Buddhist divinities were also represented. More frivolous were lacquer boxes, combs, and writing utensils suitable as gifts, and if funds were running low, there were paper umbrellas and painted fans. Food sellers were also in evidence, but Akitada ignored these and told Junichiro to select a restaurant that served decent food.

When the dwarf stopped before a large, brightly lit place called The Phoenix, Akitada balked. "Look," he said, "I know they'll pay you something to bring in a customer, but I'll be in a very bad mood if the quality of the food doesn't surpass the price."

Junichiro grinned and took him down the street to a place that specialized in fresh fish soup. It had a reassuringly local clientele, and Junichiro and Akitada found room on a bench outside where they could watch people.

While they waited for their meal, Akitada asked, "Do you remember the well-dressed man at the inn? The one who had just arrived as we were leaving?"

"You mean Master Murata?"

"You know him? How did you manage that?"

"He's a regular guest there. Comes every few weeks." The dwarf chortled. "He comes for business and pleasure."

The waitress brought large bowls of fish soup, and Akitada paid. "What sort of business?" he asked after they were alone again.

"He owns ships, I think. Very wealthy but stingy and mean." Junichiro raised his bowl, slurped, and smacked his lips. "Good! Go ahead and eat."

The soup was indeed good, and Akitada was hungry after the unsatisfactory noodle soup in Oyodo. He filed the information about the merchant away. It probably meant nothing. A ship owner might have legitimate business talking to rough characters in a harbor, and if the man was stingy, he was likely to stay in cheap places.

They devoted their attention to the excellent fish soup. Akitada saw that Junichiro had a healthy appetite in spite of his small stature.

Watching the people passing in the street, he felt some dismay at how this place had changed since he had last been here. All of these people, mostly men, were bent on pleasure. The contrast between the night-life in Uji-tachi and the most venerable and simple of shrines seemed unimaginable. What did the goddess make of all this?

Given the fact that he had encountered a murder after barely setting foot in Ise province, Akitada got a strong, if irrational, feeling that nothing good would come of his assignment, not matter how simple it seemed.

Just as he set his empty bowl down and thought about bed again, he was startled to see a very handsome and elegant man in costly clothes striding down the street. He looked remote and had pale features and a haunted look about him. He also seemed alone when Akitada would have expected a handful of servants to accompany him.

"Who is that?" he asked Junichiro.

The dwarf also gaped after the young nobleman. "That's Lord Minamoto. He has a hunting lodge up the mountain, but he never comes to Uji-tachi. I wonder what's up with him." He had finished his soup before Akitada and now looked eager to be gone.

At that moment, a red-coated police constable suddenly crossed the street and stopped before them. He merely glanced at Junichiro, who shrank back, and said to Akitada, "Compliments of Lieutenant Matsuura, sir. He wants to see you."

Akitada raised his brows. He had little confidence in the local police after watching them earlier. "You must be mistaken, Constable, "he said." I've only just arrived and have no business with the police."

"Sorry, sir. The lieutenant pointed you out to me. He waved a hand in the direction of a building on the other side of the street.

Akitada saw the flag of the local police administration drooping limply in the muggy night air. "Very well," he said with a frown. "We are finished here." Turning to Junichiro, he added, "Run along now, imp. Perhaps I'll have some use for you in the morning."

The dwarf made him a bow and hurried off after the handsome Lord Minamoto.

The constable looked after him. "Best not to encourage him. He's *hinin*. Trash. He'll steal you blind. Now, if you don't mind, the lieutenant's a busy man."

Though irritated by the constable's words, Akitada reminded himself that he was supposed to be a mere low-ranking public servant and followed the impatient constable across the street.

For a town as small as Uji-tachi, the police presence was impressive. The station building extended in the back, no doubt to make room for a jail large enough to hold all the drunks and troublemakers the town produced. Akitada was shown into the commanding officer's room, where the lieutenant he had seen earlier at the river rose to meet him.

"Thank you, Kano," the lieutenant told the constable. "Close the door behind you."

Mystified, Akitada looked around. "What's this all about, Lieutenant?" he asked.

To his surprise, the lieutenant smiled broadly at him and saluted. 'Welcome to Ise, Lord Sugawara. Beg your pardon, your Excellency! I heard you were made governor of Miwaka. My felicitations! I recognized you down at the river. It's a pleasure and a great honor to see you again."

4

The Ise Virgin

Akitada's jaw dropped. "I beg your pardon. Have we met?"

"We have indeed," said the lieutenant gleefully. "In the capital. I expect you don't remember me. I was a mere sergeant then. Superintendant Kobe always spoke with admiration about you, and I soon learned to watch out for you."

Akitada silently cursed his bad luck of running into the one person who could not only identify him, but who had apparently also made a study of his activities in the capital. He forced a smile and said, "Well, it's very good to see you also. You have done very well for yourself, Lieutenant."

"Thank you, sir. I've learned from the best."

That was true enough. Kobe was an excellent police officer. Cautiously, Akitada asked, "But did you have something specific in mind when you sent for me just now?"

Matsuura flushed. "I do apologize. It could have waited until morning, but I was so startled and pleased to see you that I couldn't wait to speak to you." He raised a hand, "Oh, I saw that you were traveling incognito. Believe me, your secret is safe with me." He flashed a smile at Akitada and rubbed his hands. "To think that you are actually here, and on the same day that we find a body!"

Akitada's heart sank. Apparently, he was expected to help solve the girl's murder. "Umm," he started, "I'm here very privately. Only for a day or so to pay my respect to the goddess. A matter of a vow, you see. I'd really appreciate it if you could keep my secret to yourself until after I'm gone."

Lieutenant Matsuura was quick to apologize again and swore to respect Akitada's request. But he looked disappointed, and Akitada relented. "It has been more than twenty years since I was here last," he said. "I was shocked to see how much the place has changed. Perhaps you could tell me a little about the area. I take it that you are in charge of keeping the peace in Uji-tachi, but what about the shrine areas and the access roads? I heard in Oyodo that you have trouble with highway robbers here."

The lieutenant admitted that robbers had been known to lie in wait for unwary pilgrims. "But it's not really my concern," he explained. "The high constable's soldiers are supposed to keep the roads and harbors safe. Though it has to be said his lordship is an avid hunter, and his men do pretty much what they want."

"I see. I suppose the governor keeps an eye on things?"

"It's the high constable who's supposed to keep his eye on things. He comes here sometimes and just arrived again. If there are complaints, he brings his soldiers. I'm afraid a town like Uji-tachi cannot absorb a lot of randy soldiers on top of our visitors. And the soldiers don't pay. So we don't complain."

"Hmm. You have your hands full, then. Who looks after the shrines?"

"The chief priest. He is a very fine nobleman. I'm thankful to say that the lawlessness hasn't extended to our august shrines or the imperial virgin."

"I'm very glad to hear it. Does the virgin still occupy her own palace? The Bamboo Palace, I think it was called?"

"Yes. They call it also the Rigu-in now, sir. And it's quite magnificent. She has her own staff, and imperial guards serve there for her protection."

"You mean guards from the Imperial Palace in the capital?"

"Yes. They serve on a rotation system six months at a time. His Majesty is very concerned about his little sister." He chuckled, then flushed. "Sorry, sir. I meant no offense. We're very proud to have such a beautiful young princess serve as our high priestess. And the young officers are very welcome in town."

"Yes, indeed," said Akitada and wondered if youth and beauty were guaranteed to please the gods. "Since I seem to be somewhat lost here, I'd be grateful if you explained where everything is. I hope to visit as many shrines as possible in the shortest time." Since this sounded less than devout, he added, "Duty calls me back to my province, you see."

The lieutenant understood perfectly and stepped up to a map hanging against the wall. Akitada saw that it was a schematic painting of the area with all the shrines, rivers, roads, bridges, and significant places represented against a background of green mountains and forests. The lieutenant pointed and explained.

"Here and here are the two most important shrines. The one at Watarai is Naiku, the shrine of the sun goddess; the Geku shrine of the goddess of farming and silk making is four miles down the road that passes through Uji-tachi. The Isuzu River runs along the road toward the coast, and here is the Bamboo Palace where the princess resides. You see it is close to the shore at Itsukinomiya where she performs her sacred ablutions."

"Ah," said Akitada, peering and measuring distances and roads with his eyes. "That is very helpful. And where is the chief priest's residence? I would like to pay my respects while I'm here."

The lieutenant pointed to a smaller residence between the shrines. "It all looks pretty empty on this map, but there are all sorts of hunting lodges on the sides of the mountains. Both the chief constable and one of the imperial princes spend time there, and of course many other noble persons."

"Yes, hmm. I hope to see more of your beautiful area tomorrow. Now I must let you get back to your duties."

The lieutenant looked disappointed. "I understand that you don't wish to be bothered while you are here, sir, but I'd be very grateful if you should happen to have any ideas about this murder. It's very troubling because we've lost two other young women recently. I'd hoped this one was just another suicide, but if someone is killing the young women, it could be a big problem."

Akitada hesitated. "He had dealt with a series of murders in Omi province not too long ago and knew that people panicked and rumors grew disproportionately to the crimes. But he could not become involved. He said quite firmly, "I have every confidence that you will get to the bottom of this crime very quickly. Should I hear anything of interest, I'll report it to you, but you must remember that I'm just an ordinary visitor by the name of Yoshimine."

The lieutenant saluted. "I won't breathe a word, sir."

∞

Akitada returned to the River Palace where the innkeeper dozed behind the counter, while his wife sat in the backroom over some paperwork by light of an oil lamp. This surprised him a little since keeping accounts was usually man's work. He cleared his throat. His host awoke, blinked and belched, then recognized him.

"Oh, is it you, Mr. Yoshimine? Some packages have been delivered and taken to your room. You'll be pleased with your purchases. Mrs. Akechi only deals in the best silks. Well above a poor innkeeper's earnings,

I'm afraid." He grinned unpleasantly. "I gave the boy ten coppers for his trouble," he added and looked at Akitada expectantly.

Akitada handed over the ten coppers, doubting very much that the boy had received anything. Having been provided with an oil lamp, he walked down the dark corridor to his room.

His bedding had been spread out. It was of dubious cleanliness and the quilts were thin and worn. He checked the packages from the silk shop, making sure that his purchases were safe. Then he removed a folded sheet of paper from inside a seam of his robe. This he unfolded and reread by the flickering light of the lamp.

It was the letter from His Majesty's secretary. While any communication from a source this close to the emperor constituted a direct order of the highest importance—and he had obeyed immediately—he still saw little that should have caused such haste. Secretary Tachibana had written, "Upon receipt of this you will make all haste to Ise, where you will contact the chief priest Nakatomi. You are to ascertain the wellbeing of Her Imperial Highness, Princess Takahime and report by special messenger to me. You are to undertake this visit without revealing your true identity or position to anyone but Nakatomi and you will destroy this letter after reading it."

That was all. There were the usual crimson seals of the imperial secretariat. He had already disobeyed in the matter of destroying the letter. Experiences in the past had taught him to distrust those above him in the government and he had kept the document in case he was about to walk into some trouble. In the matter of concealing who he was, fate had interfered in the person of Lieutenant Matsuura. But surely his errand was ordinary enough. He would ask to speak to Her Highness and then report that all was well. If it was not, he would plan accordingly.

He refolded the letter and hid it away again. Then he undressed, and lay down, using the robe with the letter as a pillow.

As soon as he relaxed, doubts began to trouble him. At first glance, all he was expected to do was to verify that Princess Takahime was alive and well. So far, he had heard or observed nothing that would suggest otherwise. But why send him on such an errand unless there was something wrong. Anything affecting the Ise Virgin was of national importance because an offense against her would be counted as an offense against the goddess, and Amaterasu held the fate of the imperial succession in her divine hands, while the goddess of farming and silk making controlled the livelihood of the nation.

He sighed. Nothing to be done tonight. In the morning he would visit the chief priest. With any luck, he would confirm that all was well.

And then home to his family.

To Yukiko.

He smiled, closed his eyes, and slept.

5

Pirates

It was a beautiful autumn morning in Mikawa, still pleasantly cool, though later the heat would return. But for the moment all seemed right with the world. Life was peaceful, food and wine were plentiful, and Hanae and Yuki seemed happy here.

In spite of all this, Tora was depressed. His world had changed. Nothing was the same any more. He had looked forward to this assignment. His master's previous appointments as governor to Echigo and Kyushu had proved to be exciting for Tora. Both times, they had faced danger together, fought powerful foes, and emerged successful. Tora had served Lord Sugawara Akitada now for sixteen years, and a strong bond had developed between them, a bond that meant they would die for each other if necessary. It had made Tora proud to serve such a man.

Maybe age had caught up with both of them. The master had remarried, doting on his pretty young wife and enjoying the easy life of an appointment that was considered highly desirable because nothing ever happened here and it was not far from the capital. And Tora, also a married man with a young son, had become restless, his usual good nature marred by bouts of pain that made his head feel as if it was about to burst. Sometimes it got so bad, he felt dizzy. He had not told anyone though he suspected that Hanae knew.

He should have been able to relax and take life easy like his master, but he missed both the danger and the challenge of the other two assignments. Even in the capital more had happened. But the worst of it was that now, as if to prove that he, Tora, had become useless, the master had gone off to Ise without taking him along. It rankled.

Having finished his morning drill with the provincial guard—he was once again Lieutenant Sashima and wore a military tunic and half armor—he walked to the main building.

The Mikawa tribunal, unlike the facilities in Echigo and Chikuzen, was a neat compound consisting of a main building with reception rooms and offices, barracks for the soldiers, stables for horses, kitchens and outbuildings. The governor's residence adjoined the tribunal compound and was equally commodious and surrounded by a pleasant garden. Prior governors had spared no funds to make themselves comfortable here.

But at the moment, Tora was headed for the governor's office in the tribunal hall. There he found Saburo watching over a number of clerks doing assorted clerical work that Tora took no interest in.

"Morning, brother," he greeted Saburo, who gave him a sharp look and answered, "Good morning, Lieutenant. What can I do for you?"

Tora jerked his head toward the door. "If you can spare a minute?"

They went out onto the wide veranda that looked across the forecourt of the tribunal.

"What's the matter?" Saburo asked. "And could you please address me as Secretary Kuruda in front of the staff? It encourages proper discipline."

"Sorry. Forgot. I've been thinking."

Saburo snorted. "Really?"

"Something wasn't right about the way the master went off. Without telling us anything. And he didn't take me along."

"He didn't take me either. But he's entitled to visit the shrines by himself if he wants to."

"There was that messenger. What was that all about?"

"Some instructions from the capital. They're common in a governor's office. Very dull stuff. I've been wading through such communications for the past four years of our predecessor's tenure."

Tora looked astonished. "Why?"

"To keep myself informed on how we are to conduct business. You'd do well to do some reading, yourself."

I. J. PARKER

Tora glowered. "Don't tell me what to do."

Reading was not his strong suit. He had been embarrassed repeatedly to find his own son correcting him. On their master's suggestion, Yuki was taking lessons with the Sugawara children. "I am to keep an eye on the populace. You can't do that by staying inside reading dusty papers."

A short silence fell.

Tora returned to his grievance. "It's not like the master to run off to visit a shrine without any warning. Her ladyship is puzzled, too. Something's going on. I don't like it. He may run into danger. He should have taken me along."

"Settle down. He's only been gone a little more than a day. He'll be back in another two."

Tora fidgeted. "Maybe so. I wish there was something interesting going on here. This is the quietest place I've ever seen. Her ladyship is bored, too."

Saburo frowned. "She's very young. She'll be happier when she has child."

Tora nodded. "It's been more than a year. We'd all been hoping they'd have another boy or girl by now. It's strange. Hanae says there's nothing wrong with her."

Saburo flushed. "This conversation is very improper, Tora."

Tora snorted. "I forgot you're not a married man. In any case, it will probably happen soon. His first lady also went for years without bearing a child. But I do wish there were some action around here."

"Be thankful for peace and order. If you really have nothing better to do, you can go talk to the police chief.

I hear a merchant showed up there yesterday complaining about pirates."

Tora cheered up. "Pirates? And you just mention the matter casually? Don't you know the master's been worried about pirate activity?"

"Well, then go and find out. Frankly, the pirates in Mikawa have little in common with the ones on the Inland Sea. They're mostly fishermen in small boats harassing other small boats."

"There are robbers on highways and robbers on the water. It's a crime and harms commerce. Anyway, if anyone asks, I'm in the city."

∞

Komachi, like Hakata, was on the coast. But there similarities ended. Komachi was on Ise Bay and a much smaller town. Its harbor served coastal traffic. All the ships were small and few were truly ocean-going vessels. The larger ones served to carry passengers across the bay or transported merchandise or tax goods because shipment by water, though threatened by weather and pirates, was still cheaper and faster than highway transport.

The town was prosperous and tidy like its provincial headquarters, and the police station was within easy walking distance from the tribunal. Tora had already made the acquaintance of the police officer assigned to Mikawa. Lieutenant Mori was middle-aged, verging on corpulence, and stiffly efficient. He did not seem overly friendly, perhaps because he feared interference from the new governor and his staff.

Tora was shown into the lieutenant's office promptly by an eager young constable. Mori was bent over some papers at his desk, but he got to his feet and made Tora a small bow. They were both lieutenants, and both considered their position the more important one, so a certain formality had existed between them from the start.

"Good morning, Mori," said Tora, returning the small bow. "I heard something about pirates. I suppose the information got lost before it got to me."

Mori said stiffly, "I reported to his Excellency's secretary."

"Ah. That explains the confusion. I'm actually the one in charge of criminal activities in the province."

Mori cleared his throat. "Really? I thought that was the function of the police."

Tora debated for a moment whether to inform the man once and for all that there was a new administration and things would be run differently in the future. He decided against it. It was not a good idea to make an enemy of this man. He might need him. So he merely said, "His Excellency takes a great interest in crime and likes to be informed at all times. Such information had best come through me, because Secretary Kuruda deals only with administrative and tax issues. Now what is this about a merchant filing a complaint?"

"I see. Have a seat," Mori said somewhat ungraciously, "while I look for the report."

Tora sat down and watched as Mori shuffled through a stack of documents. "You seem to be busy," he commented somewhat enviously.

Mori muttered, "Nothing out of the ordinary. Here it is." He held up a sheaf of papers. "Mind you, reports of piracy are as common as pebbles on the shore. You can read it for yourself." He handed the papers over.

Tora started reading with a frown. Whoever had taken down the notes used very small characters. He caught the gist but there were several passages that confused him because he could not make out the meaning of the characters.

Apparently, a rice merchant from Owari had come into the police station to announce that one of his boats had been boarded by pirates who had robbed him of money and goods to the tune of one thousand pieces of gold. Tora looked up. "He claims he lost one thousand pieces of gold? He's a liar. There's not that much gold in the whole country. I expect you sent him on his way."

"We are investigating," Mori said stiffly. "And his story is quite convincing. You did notice he said what he lost in money and goods was worth as much as one thousand pieces of gold. That's not the same as a thousand pieces of gold."

Tora flushed. Putting the documents back on Mori's desk, he said, "I'm wondering what made you trust him. What can you tell me that's not in the report?"

"Well, as I said, he came in here two days ago all outraged and accused us of not controlling our pirates. He said his boat carried merchandise ordered by customers as well as tax payments from Totomi province in addition to some personal property. I had him list everything they took. You'll find the list at the end."

"Never mind that. I assume you sent a copy to the tribunal?"

"Not yet. We've been rather busy," Mori said pointedly, gesturing at the papers scattered over his desk."

"You'd best do so now," Tora growled. "I intend to look into that dubious claim. Piracy comes under the authority of the governor. What else do you know about the man? If he's from Owari, what's he doing here?"

"He came here to meet his boat. That's also in the report."

"Yes, yes, I remember. So what he tells you about the pirates is what he's been told himself?"

"Of course."

"But can he be believed? And for that matter, can we believe what his sailors said? Did you go to talk to any of them?"

Mori snapped, "We've had our hands full dealing with a disturbance at the temple fair, so no, I haven't had a chance yet."

Tora rose. "Very well. The boat is in the harbor, I take it? I'll go see what I can find out since I have a free day. No, don't thank me. Glad to do it. Don't forget that copy for the tribunal." He flashed his brilliant smile at Mori, performed the small bow again, and stalked out.

6

The Harbor

Tora was angry with Mori, whose attitude toward a commander of the provincial guard left much to be desired, and with himself for having looked a fool by being unable to decipher the report. He resolved to return to his studies with renewed vigor to avoid such embarrassments in the future.

Since he had been unable to discover the rice merchant's whereabouts without revealing his inability to read the report, he turned his steps toward the harbor.

He had always liked harbors. They teemed with life and offered glimpses of far-away places and a chance to dream of adventures. Komachi's harbor, though, did not allow far-flung fancies. The boats tied up there plied only along the coast. Many were simple fishing boats. The biggest regular visitor was a two-masted ferry that carried travelers between Mikawa and Ise. His master had left on it, and the ship was back, tied up in the harbor. It was waiting for passengers who were already gathering on the landing.

For a moment, a wave of misery washed over Tora again. The master had gone off without him, without so much as a word of explanation beyond saying he was making a quick visit to the Ise shrine. Unlike Saburo, Tora did not believe this for an instance. First, there had been the messenger. Tora had seen him. He had been a high-ranking nobleman who had arrived on a fine horse and had been wearing expensive armor over silk robes. Such a man did not carry a casual communication from some bureau in the capital. The messenger had talked to the master and then left again immediately. And right after this, the master had announced that he wished to worship at the Ise shrine. That could not be a coincidence.

Saburo had seen this visitor and seemed patently uninterested in Tora's grievance. But Tora knew there was something afoot.

The problem of the rice merchant made up for some of his disappointment. It involved a case of piracy off the coast of Mikawa, and the master had expressed a concern about past reports of such activities. Tora saw an opportunity to prove his own abilities and possibly uncover something that might send him after his master.

The Shrine Virgin

His good humor somewhat restored, he walked along the dock scanning the boats in their berths. The fishing boats announced themselves by their rank odor. The day was becoming hot, and the stench was horrible. But someone had segregated these to one end of the harbor. Between the ferry landing and the fishing boats, transport barges were tied up. These were wide and deep-bottomed, usually carrying one mast and a square sail, now reefed up, and had no quarters for passengers because most of the space was taken up by bales, boxes, barrels, and bundles of assorted goods. One of the boats carried horses. The poor beasts stood tightly corralled, their heads hanging low.

Eventually he found the boat in question. It was one of the bigger ones there, substantial enough to carry bales of rice, but now riding high in the water and apparently empty. It seemed in good repair for having been attacked by pirates. A sailor was leaning against the mast and fast asleep, but otherwise there was no sign of life. No doubt his fellows were in town getting drunk. Tora wished he had worn plain clothes. He did not like the sleeping man's looks, though such boat people were usually rough characters. Too soon to tell if they had lied about the pirates. He walked on.

One of the many youngsters who hang around the harbor in hopes of carrying the bags of a traveler or of delivering messages between the boats and the town, strolled toward Tora, whistling through his teeth and staring at Tora's pale red guard tunic and the black headgear with the brushes over each ear.

"Morning," said Tora with a grin. "Planning on taking a trip?"

The boy, who was about fifteen or sixteen, stopped and grinned back. He had a gap between his front teeth which accounted for the keen sound of his whistling. "Wish I were," he said, looking toward the ferry. "And you, Officer? Are you going somewhere or are you arresting someone?"

"Just getting to know the place. You want to earn a few coppers by being my guide?"

The boy cocked his head. "How many coppers?"

"Hmm, five?"

"I can make ten running an errand into town."

"All right. Ten, then."

"I'll have to leave after the ferry goes."

"That's not much time," Tora said, seeing sailors loading baggage onto the ship."

"Plenty of time. Take it or leave it."

"You strike a hard bargain." Tora counted out ten coppers from the string he carried inside his sash.

The boy grinned and shoved the coins inside his shirt. "I'll let you buy more of my time if you want."

"Thank you, but at this rate I'll be a poor man before the sun sets. Very well, tell me about the harbor. What about that ferry? It goes to Ise across the bay, I think."

The boy nodded. "And then up the coast to Owari and back to us. There's another ship that goes the opposite way."

"Every day?"

"No, silly. Every other day. It takes a day one way and a day coming back, though the wind has to cooperate."

Tora frowned at him. "Watch your tongue, youngster. What about these boats here?"

"They carry goods."

"What sort of goods?"

"Oh, anything. Rice, silk, ramie, hemp, horses, dye, whatever people use."

"I saw the horses."

"They come from up north and most go to the capital."

"Tax goods, too?"

"Sometimes. They need special permission to go by water."

"I see. And the others don't need permission?"

"They all need permission, but for tax goods, they need special papers."

"And who checks the permissions?"

"The harbor master." The boy pointed toward a small building next to the post station. The post station was flying the usual flag and seemed busy this morning with ferry passengers.

"Is there a lot of trouble with pirates? I heard some talk in town."

The boy nodded. "A fair amount, but mostly small stuff until now."

"Oh?"

The boy turned back and pointed to the boat with the sleeping sailor. "That one came in two nights ago. They'd been attacked between here and Totomi. They said the pirates came from shore in many boats and killed one of the sailors. They took everything that was on the boat."

"Shocking! How do you know this?"

"I work here, and people talk. The owner was here yesterday, shouting at the sailors about losing his fortune. Next a couple of constables came down and took a look."

"Ah!" Tora shook his head. "I bet that makes the other boatmen nervous. I wonder why the owner blamed the sailors. They couldn't help it if they were outnumbered."

The boy chuckled. "If they told the truth. Some boatmen just claim that pirates boarded them and took some of their cargo. Never this much, though, and never a whole cargo of rice."

"Do you know where the owner went? I might want to talk to him."

"He was staying at the post station. Not sure if he's still there. He could've gone back home on one of the ferries."

They both turned to watch the ferry and the loading of its passengers. They seemed almost ready to set sail. Already, sailors were scrambling about, and the passengers that had been waiting on the dock had gone on deck and disappeared into the small building that was the passenger cabin.

"Well, I suppose that means my time is up," said Tora. "I think I overpaid."

The boy folded his arms protectively across his chest. "A deal's a deal," he said. "But I could give you a bit more time."

"No, thanks. I'll have a talk with the harbor master. But you owe me, if we meet again."

The boy nodded with a grin, no doubt thinking that was not likely to happen, and they parted company.

The post station was settling down to normal business after dealing with the ferry. Tora looked it over and noted the adjacent lodge and stables. Then he entered the harbor master's office. One of the two clerks in the front room ran to announce him, and a moment later the harbor master, a short man with a goatee and the formal black robe and hat of officials everywhere, bowed Tora into his office.

They had met before when harbor master Osumi had reported to the tribunal with the monthly account of shipping in the harbor, but this was Tora's first visit to the station.

Having seated himself, he said, "I won't trouble you long, Harbormaster, but we've had a report of a pirate attack and I find the boat in question is still docked here. Have you talked to its master?"

"Yes, Lieutenant. He told a shocking tale. They were off the southern coast of Mikawa, just making the turn into Ise Bay, when suddenly some ten or twenty longboats shot out from among the rocks and inlets of that rough coast. There were at least five armed men in each boat, and the first boat hailed them, telling them to reef the sail and drop an anchor. The boat master ignored this and tried to run down one of the boats. But the pirates had bows and arrows and also swords and knives. They killed one of his men with an arrow, and he obeyed. They came on board and started checking the goods. Meanwhile more boats joined them. They unloaded everything to the other boats, then got back into their boats and left. The boat master said it was all over in less than an hour."

Tora frowned. "That's not good. That part of our coast is quite a distance from here. It may take time to get some soldiers to that area. Did you talk to the owner of the goods?"

The harbormaster rolled his eyes. "Dear me, yes. He stormed in here the very next day and wanted me get started on his paperwork."

"Paperwork? What about the pirates and the dead sailor?"

The stationmaster spread his hands. "Not his concern. That's for your governor to take care of. He wanted me to give him something to prove he'd lost his whole cargo."

"And did you?"

"I walked back to the boat with him and talked to the sailors. They said pretty much the same thing." The harbormaster paused. "Mind you, they are pretty rough characters. Frankly, I wish they were on their way back to where they came from. Already there has been a fight in a wine shop and I hear one of the brothels had to call the constables."

"Hmm," said Tora. "They seem to be pretty flush with money if they are doing much drinking and whoring after having been cleaned out by pirates."

"My thought exactly. But maybe the owner paid them off."

"Maybe. Where's this owner now, and did he give a name and a hometown?"

"He said he was staying at the post station lodge. His name is Takanami Masayoshi, I think." Osumi reached for a ledger and found the entry. "Yes, Takanami Masayoshi, rice merchant from Nakashima in Owari province."

"Thanks. I'll see what I can find out. I guess we'd better do something about those pirates."

Tora left the harbor in excellent spirits. Finally something he could get his teeth into. He would organize an expedition of provincial guards and local men and head south to wipe out that nest of vipers who were terrorizing local shipping.

But the first step was to return to the tribunal and get Saburo's help in deciphering the report from the very unhelpful police chief. Something did not ring quite true. He was not at all convinced that merchant Takanami had been completely truthful. For that matter, his double name meant that he was a man of rank, perhaps some local nobleman. No matter. If he was a crook, Tora would make short work of him.

7

The Merchant from Owari

Before leaving the harbor, Tora stopped by the lodge that adjoined the post station and asked to see the register. He saw the name Takanami but was told the merchant was no longer there. The clerk was not sure if he had left on the ferry or decided to move to one of the inns in town.

Tora assumed the latter. For one thing, the post station lodge offered only the simplest accommodations, a large room under a roof. Travelers of all kinds huddled together there to save money. A man who had just lost the equivalent of one thousand pieces of gold would hardly settle for this for more than one night. More importantly, since he was so eager to get proof of his losses, and the police were not finished investigating, he was surely still in town.

He walked back to the tribunal and put his head into the main office. Saburo was perusing documents, so Tora asked, "Did Lieutenant Mori send over a report?"

Saburo looked up. "Yes. Just a short while ago. Why?"

Tora preferred to see both Saburo and the report privately and came in. "I think it concerns pirates. Could we talk about it?"

"Very well." Saburo found the document, and they went next door to a small room under the eaves that held mostly provincial archives.

Saburo handed over the report. "What's so urgent?"

Tora unfolded the paper and frowned down at it. "It's about this merchant from Owari who claims his goods have been stolen by pirates. Rice and gold."

Saburo's brows shot up. "Gold? How much gold?"

"I don't know." Tora was still trying to decipher the list of stolen goods. "The whole loss is said to be one thousand pieces of gold." Frustrated he handed back the piece of paper. "Here, you read it. I can't make out those chicken scratches."

Saburo stared at him. "One thousand pieces of gold? How can that be? Who has that much money except the emperor?"

"Well, that covers the value of the rice, too, but I think the whole thing is a lie."

"But why make up such a crazy lie?"

"I don't know, but he seems desperate to prove he's been robbed."

"I see." Saburo pondered this a moment, then read the whole report carefully.

Tora became impatient. "I got the gist. I need to know what this Takanami said exactly."

"Well, he told the police that he was meeting the boat here, and the boatmen told him of the attack and of one man being killed. They showed him the empty boat. They said it happened south of here."

"Right. I got that. What else?"

"Well the rest is just a list of goods he was robbed of."

"Read the list."

Saburo sighed. "You know, you really should read better, Tora. Now that the master is rising in the world, so are we and our duties are getting more complicated. Your sword or your fighting sticks aren't much good anymore."

Tora gave him a look. "He took me on because of my courage and my skill with the *bo*. And my sword has come in handy on a number of occasions, one of them involving you. Nobody said anything about reading."

"Never mind." Saburo read the list aloud.

" 'Four hundred bales of highest grade rice: value five hundred pieces of gold. Forty bolts of fine silk and silk gauze: value two hundred pieces of gold. Sixty bales of floss silk: value one hundred pieces of gold. Ten barrels of oil: fifty pieces of gold. Personal property: one money chest containing one hundred pieces of gold, and half that value in gold dust, plus one hundred and fifty large silver coins.'" Tora whistled. Saburo paused to add up the figures and nodded. "Yes, that's more than one thousand pieces of gold. Quite right."

Tora snorted. "Nothing about this is quite right. It's a lie. Who's to prove that's what he lost? Who's to say there was anything of value on the boat except maybe a payoff to the boatmen and he made that after they got here."

"Perhaps, but what about the dead sailor? Or was there a dead sailor?"

"It's all a pack lies from beginning to end." At least that was Tora's gut feeling.

"Then there are no pirates?"

Tora looked less certain. "Well . . ."

"What are you going to do?"

"I suppose it's got to be investigated. I'll have a talk with the merchant if he's still in town. And maybe we need to look into this claim of pirates. Would you write to the Owari tribunal and ask them about Takanami?"

"Glad to. Before you leave for town again, the gardeners have arrived at the residence. I'm too busy to check on them. Will you make sure they do a good job?"

Tora grinned. "My pleasure." They bowed to each other and parted.

∞

Tora walked through the small gate in the high wall that separated the tribunal compound from the governor's residence. He was immediately in a different world. Tall trees shaded shrubberies and stone paths leading to a fine house with sweeping tile roofs, broad verandas, and several pavilions. The air was pleasantly cool in the shade, but Tora frowned at the overgrown vegetation under the trees and had to duck under a low-hanging branch of a pine. Its needles were brown; the branch had broken in one of the frequent storms that lashed the Mikawa coast. There was plenty of work here for the gardeners. Where were they? He did not hear the sound of saws. The previous governor had been too tight to maintain the property during his last year in office. He had left the repairs to his successor. A good thing that the master had the income these days to provide a comfortable home for his high-born lady.

Pushing on toward the northern pavilion, the residence of Lady Yukiko, he finally heard voices and the laughter of his mistress. She had a very pretty laugh, and he assumed she must be playing with the children.

She was not.

When Tora emerged from the overgrown part of the garden near the back of her pavilion, he stopped, shocked by what he saw.

Lady Yukiko stood among some eight scruffy-looking men who were leaning on shovels or watching with their arms crossed. She had covered her silk gown with a hemp apron, gathered up her hair and covered it with a hemp cloth, and held a plant in hands that were black with earth. And she was laughing with the gardeners.

He was still gaping when she saw him. "Tora!" she cried. "Come see my chrysanthemums. I shall have a chrysanthemum garden this autumn. We are planting them right here under this maple and over there under the Ginkgo tree. The bronze and yellow ones will be under the maple, and the white and purple ones near the yellow Ginkgo. The garden will all be a blaze of colors in another few weeks. Akitada will be so amazed!"

Well, it was not precisely what was needed most urgently in this garden, but Tora warmed again to his new mistress. She had a way with her that lifted a man's spirits even when he had a headache. No wonder the master doted on her.

He approached, bowing to Lady Yukiko—perhaps more deeply than usual to remind the gardeners of the respect due to this pretty young woman—and said, "It will be quite beautiful, my lady. Will all these men be required for the chrysanthemums?"

"Why? Do you need them elsewhere?"

"Well, there's the matter of cleaning up the shrubberies. They are in a shocking state. A dead branch is hanging over the path to the tribunal. It will knock the master's hat off if he passes under it without paying attention."

She burst into a peal of laughter. "Oh, I'd like to see his face. But you're quite right. We cannot have my husband suffer injuries to his dignity." She turned to the gardeners. "What do you say? Can some men be spared for the branch?"

"And some other clearing work," Tora added quickly.

They decided they could spare two. These departed, looking unhappy. The others started digging the soil around the two trees, and Lady Yukiko asked, "Any word from Ise?"

"No, my lady. But it's too soon. Perhaps tomorrow. A ferry runs between the provinces."

"Oh, how I wish I could have been on it!" she cried and turned to look in the direction of the sea. It could not been seen from here—the trees blocked the view— but her longing transformed her pretty face, reminding Tora of his own disappointment.

He felt himself melt again. She loved her husband and missed him already. Lord Sugawara Akitada had been lucky in his wives. Lady Tamako, his first wife, had given him his two children, four if you counted the baby that had died with her and Yori who had died at five from smallpox. Lady Tamako had been much quieter than Lady Yukiko, though very friendly and kind to all of them. She would never have laughed with gardeners or—heaven forbid—revealed her feelings for her husband to Tora or anyone else. She had had exquisite manners at all times. Lady Yukiko still quite often behaved like a young girl, one who had been spoiled by her doting parents. But you could not help smiling and feeling your heart lift at her lively spirits. No, everything considered, the master was a very lucky man.

And would be luckier still once there was another child.

He had arrived at this conviction when Lady Yukiko said fervently, "I want to travel. I want to see the world. I want to go everywhere. Women should not have to be confined to their homes while men get to have adventures, meet people, and see all sorts of sights."

Tora gulped. "It wouldn't be safe, my lady."

"Nonsense. I'm not afraid. You cannot really live unless you leave your house." She gestured toward the gardeners digging in her plants. "It's not enough to admire the chrysanthemums and maples every autumn," she added, her voice suddenly forlorn.

Tora voiced his earlier thought. "But women are happiest raising their children."

A shadow passed over her face. "So men like to think, Tora." She turned away. "Besides not all women are alike."

He did not know what to say, so he muttered, "I'm sorry, my lady."

Her smile returned. "No need to feel sorry. There's always tomorrow, and my lord will soon be back with us."

Tora bowed. "Yes, indeed. Is there anything I might do for you?"

"No Tora. Thank you. I'll see to it that these men make the rest of the garden presentable also."

Tora bowed and went to see his own family.

Since Yuki was at his lessons in the main house, only Hanae was home. She was sewing some garment but jumped up to hug him. "Back already? You missed me?" she cried.

He laughed and nuzzled her neck. "Don't you know that you should greet your husband with more respect? Lady Yukiko and Lady Tamako always bow to the master."

"Ah," she said, wriggling away, "you came home to find fault. And here I thought . . . well never mind what

I thought. You probably would find that disrespectful also." She pouted.

"Never," he cried, reaching for her.

"Ouch! Tora, you're wearing your armor."

He released her. "Sorry. I came home to change anyway." He grinned at her. "Come, you can help me."

∞

Tora left an hour later, smiling contentedly. What a lucky man he was! Perhaps even luckier than his master. Hanae doted on him and was content to be his wife and the mother of his son. He hoped Lady Yukiko would learn something from her.

He found the merchant quickly.

Takanami Masayoshi and a servant were installed in the best inn in Komachi's center. The presence of a servant, not previously mentioned, suggested again that the man was not just any citizen of Owari even if he was a merchant. This was not altogether surprising since a number of noble families had recognized the advantages to be gained from trade. Several great houses, like the Fujiwara and the Tachibana, were regularly engaged in lending rice to farmers in return of a large portion of their harvest. Rice storage and distribution were probably the biggest businesses in the country, and this particular noble merchant had evidently also invested in transport.

Tora had changed into his ordinary clothes, a neat blue cotton robe with a black sash and his black hat. When he arrived at the inn, he was received with some courtesy, but the maid sent to Takanami returned to say their guest was too busy to see people.

Believing this due to his ordinary appearance, Tora sent the maid back with one of his cards identifying him as commander of the provincial guard.

This time, the maid returned to take him to a room where Takanami sat at his ease on a cushion, some paper work and writing materials by his side. The room was upstairs and gave onto a narrow balcony that overlooked the main street of Komachi below.

Takanami was middle-aged and had a round face, dandified mustache, and heavy-lidded eyes. He wore clothes of heavy silk. When Tora entered, he did not rise and regarded him with a frown. "You're from the tribunal? What do you want?" he snapped.

Offended by this rudeness, Tora merely nodded and seated himself uninvited. "Why did you leave the post station lodge?" he said in lieu of a greeting. He could be just as rude as Takanami.

"Because it's an awful place. You people should do something about it. The people who stay there are all porters. They smell."

Tora raised his brows. "I was told you're a merchant from Owari."

Takanami flushed. "We are an old, land-owning family in Owari. The rice business is a sideline."

"Really? The police chief said you were robbed of one thousand pieces of gold. The tribunal takes an interest in large gold shipments. Do you carry the proper permits?"

The merchant-nobleman made a dismissive gesture. "If that's what he's told you, he's a fool. There was some gold, my personal property, but most of the value of the goods was in rice and silk and such commodities. Most of it was destined for the capital."

"These goods had been purchased by you or in your name?"

Takanami fidgeted. "Not all. Some were tax goods I provided transport for."

"You are also in the transport business? You must be carrying several permits then. Might I see them?"

Takanami handed over a small package containing a number of permits issued by authorities in Owari and in the capital, all properly signed and bearing the seals required. Tora had seen and handled enough permits in his day to accept these as authentic. But his suspicions had increased. He did not like the man.

In the end, he had him write out the list of losses again, then said, "I expect you and the boat will remain in Mikawa for the time being?"

The merchant blustered, "Believe me, I would already be gone if your authorities weren't so slow in certifying the attack on my boat. I have to explain to my clients and to the government what happened to their goods."

"Ah. Well, they have to prove your story first. It all depends on whether the pirates can be found with your goods."

Takanami turned purple. "What do you mean? You have my statement and that of the boatmen. Are you suggesting I lied? Why do you need the pirates?"

Tora tucked Takanami's list into his robe and got to his feet. "Among other things, we try to return stolen property to its owners. I hope you will enjoy Komachi, sir."

8

The Lost Jewel

On the morning of his second day, Akitada was up early. Somewhat to his surprise, Junichiro was nowhere in sight. A very pretty young woman was behind the counter. She wished him a good morning and asked if he had slept well. This was such a pleasant change from the rude male who had been working the night before that he thanked her with a smile and said he was on his way to the shrines.

"Oh, very good, sir. You may catch one of the ceremonies at Geku. Do you know the way?"

"Yes. I've been here before." He paused, impressed by her courtesy as much as by her prettiness, and added, "I arrived yesterday but didn't see you."

She looked pleased. "I'm Keiko. I only got here my-self last night. I'm visiting my mother." Seeing his blank look, she added, "She owns this inn."

"Oh. Well, I'm glad to have met you, Keiko."

She wished him a pleasant day, and he walked out into the sunshine.

It was not too warm yet and the fragrance of the ev-ergreen forest that clothed the mountains on either side of the river filled the air. Akitada had decided to fast in order to approach the *kami* properly. Cleanliness, both physical and spiritual, was mandatory for shrine visits. He had bathed the night before, but would also per-form the required ablutions before entering the shrine precinct. He had not engaged in sexual intercourse and, while he had witnessed the retrieval of a dead woman, he had not been anywhere near her or touched her.

He walked to Uji Bridge. It spanned the river and led to the shrines on the other side. There were many shrines in the forest and on the mountain sides, but the main ones were Naiku and Geku.

Though it was still early, other visitors were also crossing the river. This crossing over water marked the passing of the boundary between the ordinary world and the sacred one.

On the other side of the bridge was a landing, and there the shrine visitors performed their ablutions at stone water basins. He waited his turn, then rinsed his hands, took a drink from the bamboo ladle to rinse his mouth, and spat the water on the ground. The road wound through a forest of giant cryptomerias. He passed several halls used for purification ceremonies, prayers, and the preparation of food offerings. Then he walked under the first of two red-painted *torii*.

Naiku, the shrine sacred to the goddess Amaterasu, was of extraordinary plainness, just a small, slender building made of weathered cypress wood behind tall cypress fences. Only the emperor was permitted to enter the shrine proper, which contained the most inviolable treasures of the nation, the sacred mirror in which to reflect Amaterasu, the tutelary goddess of the Yamato clan of the imperial family, and the sacred sword.

It was said that the mirror reflected both good and evil, both right and wrong, and that it was always fair and impartial.

He reflected that this made it also a symbol of his own calling, of providing justice that always weighed both sides and applied the laws impartially. And the sword surely represented the power of enforcing justice.

A strange kind of peace filled Akitada. He was not a very religious man and positively disliked Buddhism, but here he felt close to his origins and to his country. These were his own gods, forever present in the mountains, the sky, the plants, the waters of these beautiful islands.

He wanted to linger, but somehow the imperial secretary's letter had taken on a new and ominous significance since he had set foot on sacred ground. So he performed his obeisance and silently asked for guidance in his work. Then he turned his steps in the direction of the chief priest's dwelling.

The priest was a descendant of the Nakatomi family, once part of an early imperial branch. Nakatomi males were hereditary head priests at the Ise shrines and represented the emperor in their duties. The head priest only performed the ceremonies on high holy days. Other, lower-ranking priests undertook the daily duties.

Akitada had seen several of these as he walked. And there were also some of the charming shrine maidens about. These were mostly daughters of the priests, dressed in their red and white silk costumes with their long hair flowing down their backs.

Nakatomi lived in a spacious villa that would have been adequate for a retired emperor. Akitada was admitted, gave the Yoshimine name, and asked to see the priest on behalf of his Excellency, Tachibana Nakahira.

Somewhat to his surprise, the servant returned quickly and led him to a large room overlooking a garden. *Tatami* mats were spread on the dark, glossy floor and green reed blinds covered part of the open doors to a veranda.

A slender elderly man with thick white hair came to meet him, examining him with sharp eyes. "So you are Sugawara Akitada," he said in the friendliest manner. "How nice that his Excellency sent you."

Akitada bowed politely and said he was greatly honored that Nakatomi should have heard of him.

The priest smiled a little and asked, "You have visited the shrines?"

"Only the inner shrine, sir. I did not want to delay seeing you."

The priest nodded and gestured to some cushions. He turned quite serious. "I'm afraid what I have to tell you is shocking. In fact, it may already be too late."

The Shrine Virgin

They seated themselves near the open door over-looking the garden and the distant mountains. The summer morning was fragrant and peaceful. Akitada did not know what to make of the priest's words and, since Nakatomi had fallen into a mournful silence, he asked, "Has something happened to Princess Takahime?"

The priest regarded him sadly. "You might say so. I suspect that she is gone, perhaps dead."

The words hung in the silent air. Gone? Dead? Akitada shivered. He could not imagine a disaster of greater magnitude befalling the nation. Even an attack on the capital might have a more hopeful outcome than the death or defilement of the Ise Virgin. She was the guardian of the sacred mirror and sword upon which rested the imperial rule. Divinely descended and cho-sen by the gods, the Yamato line of emperors, unbro-ken since the very beginning of time, took its legitimacy directly from the ancient gods. If through the high priestess of Amaterasu the gods had been offended, disaster would strike the land and destroy its people.

In any case, the majority of His Majesty's subjects believed so. Their panic would rise with every small disaster. A storm would be blamed on the anger of the goddess, a poor harvest would be seen as direct pun-ishment, every disease would be visited on them through her anger. Their entire happiness rested in their trust in the blessings of the gods.

But the priest merely suspected that she was gone.
Akitada asked, "What makes you think so?"

"She has not appeared in public for many weeks. I have not seen her on my visits to her palace. She has not officiated at important ceremonies. Dear heaven, I'm afraid she must be dead! How else would you explain it?" Nakatomi shook his head. "I don't know what we will do."

Akitada suppressed another shudder and wondered if the priest was not exaggerating. He asked, "How could such a thing have been kept quiet?"

The priest did not meet his eyes. "I took some steps to make sure her duties were performed as usual. We were able to fool people so far, but it cannot last. And it is a sacrilege, of course. This is why I traveled to the capital and informed His Majesty. It was decided to bring in someone from the outside, someone who could not be involved in any way. They chose you."

Akitada's head reeled. "I still have a hard time taking it in," he said. "What do the princess's people have to say? Surely they must know something. It is my understanding that she resides in a large household with many attendants and servants, and that her palace is heavily guarded."

"That is so. But as for being heavily guarded, I doubt the young gentlemen of the Imperial Guard take their job very seriously. The nature of their assignment here seems to encourage them to live a life of leisure and debauchery. Uji-tachi with its brothels and gambling dens is a major attraction, as are hunting and fishing."

Akitada recalled the elegant nobleman from the night before. He had been walking toward the pleasures of Uji-tachi with a fierce look of determination on his handsome face. He considered the general lack of discipline for a moment and asked, "Is it possible that the princess left of her own accord?"

The priest sighed. "I think so, but her senior lady-in-waiting denies it."

"What explanation does she give then?"

"Oh, she denies that she is gone. She claims the princess is ailing." The priest clenched his fists and said angrily, "The woman is lying. I know it. She's a horrible creature, an evil woman who should never have been allowed close to Her Highness. Whatever happened, she was the one who made it happen!"

Taken aback by this outburst, Akitada asked, "Who is she?"

"She is known as Tamba Shikibu. She is married to the governor of Tamba and a daughter of Tachibana Moroe. A thoroughly depraved female." He glowered. "Really, I sometimes wonder at the lack of propriety among court ladies, but you would expect an older woman to have more sense. Even in these sacred surroundings, the princess's attendants are allowed a degree of freedom that is shocking."

This made Akitada ask, "You suspect a romantic entanglement?"

The priest threw up his hands. "Who knows? Anything is possible. And don't ask me for details. I'm completely in the dark. Speak to that woman." He paused, then muttered, "Though she'll lie, of course."

Akitada thought there had been a great deal of lying going on already. In fact, his own presence here was based on a lie. He asked. "How exactly have you managed to keep this covered up? Did you use a stand-in?"

For the first time, the priest smiled a little. It made him look gentler. "My daughter Nobuko took the princess's place for the Tsukinamisai."

"Your daughter?" Akitada regarded the elderly man and wondered how such a substitution could have succeeded. Princess Takahime was in her early twenties and by all accounts beautiful, though that could be an exaggeration. All imperial descendants were automatically endowed with perfections.

"My daughter is twenty-one," said the priest, guessing his puzzlement. "She's the child of my old age, the one neither my wife nor I expected. And she is, of course, a shrine maiden and very familiar with the princess's duties."

"You are to be congratulated," Akitada said, wondering if someone would someday look with the same surprise at his children by Yukiko. She had not given him a child yet and it was altogether possible that he would be taken for its grandfather. "How many people know what has been going on? There is your own household, and then the princess's establishment. And what about the other priests and attendants at the ceremonies?"

"I cannot speak for the princess's palace, but here only my wife and daughter are aware. I have been most careful to announce that Her Highness would travel with my wife to and from her palace. The driver is unaware who enters the carriage at my house."

The Shrine Virgin

Akitada nodded. It seemed just possible, though surely this could not go on forever. He was becoming very curious to meet Lady Tamba. "Can you write me a letter of introduction that will admit me to the Bamboo Palace?"

The priest rose to go to a small carved desk. Taking a sheet of paper and rubbing some ink, he wrote, pausing now and then to tap the handle of the brush against his nose. When he finished, he waved the letter about to let the ink dry, then brought it to Akitada.

"See if you approve," he said.

Akitada read, "On behalf of His Majesty, I introduce to you Lord Sugawara. He has travelled far to bring a message to Her Royal Highness from her August brother."

The note—on paper every bit as fine as his own letter from the imperial secretary—was addressed to Tamba Shikibu.

"It will do very well," Akitada said as he gave it back to be folded and sealed. "Am I to assume that I may now use my own name?"

The priest started. "No, by no means. It would cause people to wonder. The Tamba woman doesn't matter. She has her own secrets to keep and won't talk."

Akitada nodded. "True enough. But you should know that I have been recognized already. The police lieutenant in Uji-tachi used to work with Superintendant Kobe in the capital. Of course I've have sworn him to secrecy. He seems reliable."

The priest sighed. "It can't be helped, but we must be careful."

Akitada rose. "I agree. If there is any news, I'll return."

The priest came to put a hand on Akitada arm. "I'm very glad you're here.," he said. "It's an enormous relief to know that someone else now bears some of the burden. I don't mind telling you, I've been nearly out of my mind." He squeezed Akitada's arm gratefully and added, "But remember, don't trust that Tamba woman."

∞

No wonder the high priest had panicked and reported to the emperor. If he was indeed right, and Akitada tended to believe him because he had seemed a rational man, then the situation was dire. Some weeks ago, perhaps as much as a month, the princess had disappeared. Akitada agreed with the priest that it seemed inconceivable that she could still be alive after all this time.

Akitada's thoughts returned to the bodies of young women that had been fished from the river on what appeared to be a regular basis. Had they all been identified? Had it occurred to the priest to examine them?

He had not mentioned such a thing, perhaps because he did not want Akitada to consider her dead. Or perhaps he knew something more about the disappearance that would explain the absence but could not be divulged. Akitada sincerely hoped this was the case. He also hoped that her ladies-in-waiting would know what had happened to her.

As Akitada pondered what he had learned from Nakatomi, he came to a crossroad. Signs pointed either ahead to Geku, the outer shrine, or to Naiku where he had already been. He decided to complete his visit of the two most important shrines before noon and call on the ladies in the Bamboo Palace after eating something. His stomach rumbled, but he did not want to waste the day's abstinence, so he continued to the shrine dedicated to Toyouki, the *kami* of agriculture and crafts.

He caught the end of the morning ceremony. It was performed twice daily by Shinto priests in pure white robes and shrine maidens in their red skirts and white jackets. He watched them appreciatively because this shrine celebrated all the things that people needed to sustain life and culture. The god blessed rice farming, salt-making, fishing, silk production, weaving of both silk and hemp, and pottery making. It struck Akitada again that anything befalling the Ise virgin would wreak havoc in many lives by bringing devastating droughts, earthquakes, storms, and diseases. Deaths and starvation would bring about rebellion and war, and the nation would be shaken. Humbly, he made his own prayers to the god before returning to Uji-tachi.

He would do his utmost to return the lost jewel to its shrine.

p^2

9

The Dragon Lady

Back in Uji-tachi, Akitada returned to the place that served the excellent fish soup and fortified himself with two large bowls of this before setting out for the Bamboo Palace. Since he had done a significant amount of walking these last two days, he rented a horse for the journey. The beast was elderly and certainly did not make a good impression, but then neither did he in his plain black robe and the cap of a minor official.

The palace was indeed quite impressive, though the buildings had been kept simple in keeping with the ancient shrines. But there were halls, pavilions, galleries, and outbuildings tucked away behind a tall wooden fence, and the large gate was manned by guards in the imperial colors.

Akitada was stopped, gave his false name, and said that he had come from the chief priest with a letter for Lady Tamba. This produced grins and made it clear that the hostilities between the senior lady-in-waiting and the chief priest were known to all. It also proved the soldiers' lack of discipline the priest had mentioned. Their sneers made it clear that the chief priest was not held in great esteem. However, Akitada was admitted and allowed to dismount while someone went to announce him.

He looked about him, trying to gauge the mood here. If they knew the princess was gone, they did not give any sign of it. Neither did they seem overly downcast by any illness that might have befallen her.

A servant returned to take him to a reception room in the main building. This was large and empty. He waited, pacing back and forth. Somewhere in the distance he heard women's laughter, and was struck again by the normalcy that seemed to prevail.

He had quite a long wait, which he ascribed to the hostilities between the chief priest and the senior lady-in-waiting. Finally a door opened in the back of the room, and an old woman with a white-painted face and painted eyebrows appeared. She wore the court robe of many layers of silk but was frail and walked up to him with small shuffling steps to peer over her fan with rheumy eyes. Akitada was somewhat astonished that the chief priest should have been so outraged by someone who was so clearly feeble, when the old lady said in a cracked voice, "You are to come!" and turned to shuffle away again.

The Shrine Virgin

Akitada followed her out of the main hall and along a series of galleries through some beautiful gardens to a pavilion. The old lady finally stopped, gasping a little from the exertion, and gestured at the door. "Go in," she croaked.

Akitada bowed his thanks. Great age always deserved this honor, even when he did not know what function this woman had. Then he opened the door and stepped inside.

The room was large and luxuriously furnished. Painted screens, *tatami* mats with silk trimmings, green reed shades with brocade ribbons, an assortment of smaller furnishings, such as lacquer clothing trunks, bamboo book racks with books, braziers, lamps, desks, comb boxes, silver mirrors, and other oddments made it a suitable place for an imperial princess.

But there was no princess. The only woman present was middle-aged, tall for a woman, but also fat, to judge by her round face, for her voluminous gowns and the fact that she was sitting made it hard to tell. Like the old lady's, her face was painted. Unlike the old lady, she disdained to hide behind a fan. Instead, she fanned herself with it angrily.

"So you come from that man!" she snapped. "What new torment has he invented for me?"

Akitada bowed. "Do I have the honor of speaking to Lady Tamba? Tamba Shikibu, the senior lady-in-waiting to her Imperial Highness?"

She compressed her lips. "Yes. Be quick about it. I'm very busy."

Clearly her anger was directed against the chief priest rather than against him. It occurred to Akitada that the level of hostility between these two important guardians of the Ise Virgin most likely defeated the purpose of providing proper guidance to the young woman through the wisdom of elders of both sexes.

Not having been invited to sit down, Akitada cleared his throat. "It is true that I came here after speaking to the chief priest; however, my purpose is with you and my charge is from His Majesty. I am to speak to Her Highness and report back to His Majesty."

She started. "Impossible. She can see no one."

"Madam, I urge you to reconsider. You are refusing an imperial order."

She bit her lip. "My duty is to the princess. I will not allow any man access to her. I would rather die than have her exposed to improper eyes."

The dragon lady protecting her jewel! It might have been amusing, given the general laxity the priest had complained about, but Akitada would have none of it. He sighed, undid the seam of his robe and drew out the secretary's letter. "Allow me," he said, presenting it to her with both hands.

She stared at him, then dropped the fan and took the letter in both of hers. Unfolding it, she read. It was impossible to see her changing color under all that paint, but her jaw sagged. She raised her eyes and stared at Akitada. "No," she gasped. "No, I can't. It's impossible. She's ill, very ill. She cannot be seen by a man." She drew a deep breath. "How dare you suggest such a thing?"

The Shrine Virgin

Akitada walked to the nearest cushion and sat. "Madam, I am charged by His Majesty. I am also a married man with children of my own. I assure you Her Highness is quite safe with me, but of course, you may stay to make certain of it."

She flushed and looked helplessly around the room. "It is cruel to torment the poor ill child so. She's had a very bad night. Perhaps you could come back tomorrow."

"What illness is troubling the princess? Has she been seen by a physician?"

"No physician, no. Lady Ayako no suke is knowledgeable about herbal medicines. I assure you, Her Highness is well taken care of."

"May I have my letter of introduction back?"

She looked flustered, then refolded it with trembling fingers and passed it back. Akitada tucked it away again. "I'm here incognito. It was thought safest not to cause people to wonder what's amiss. But something *is* amiss, and I intend to get to the bottom of it." He rose, made her a perfunctory bow, and added, "I shall return tomorrow."

Closing the door behind him, he stood outside in the gallery for a moment. He thought he heard her moaning and pacing inside.

So, the princess *was* gone, and Lady Tamba clearly had no idea how to get her back. He wondered what she would do next. He would be back the next day. She could not keep denying him.

A dry cough made him jump. The frail old lady had been crouching around the corner of the pavilion. She was muttering under her breath.

Akitada asked, "I'm sorry, I didn't hear what you said."

She struggled to get up and he gave her a hand. She felt light as a feather. She looked at the wall of the pavilion and shook her head. "I told her! But would she listen? Not her! Never did listen to her mother. Now she weeps. Stupid girl. Nothing worse than raising headstrong daughters." She shuffled past him and went inside.

Akitada would have been amused by the thought that the dragon lady was about to get another lecture from her aged mother, but concern for the princess removed all humor from the situation. He walked away, found his way to the courtyard, and got back on his horse without having the faintest idea what he should do next.

Again the sick fear rose in his stomach that the princess was dead, had been dead perhaps for weeks. If so, what was to be done? It would be for the emperor to decide. An investigation into her death—from illness or murder?—would only achieve the public catastrophe he had been sent to avert. But her absence could not be hidden much longer, and the idea of a permanent substitution was unthinkable. He had failed before he had even begun.

He had not left the Bamboo Palace far behind when he encountered another rider. He recognized him as the same aristocratic male who had passed him on the street in Uji-tachi. On this occasion, he looked, if any-thing, even more distracted. In fact, he looked frantic. Akitada reined in his horse. Anything that seemed out of the ordinary here aroused his curiosity and suspicion.

"Forgive me," he called after the horseman, "are you by chance headed for the Bamboo Palace?"

The young man halted his horse. "Yes, why?" he asked, eyeing Akitada suspiciously.

"I wondered, because I tried to see the princess. I was told she was ill."

"Ill? Then she—" He broke off and looked toward the palace. "I must go," he muttered, and spurred on his horse.

Strange.

Since Akitada could think of nothing else to do with the rest of this day, he decided to find out who this young man was.

∞

According to Junichiro, the young nobleman was a Lord Minamoto, but they were a very large clan. The dwarf had also seemed interested in him. In fact, Akitada had been under the impression that Junichiro had left him to follow this Lord Minamoto. Perhaps the dwarf had only hoped to earn more money from some-one who was clearly much richer than Akitada, but Junichiro kept himself well informed about the local inhabitants and should be able to tell him something beyond the fact that the young man's name was Minamoto and that he was a hunter.

He hoped to find Junichiro hanging about at his inn, but the dwarf was not there. Neither was the pretty maid. The entrance was empty, and the counter unattended. He called for service, but to no avail. From the back he heard voices raised in an angry argument. It sounded like a domestic quarrel between a man and his wife. He was about to leave again to start searching the town for the dwarf when the voices stopped and a door slammed. After a moment, steps approached and the landlady appeared.

She had been weeping and her color was still high from the quarrel with her husband. Akitada had not liked the man and felt sympathetic as she dabbed at her face with a sleeve and muttered an apology.

"I wondered if Junichiro had been by and asked for me," he said.

"I don't know, sir. My daughter was here earlier." Fresh tears welled up.

"Yes. I met her. She was very helpful. Could you ask her if she has seen Junichiro?"

She shook her head. "Keiko's gone. It was only a short visit." It sounded forlorn and final.

"I'm sorry. Well, I'll have a look around. Perhaps I'll find him. If he comes here, will you give him a message that I'm looking for him?"

She pulled herself together. "Yes, of course, sir. I'm very sorry I couldn't be more help. Junichiro may be at one of the other inns. He earns a bit of money offering to show visitors around."

"Yes, I know." He, too, had fallen prey to the dwarf's enterprising methods. "I hope he isn't dishonest."

She smiled a little. "No. Junichiro isn't a thief, but he can be a nuisance, sticking his nose in everybody's business."

Akitada thanked her and went back outside. So Junichiro was inquisitive. No doubt, this was part of his success. He found out things and used the information to earn a few coppers here and there. It was what made him useful to Akitada—and also what would make him dangerous.

As he stood outside the inn, he heard shouts in the distance. In a moment, the people walking on the street hurried aside, leaving the thoroughfare empty. Akitada looked down the street and saw soldiers riding toward him. The one in front carried a flag with the characters for "High Constable" painted in black on white ground. These soldiers, some twenty of them, were followed by an open sedan chair carried by eight strong bearers. In it sat a middle-aged man with a mustache and protruding eyes. He wore the formal clothes of a senior official. The bearers trotted past quickly and people bowed. The high constable ignored them. Another twenty soldiers followed, and then the procession was gone. Everyone returned to the street, and Akitada went in search of Junichiro.

Finding him turned out simpler than he had feared. Junichiro was outside the Golden Dragon, talking to a man and his wife and gesturing along the road. The man listened, then firmly shook his head and drew his wife away with him. Junichiro looked after them, then raised his shoulders resignedly and made for the entrance of the inn.

"Hey, Junichiro!"

The dwarf stopped, saw Akitada, and waddled toward him, grinning. "There you are, master," he cried in his high voice. He grasped Akitada's sleeve and looked up at him. "I've been looking everywhere for you. The girl at the inn said you'd gone to the shrine, so I waited at the bridge, but you didn't come back. Where have you been?"

Akitada wisely did not answer that. He smiled down at the little man. "Just sight-seeing," he said vaguely. "What about you? When you left me yesterday, you were running after Lord Minamoto, weren't you? When I didn't see you at the inn this morning, I was afraid you'd got in trouble over it."

"Oh. No, I'm all right. He's always nice to me. I was hoping for a few coppers, but he didn't have any time for me. He stopped at the Golden Dragon to ask some questions and then rushed away again."

"Hmm, well, I'm glad you're all right. After you left I thought there was something familiar about him." Akitada frowned as if trying to remember. "Minamoto," he mused. "I wonder which Minamoto he would be. You said he comes here to hunt?"

"Yes. He's very rich, that one. He owns a lot of land on the mountain and used to bring his friends along to hunt grouse and pheasants. I think he must be a wonderful bowman."

"Well, that doesn't ring a bell. What is his first name, do you know?"

Of course, the dwarf knew. "Sadamu," he said.

Minamoto Sadamu!

The Shrine Virgin

Akitada said the name aloud a couple of times, and an image rose in his mind, the image of a young boy of eleven with a tear-stained face and a fierce look. "Sadamu?" he said again. Could it be?

Junichiro was all avid interest. "Do you know him? How did you meet?"

"It was a long time ago when he was still a child and grieving for his grandfather. How strange that we should meet again here and now!"

The memory of the grieving child had been joined by that of the child's great uncle, Bishop Sesshin, an imperial prince who had become a monk and had been one of Akitada's benefactors. The imperial link could well be significant under the present circumstances. If so, Sadamu might well be helpful. Akitada was so intrigued by the possibilities that he had become less than cautious about talking to the dwarf, who still waited to hear all about his "master's" memories of the great lord.

Pulling himself together, Akitada smiled at him. "Ah, memories! That was a very long time ago. He would not remember me. Even then he was one of the good people, and now he is a great lord, as you say." He sighed. "Blessings follow the great, while the rest of us must struggle along as best we can. Come, I'll buy you dinner again if you can recommend some other delicacy."

The other delicacy was fried abalone and the meal elicited two further pieces of information. One of these was the location of Lord Minamoto's hunting lodge; the other concerned the friendly maid at his inn. Junichiro had watched her departure earlier in the day and said she had been weeping. "Had a fight with her mother," he explained.

"How do you know?" Akitada was surprised by this because he had just spoken with the mother who had seemed sad that her daughter had left.

"Because I heard the mother shout after her not to come back."

This was puzzling, but Akitada was eager to be free of Junichiro by then. He had made up his mind to renew his acquaintance with Sadamu and did not want Junichiro or anyone else to know.

10

Forgotten Favors

Akitada and Junichiro parted at the door to the River Palace. Inside, the ill-tempered innkeeper was signing in new guests.

He seemed in passable humor tonight and even gave Akitada a nod. "Staying another night, sir?" he asked in his rough voice.

"Yes, and possibly longer."

The man bared his teeth in what Akitada took to be a smile. "I don't blame you, sir. I'd like to be so lucky myself. There are some fine girls in Uji-tachi." Seeing Akitada's face, he added quickly, "No offense. Just wishing the gentleman a good time."

"Thank you. Have some tea sent to my room."

Akitada could not imagine what the pretty girl's mother could have seen in that lout who could barely write. Perhaps his skills lay elsewhere.

In his room, he sat down by the window overlooking the slow-flowing river and thought about the missing princess. Unless she was still in the Bamboo Palace, as her lady-in-waiting claimed, she must have left without being noticed. Perhaps such a thing was possible after dark. The guards probably never left the main gates to the compound. But in that case she would have done so of her own free will. And then? Where would she have gone? And on foot? It was unthinkable.

Again the image of the dead girl at the river rose in his memory. A young woman wandering about in the forest in this area could have run into serious trouble. What had Junichiro called those highwaymen? The prowlers. Robbers who worked after dark taking the money of incautious visitors. What they might have done with a young woman walking alone was unthinkable.

He reminded himself to ask Lieutenant Matsuura about the prowlers.

His tea arrived, brought by his hostess herself. She, too, looked more cheerful. She had added a sweet rice cake to his order, and he thanked her. Still puzzled by the sudden departure of her daughter, he asked where the girl lived.

A shadow passed over her face. "Keiko works for a family in Mikawa. She was here only for a short visit."

"I see. Thank you, Mrs. Inabe."

The Shrine Virgin

Alone again, he sipped his tea, leaving the rice cake for later. When he thought it late enough, he took out his writing utensils, rubbed some ink, and wrote a brief note, which he tucked in his sleeve. Then he put on his sword, borrowed a lantern from the inn, and set out for the Minamoto hunting lodge. He tried to remember Lieutenant Matsuura's map. The distance was significant, but he thought it should be manageable.

His recent thoughts about the prowlers made him uneasy on his journey across Uji Bridge, past the now deserted shrine and into the large forest that clothed the side of the mountain. He was glad of his sword, but wondered how many men he might have to defend himself against. It seemed the prowlers worked in bands.

Somewhat to his surprise he reached the rustic building inside its cedar fence without encountering anyone or getting lost. The gate was closed, but he saw a dim aura of light on the other side and used his fist to pound on the wooden boards. For a long time nothing happened and he knocked again. Then a door slammed somewhere inside, and wheezing voice cried, "I'm coming, I'm coming! What's the rush?"

The gate creaked open, and a bent old man with a thin white beard held up a lantern and peered up at him. "Who are you?" he demanded. "What do you want? It's nighttime."

"I'm an old friend of your master's. I've come to pay him a visit."

"I don't recognize you." The old man stepped closer. "No. Never saw you before in my life. You'd better run along. His lordship's in a very bad mood."

Akitada took the note from his sleeve. "Take this to him. I'll wait here."

The old gatekeeper took it and slammed the gate shut again. His retreating steps were accompanied by muttered complaints about disturbing honest people in the middle of the night.

It was not long before the steps returned and the gate opened again.

"Come in, then," the old man said ungraciously. "It's getting so a man can't get any sleep around here. Comings and goings. Day and night."

Akitada said nothing. He looked around curiously. It was too dark to make out much, but the single dwelling appeared of comfortable size, though it had more the appearance of a hermitage for one rather than a place to entertain groups of friends. There was a modest stable and another small building, perhaps the place where the gatekeeper had hoped to lay his head. But this was all, and all was of the simplest materials, unfinished wood, bark roofing, and a courtyard of plain dirt and trees.

They climbed the steps to the veranda slowly, the old man wheezing badly. Once there, he pointed to the simple door. "Go in," he said and turned back.

Akitada was beginning to wonder if he had indeed the correct Minamoto Sadamu. First names often ran in families, and the Minamoto clan was large. More to the point, the boy Sadamu had had imperial blood, recent imperial blood. He had been removed from the succession by only one generation. It seemed unlikely that he would live here.

He opened the door and hesitated on the threshold. The room he looked at was a large open area. It had a rustic fire pit without a fire, and the walls he could see were covered with hunting paraphernalia. He had never seen so many bows except in the armory of the Uesugi fortress in Echigo. There were also basket quivers of feathered arrows, and many knives, probably used for dealing with dead prey.

In the middle of the room stood the tall young man Akitada had seen twice before. If he had not been young, Akitada might have thought him seriously ill. He was unnaturally pale; his eyes glittered feverishly and were red-rimmed, and there were dark shadows under them. In his hands was a woman's fan that he handled absentmindedly. Akitada guessed that he wasted his health with late nights, probably with some of the women of Uji-tachi. He searched in vain for the features of the boy Sadamu.

But it was so after all. This elegant young nobleman was Sadamu.

He said in a voice that was both tight and sharp, "Are you really Professor Sugawara? But it cannot be. What are you doing here? Why have you come?"

Clearly Lord Minamoto was under some sort of strain. Akitada could hear it in his voice and the curiously unfriendly greeting. Out of his confused set of questions Akitada cautiously chose to answer one. "I'm paying a visit to the shrine and heard you were here. How are you, my lord?"

Minamoto held the fourth rank, well above Akitada's rank. Given his reaction, Akitada began to regret his decision to pay this unannounced visit. Still, he had been fond of the boy Sadamu, and the adult would surely remember the service he had done him.

The young nobleman came closer. "Yes," he said in a tone of wonder, "You really are my old professor. After all those years! You have changed." He suddenly recalled himself. ""Forgive me, but your sudden visit has confused me a little. I, er, expected someone else. Will you take a cup of wine?"

Akitada also felt confused. He was not sure what he had hoped for in meeting his former pupil again, but it had not occurred to him that he would be unwelcome. The comment that Sadamu expected someone else made it clear that he should not have come here uninvited. And the reference to an "old professor" was not only less than friendly but positively humiliating. For a moment, Akitada saw himself as a seedy elderly academic who was seeking favors from a wealthy and powerful nobleman because he had once been his teacher.

He stiffened immediately and said, "No, thank you. I hope you forgive the untimely intrusion. In my surprise I made the mistake of rushing off immediately to pay my respects. My apologies." He bowed and turned to leave.

"Wait!" Lord Minamoto sounded distracted. "Please," he said, waving the hand with the fan, "don't go away angry. Soon, perhaps tomorrow, I'll call on you. You are staying in town?"

Only slightly mollified, Akitada nodded. "I'm staying in the River Palace. You will have to ask for Yoshimine Takatsuna."

Minamoto stared at him blankly. Good, he thought. Let him wonder what I'm up to. He will not call on me. That was merely a polite lie. Our paths have diverged. He is a great lord now and has no time for me. Well, let it be so. I don't need him.

The gatekeeper was waiting for him. Glaring at Akitada, he said, "Old friends, eh? Looks like he didn't remember you."

Akitada flushed with anger and opened his mouth to reprove the old man. But he bit his lip, reminding himself that he must play an ordinary and humble man a while longer.

11

A Face from the Past

Tora returned to the tribunal to share his information about the Owari merchant with Saburo. "Clearly there is something illegal going on and it's big," he summed up. "The master mentioned his concern about local pirates to me and this is just the opportunity to teach them a lesson. I'm thinking of using the provincial guard and some conscripted fellows used to fighting and go down the coast to find them. And if we find the stolen goods, all the better, though I still don't trust that merchant."

Saburo had listened attentively and now pursed his lips. "The merchant does sound like a suspicious character. That claim of losses strikes me as excessive. Have you investigated him? Is he regularly involved in such shipments?"

Tora said impatiently, "I'll look into it, but the pirates are more urgent. If we don't go after them now, they'll sell the goods and we won't have any proof."

"Tora, you cannot conscript people for such an undertaking. Only the governor can do that. It will have to wait until the master returns. Meanwhile, I'll send some letters to Owari and Totomi and ask them for information about Takanami. What did you say his first name is?"

"It's Masayoshi. But, Saburo, we can't wait for the master. We have to be quick. If I can't conscript, I'll hire some extra men."

"You have the money?"

Tora glared. "Of course not. But you do. You're sitting on the provincial treasury."

Saburo drew himself up. "I shall not issue funds without the master's approval."

Tora muttered something crude and stalked out, slamming the door behind him.

Saburo shook his head, sighed, and returned to his labors.

The next morning, he still felt troubled by the disagreement with Tora. Their having been brought to Mikawa together had made him happy. They had begun to explore the town and share their evening rice and a cup of wine or two in the local establishments.

As soon as he was dressed, he went in search of Tora. He found him in the quarters he shared with his family, in full spate of complaint to his wife Hanae.

"There you are," he greeted Saburo with a glare. "Have you changed your mind?"

Saburo sighed. "Look, Tora," he said, "you've got to understand. I can't just reach into the provincial money chest whenever I feel like it. I would become a thief. Remember, he who touches vermilion gets his hands red."

Tora was outraged by this. It did not help that proverbial wisdom had been the method used by old Seimei to restrain the young and rash Tora in years past. He snarled, "Are you calling me a thief? That's it. Leave my house."

The house was not really his, but Saburo, deeply shocked, turned to leave. Hanae cried out, "Oh, Tora, how could you say such a thing? Please, Saburo, do not take offense. He didn't mean it."

Saburo looked at her sadly. "I must go, Hanae. Good bye."

That evening, he left the tribunal alone and walked into town as the sun set over Ise Bay. It had been a beautiful day, if somewhat hot, and the sea in the evening sun was a beautiful sight, but the quarrel with his friend had upset him deeply.

Tora had changed. There was an impatience about everything he did or thought about doing. And he often looked distracted and unhappy. This was not like the Tora of the past, who had been unfailingly cheerful and optimistic. Saburo decided to forgive him and to be very gentle with him in the future. Something was not right. It might be as well to speak to the master about it.

But Tora's moodiness could have something to do with what had happened in Otsu last year. And that he could not share with the master. That was a secret only he and Tora knew about, because they had disobeyed a direct order and gone into the mountains to kill four murderous *sohei*, one of whom had tortured Saburo many years ago, leaving him disfigured and an outcast. The bond of secrecy placed special obligations on both, and Saburo knew that Tora would eventually come to apologize.

Meanwhile he was on his own on this beautiful evening. He strolled about, eyeing various establishments that seemed to promise a good meal. He rejected several that looked too expensive and settled for a very modest place near the harbor. Appetizing smells of seafood emanated from inside where he saw ordinary laborers, porters, fishermen, and boatmen enjoying a noisy meal. He liked what he saw and smelled and entered.

Saburo was very careful with his money. Not only had he been abjectly poor at one time and had disliked the state extremely, but he now had his mother to support in the capital. He found a seat, ordered, and looked around him. At first he thought he was the only customer who was not in work clothes, though his blue robe was indeed what he worked in. Then he saw another man who wore a robe rather than short pants and a shirt like the harbor workers. His robe was brown, plain, and not particularly clean, and his short gray hair stood up stiffly while Saburo's was long, tied in back, and twisted up neatly. The man in the brown robe was half turned away from him as he talked to two young boatmen sitting across from him. The boatmen had a rough and dangerous look about them.

There was something curiously familiar about the man in brown. As Saburo ate his fish stew, which was fresh and good, he watched the other man, racking his brain where he might have seen him.

The hair finally gave him a clue. It looked a lot like the hair of a former priest, growing unchecked after years of having been shaved off. So this man had been a priest or a monk.

Saburo's past was filled with monks, and the memories were mostly bad. He did not feel good about this man either but had no clue who he was until the three finished their meal, and the man in brown got to his feet and turned.

He recognized him immediately.

He had been a *sohei*, though not quite like the brutish characters he and Tora had encountered on Mount Hiei. This man had been trained with Saburo on Mount Koya. He had been one of their warriors while Saburo, being smaller, weaker, but much more agile, had become a spy for them. The man-in-brown's name had been Hozo then, and he had had a reputation for extorting money and seducing the womenfolk of local peasants. In those days, Saburo had still kept faith in the way naïve, young men will, and yet it was Saburo they had sacrificed in the end, while Hozo remained, garnering honors and titles in the process.

Life had a way of stripping men of their dreams and their trust.

But now it appeared that Hozo, too, had left the religious life and had fallen on hard times. Nothing about his appearance and companions suggested that he had changed much. And Saburo did not trust him. Where Hozo was, there was trouble of some sort.

He paid quickly and followed him.

It was getting dark outside and lights were blinking on here and there. In the flashes of illumination from some doorway or other, Saburo saw that Hozo's brown robe was not only dirty but torn in places. And his boots had also seen better days. Given Hozo's appearance, he was surprised when the fellow walked into the best inn in Komachi.

He reappeared almost instantly, being seen out by a man who was most likely the innkeeper. Hozo shook a fist at him and then made himself comfortable, leaning against the inn's wall. Saburo shrank into the shadows between two buildings and waited.

It was not long before a fat man appeared, looked around, and then went to join Hozo. They spoke briefly, and the fat man passed something to Hozo, then went back inside. Hozo tucked the small bundle inside his brown robe and started walking again.

Saburo was torn for a moment. Should he find out who the fat man was or follow Hozo? He decided on the latter. The meeting at the inn had raised a number of interesting possibilities in his mind. Could the fat man be Tora's merchant? Could the tough-looking boatmen Hozo had shared a meal with be the boatmen from the merchant's boat? Surely the fat man had passed Hozo money. The parcel had looked a little like a money purse. Or of course it could all be nothing, but given what Saburo knew of Hozo, his former compatriot definitely had been up to no good.

Hozo strode along purposefully and they soon left the lights of the town's center behind. If Saburo was not much mistaken, Hozo was headed for the coast road that followed the bay southward. He was beginning to wonder what he was getting into when they left the houses behind and came into the open. There was no traffic on the road at this time, just the two of them walking. Hozo was bound to realize he was being followed. Saburo slowed to put more distance between them, but eventually even that was inadequate. He stopped, ready to turn around and go home.

Then he saw it in the distance: a small point of light, very faint and blinking on and off, as if hidden behind trees that moved in the sea breeze. He strained his eyes but saw nothing. Even Hozo had disappeared from sight.

Saburo sat down beside the road to rest and wait. The walk had been brisk and he was tired. He was irritated, because Hozo had appeared to be in better shape. Saburo's life had changed drastically since he had entered his master's service. He now spent almost all of his time bent over paperwork. He grimaced. It was time to get some exercise. Perhaps Tora could be prevailed upon to teach him some of his skills with the fighting stick. There had been a time in Saburo's youth when he had been passably good with the *naginata*, a weapon that was essentially a fighting stick with a sword at its end. It had been a long time ago. And he had never had the strength of the other *sohei.*

With a sigh, he got back on his feet and walked toward the blinking light. In time he could make out a black mass of trees. The light was in the center of these. That signaled some human habitation, and soon Saburo saw what looked like a sizable walled and gated compound. He studied this cautiously from a distance, never getting close enough to alert some dog. In the process, he now realized that it was a large estate with several smaller peasant dwellings scattered in the vicinity.

Saburo had not been in Mikawa long enough to have familiarized himself with its geography or inhabitants, but he marked the place in his mind in order to find out what it was and who it belonged to.

Of course, Hozo could have kept walking on the coast road, but he did not think so. He thought he had come here, or possibly to one of the smaller buildings.

In any case, his pursuit had not been a total loss. He now had something to tell Tora, and the tale would reestablish them in their old, comfortable friendship.

12

Junichiro's Talent

A kitada was still angry and humiliated the next morning when he rose before dawn. He had made the return journey safely but painfully. It had turned out to be a long walk after all. Most of the night, he had tossed and turned, berating himself for his mistake in paying this embarrassing visit.

It did not help his mood that he was no closer to finding out anything about the princess. In the end, he decided to return to the Bamboo Palace and insist that Lady Tamba produce her. And while he was at it, he intended to ask why Lord Minamoto had called at the palace the day before.

Perhaps out of pique over his reception by Minamoto, he began to toy with a notion that the young nobleman was somehow involved in the situation. Given the lax discipline at the palace, and the fact that Minamoto was just the sort of young man to break a young woman's heart, he thought the theory was not unreasonable. Proving it and producing the young woman was another matter though.

As he was leaving, the reception area was empty, but someone had opened the door and swept the path. The sound of his steps brought Mrs. Inabe bustling from her backroom.

"Good morning, sir. You're early. Can I fix you a bowl of rice gruel before you leave?"

"No, thank you, Mrs. Inabe. I couldn't sleep and decided to take a walk. Do you happen to know where Junichiro lives?"

"He has a little shed on the river, about half a mile from Uji Bridge, sir. But it's not much, and I'm sure he'll turn up here soon."

Akitada thanked her and set out. It was getting light and the first birds were already awake. The morning was pleasantly cool and the exercise drove the fog of dejection from his mind. By the time he saw a derelict-looking wooden structure leaning over the river bank, he was in a better mood. The small building tilted out over the water, and for a moment Akitada thought it was slipping. He sped up and reached the door, or rather a torn curtain covering the entrance.

"Junichiro?" he called out, feeling a little guilty for waking the dwarf before the sun was up. He need not have worried; the curtain was pulled aside and Junichi-ro's round head with its spiky red hair appeared. "Is that you, master?" he asked, blinking. "What's up?" He stepped out and peered at Akitada in surprise.

"Sorry to come so early. I couldn't sleep and wondered if you might like to share my morning rice."

The little man's face lit up. "You came to buy me my morning rice?" he asked, his eyes moistening. "That's very kind, very kind indeed."

Akitada guessed he had never been treated to a meal in this fashion, and chuckled. "I hate eating alone and I want to talk. Did I wake you?"

"No, master. I was looking over my drawings before taking them to town to sell to visitors."

"Drawings?" Akitada asked.

"Come, I'll show you." The dwarf hesitated for a moment, looking from Akitada to the low lintel over his doorway. "Best go around," he said, and hopped down to take a narrow path to the river.

Akitada followed, intrigued by the dwarf's dwelling and his "drawings", whatever they were. They reached the back of the little shed, and he saw a veranda overhanging the river. Against its simple railings leaned a number of fishing poles. And at the end of the path, a small boat bobbed in the current.

Junichiro saw him looking and said with a laugh, "I eat a lot of fish."

He took some steps up to the veranda. Akitada eyed them dubiously. Since he had not brought a change of clothes, he could not afford a tumble into the Isuzu River.

"It's strong enough," said Junichiro, again guessing his thoughts. "A carpenter helped me, and he was a fat man. If it supported him, you shouldn't have a worry."

Akitada climbed up, and there on the boards lay a small pile of paper, weighted down with a rock. Junichiro took off the rock and spread out the sheets. Each of them was a drawing, and they were all different. Some were pictures of deer grazing, some of fish jumping in water, some of ducks flying up from the river. Akitada saw a fox, two doves on a flowering branch, and several drawings of spotted puppies. Junichiro had drawn the outlines with black ink, and then he had used colors to fill in the pictures, preferably bright ones. Each sheet also had a picture of *torii*, the red-painted gateways to the shrines of the *kami*.

Junichiro pointed to one of the *torii*. "That's to show it's from Ise shrine," he said. "The customer gets a pretty picture and a reminder of where he's been, you see."

"Yes. I see. Very clever. These are very good, Junichiro. Do you sell a lot?"

"A few. They're only a couple of coppers. Do you really like them?"

"Yes. Very much. I think they are worth more."

Junichiro chewed his lip. "Maybe, but then I won't sell as many. Take one! Anyone you like. There's no charge."

"Thank you, but I shall insist on paying." Akitada spread out the drawings to make his selection. He had rather liked the deer, but there had been a frog with an amusing expression that had reminded him of someone. He searched through the drawings, found the frog and recognized the merchant at his inn. Strange how that man kept popping up. He said with a smile, "He looks like a guest at my inn."

Junichiro chortled. "Murata. I thought of him when I was drawing the frog. He's not a nice man."

Akitada had already deduced that Murata had resisted the dwarf's solicitations. Perhaps he had also called him names. "I didn't much like him either. What is he doing staying in The River Palace if he's so wealthy?"

The dwarf put a finger to his nose. "Maybe he has friends that don't like to be seen going into those other places."

"Ah!" This fit nicely with Akitada's own observation of Murata talking to the two hoodlums at the harbor. "You mean criminals?"

"Let's just say I wouldn't want to meet them on a dark night in the woods."

Akitada had unearthed a new drawing from the bottom of the pile. Unlike the other images, this one was of a young woman. "Who is this?"

The dwarf snatched the picture from his hand. "Nobody. I was just doodling."

"No," said Akitada. You took pains with this one. Is it the murdered girl? It looks a bit like her. Only in the drawing her hair is loose and her face is painted. Did you know her well, Junichiro?"

But the dwarf would not meet his eyes. He sat looking down at the picture, his round, ugly face a mask of sorrow.

Akitada waited a moment, then said, "You said she was nice. Junichiro, if you know something, and I think you do, you need to tell the police. If you know who killed her, you may be in danger."

Junichiro looked up then. His eyes were full of tears. "Thank you, master, for caring about me. She cared about me, too. That's why I said she was nice. But I know nothing. Only, I hope whoever did this to her burns in hell forever."

"Why is she dressed like this in your picture?"

"I don't know. I went by her place, and she was putting on these fine clothes, and her face was made up like the faces of the girls working in the brothels. I was afraid she'd started working there and begged her not to do it, but she said she wasn't." He shook his head. "Only she must have been, because now she's dead."

Akitada found the grazing deer and added them to the frog. He offered to buy the girl's picture, too, but the dwarf would not part with it. He did accept a small piece of silver for the two drawings with many thanks, and then they walked back to town for some rice gruel with pickled plums.

∞

A few hours later, Akitada arrived back at the Bamboo Palace. He had rented a horse again because his legs still hurt from the night before. On this occasion, it struck him that Lord Minamoto's hunting lodge was much closer to the palace than to town. He wondered why the young man had not walked.

Of course, the bigger question was what business he had had there in the first place.

Akitada was admitted as before. The young guards in their resplendent uniforms cared little about his purpose there. In the guardhouse a game of dice was in progress, and while the gate guards had not joined it, they hovered near the door to watch.

But next, matters became more difficult. A servant appeared and informed him that Lady Tamba was indisposed and could see no one. Akitada nodded, then stepped around the servant and entered the main hall. The servant ran after him, plucking at his sleeve. They were out of sight of the guards by now and Akitada stopped.

"Look," he said, "I know you are simply doing your job, but you will not stop me. And you must not pull my sleeve. Understood?"

The servant shrank back, and Akitada found his way to the pavilion where he had last spoken to Lady Tamba. There he paused at the door. The servant, looking anxious, was at his heels. "Announce me. You may claim that I forced my way in."

The servant scratched at the door. Lady Tamba's voice, sounding quite strong, asked him to enter. He did and stood aside for Akitada to follow. "The gentleman forced his way in, madam," he said.

Lady Tamba was not ill. She was partaking of what looked like an ample meal of rice gruel and fruit. With her were her aged mother and a maid.

Lady Tamba dropped her bowl of gruel. The glutinous white paste spilled across her tray table and the skirt of her gown. The maid cried out and scurried over to clean up the mess.

"You!" snapped Lady Tamba, pushing the maid aside. "How dare you! I shall complain to His Majesty.

Get out! You're not welcome here! And you!" She turned her eyes on the shrinking servant. "You will go tell them at the gate that this person shall never be admitted again!" She paused. "And then you're dismissed!"

The servant muttered something rude and disappeared.

Akitada suppressed his laughter at the scene. He was here on serious business in spite of this woman's ridiculous behavior.

He approached with a bow just as the old gentlewoman said, "Stupid girl! You're making things worse!"

For a moment, he thought she had addressed the maid, who had difficulties removing the sticky paste from her mistress's gown, but he saw she was looking at her daughter. He said, "Indeed, Lady Tamba, you *are* making things a good deal worse for yourself. I am here on His Majesty's orders. That means you will cooperate or find yourself and your family in serious trouble."

"You hear that?" demanded her mother. "There goes your husband's promotion."

Lady Tamba blinked. She glanced at her mother, then at Akitada. "Very well," she said irritably. "I didn't mean to be rude. It was the shock. You see the commotion you've caused by your sudden arrival." She gestured to her gown and the kneeling maid. I must change. Then I'll speak to you."

Akitada bowed. "I shall wait outside," he said politely, wondering if she intended to flee the palace altogether to avoid the interview. He decided against it. Her mother was a sensible woman and would not permit it.

The Shrine Virgin

Outside her pavilion he leaned on the railing and looked out over the garden. It resembled many gardens of great houses he had visited. An artificial stream meandered among mossy banks, while shrubs and trees formed small groves, and paths appeared and disappeared among them. Summer was nearly over and there were few flowers left, but the scent of pines and cryptomerias perfumed the air. As he enjoyed the view and the fresh air that would become too warm for comfort later in the day, a young woman appeared on the path that skirted the pavilion. She saw him and stopped in consternation. She was a pretty creature and, by her attire, a young noblewoman rather than a maid. They regarded each other, and she raised a dainty hand to her mouth and giggled. He smiled back. She made a charming picture in her pink and pale green silks and reminded him of Yukiko, filling him with sudden longing for his wife.

He said, "Good morning, my lady. You are a delightful apparition in your beautiful garden."

Her eyes twinkling, she made him a very small bow. "Forgive the intrusion, please. It's very embarrassing, but I didn't know that Lady Tamba had . . . an admirer."

Well, perhaps it was a strange situation to find a man outside Lady Tamba's pavilion so early in the morning. It could make people assume that he was the lady's lover, departing after a night in her arms. The notion made him laugh.

She giggled again and came a little closer. "I'm Ayako," she said, "and you?"

"Lady Ayako, it isn't seemly for you to demand the name of a man who is a total stranger. In fact, you shouldn't be here at all talking to me. What would Her Highness say?"

She had stopped below him and was looking up. "She would order you to give your name." She cocked her head. "What business do you have with Lady Tamba?"

Though she was pretty, Akitada began to find her behavior extremely forward. It was probably another example of the reprehensible laxness that characterized the princess's household.

"I thought you already knew my business," he said lightly.

"Nonsense. You're far too young and good-looking to have fallen for the old bat."

"Flattery, Lady Ayako? Surely that's beneath you."

"I think you came to see the princess. Am I right?"

Before he could answer, the door of the pavilion opened and the maid appeared, her arms full of stained silk and empty gruel bowls. Lady Ayako ducked into the shrubbery, and the maid said, "Lady Tachibana said you may go in now, sir."

So Lady Tamba's mother was a Tachibana—like His Majesty's secretary. It explained a good deal.

13

Lady Tamba's Confession

He saw immediately that the situation had changed. Lady Tamba's face was streaked with tears. Her fan, held in shaking fingers, could not hide the ravages they had left behind. Her mother sat beside her, looking grim-faced. No one else was present.

Akitada approached warily and cleared his throat. The only result of this was more tearful agitation from Lady Tamba and a sound like "pshaw," from the mother.

"Have you changed your mind, Lady Tamba?" Akitada asked.

This produced a shaking of the head. Lady Tamba's mother pursed her lips and poked her daughter in the side. "Tell him," she commanded.

"I can't, Mother," wailed Lady Tamba.

"You must. You've been very foolish, but it's all over now. Tell him."

"I . . . I . . . was not quite truthful," murmured the daughter, hiding behind her fan.

"In what way, madam?" Akitada asked coldly.

"About Princess Takahime. She's not ill."

"I see. Then I must speak to her."

"You can't." She wailed, "Oh, Amida, how could this happen?"

Afraid of what he was about to hear, Akitada asked, "What happened?"

The old lady made another sound of disgust. "She means the princess isn't here. She's gone."

Finally here was the truth, but it offered only confirmation of disaster. "Where has she gone and why?" Akitada demanded.

"The silly girl thinks she's fallen in love," snapped the old one.

Akitada frowned at her for such blatant disrespect for the emperor's sister. "Princess Takahime is the consecrated Ise Virgin," he said pointedly. "She cannot fall in love." He was aware of how ridiculous this must sound and flushed a little.

Old Lady Tachibana gave a mocking cackle. "You're as foolish as that priest. The girl is young and she met a good-looking man. What else should she do but fall in love with him. People don't change just because they serve the gods. She decided she did not want to be the Virgin any longer,"—here she gave another short cackle—"and left. There you have it, the whole dirty tale. Now leave us alone."

"Alas, I cannot." Akitada located a cushion and seated himself. Both women glared at him. "Now," he said, "you will answer some questions and the first concerns the young man. Who is he?"

They looked at each other. This time it was Lady Tamba who spoke. "I cannot be blamed. It was the most harmless visit. How could I know what would happen? He came to pay his respects to his cousin. A family member! It was quite proper, and she was never alone with him."

Akitada stared at her. He was beginning to have a troubling suspicion and was getting very angry. Before he could insist on a name, the old lady said, "He's the Minamoto who has the lodge up the road. They grew up together. My daughter's only mistake—though mind you, it was a very stupid mistake, as I told her—was to think them a charming couple and let them spend time together."

Akitada said, "I know him. Do I assume she is now with him?"

Again they looked at each other, and Lady Tamba started sniffling again. Her mother said, "She was."

"She was? What do you mean? Where is she now?"

Lady Tamba burst into tears and wailed, "We don't know."

Akitada sat aghast. After a moment he asked, half hoping, "How do you know that she is no longer with Lord Minamoto?"

"Because he came here yesterday to ask if she had returned."

And there it was, the full disaster. For a moment, Akitada considered reporting the truth to the imperial secretary and returning home. Let the court decide what was to be done with a pair of wayward lovers.

But the moment passed and pity for the princess, lost somewhere or dead, took over. And his anger returned. He was angry with the foolish women who had allowed the affair to blossom, and furious with Minamoto who had seduced an Ise Virgin, offending thereby both the gods and his emperor, and had next allowed her to become lost, the gods knew where.

He got to his feet. "I don't know what will happen next," he said heavily. "The first step is to find Her Highness. I shall come back if there is news or if I have further questions. Meanwhile you are not to speak to anyone about any of this. Do you understand?"

Lady Tamba nodded tearfully. Her mother said, "I hope you have the brains to find her, young man. And be quick about it."

∞

A seething Akitada strode out of the pavilion, slamming the door behind him. He was going to confront Minamoto to tell him what he thought of him. Then he would obtain the sordid details of how the princess could have become lost without Minamoto's knowledge. Preoccupied with thoughts of the culpable lovers, he did not notice right away the light steps and silken rustle that followed him. When he did, he turned.

It was Lady Ayako.

She ran up to him quite boldly and said, "Meet me after dark at the Tanoe shrine. I'll tell you how it happened." And as quickly as she had come, she turned with a flutter of silken gowns and was gone again.

Akitada looked after her, shaking his head. He wanted to know what this was about, but a meeting at a dark shrine somewhere in the forest was not advisable. What possessed this young woman to conceive of such a thing? Apparently, she had as little care for her safety as the princess had had.

There was nothing he could do about it, so he got back on his horse and rode to Minamoto's hunting lodge.

There, his frustration grew further. The old gate-keeper opened the gate. It was daytime on this occasion, but the old man seemed even more put out by the visit than he had the night before. He glared at Akitada and snapped, "No use coming here again! There's nobody home. Go away!"

He was closing the gate again, but Akitada urged his horse forward. The old man stumbled back and fell as the gate flew open. Cursing under his breath, Akitada swung himself out of the saddle and went to help him.

"Sorry, old man," he said. "Are you hurt?"

The gatekeeper glared. "What do you care? Ride an old man down like so much cord wood. The young don't care."

Akitada extended a hand to help him up, but the old man waved it aside. "Don't touch me, you brute. Do what you want. I'm too old for this job. I told him to get someone else, but he doesn't listen. He just looks and mutters and rides away again."

Akitada sighed. "Where did your master go?"

"You know as much as I do." The old man felt his hip and grimaced. "Probably more." With infinite care he began to struggle to his feet, failing twice before Akitada grasped him under the arms and stood him up. He stood swaying for a moment, then angrily brushed off Akitada's supporting arm. Without another word, he limped to his small house.

Akitada took the steps to the lodge, calling out for Minamoto. He got no answer and pushed open the door to look in. The room was empty.

He returned, walked his horse out through the gate and closed it behind him, then he got back in the saddle and rode to Uji-tachi.

So far he had been foiled or hindered at every step he took. Most of it was due to human stupidity and carelessness. Even the elderly seemed to lack the good sense and probity that demanded respect. In a very sour humor he reached the village and rode to the police station. Since his identity was already known to the lieutenant, he might take him into his confidence—up to a point, for the princess's disappearance was not his to divulge.

But here he ran into more trouble. According to a constable, Lieutenant Matsuura was dealing with the murder of another young woman.

The Shrine Virgin

Akitada's heart lurched in his chest. Had he reached the end of his search already? Was the princess dead? The sense of failure nearly overwhelmed him.

Taking a big breath, he asked, "Can you tell me about it, Constable?"

"What's to tell?" said the man, giving Akitada a suspicious look. "What's it to you anyway? Have you lost a daughter?" He laughed. "Or maybe your girlfriend?"

Age becomes flexible when you are past forty. Lady Tamba's mother had called him "young man," but this young, and very rude, constable thought him old enough to have a grown daughter.

Akitada gave him a cold look. "What's your name, Constable? I'd like to tell Lieutenant Matsuura about your helpfulness. Tell him Yoshimine Takatsuna is here to see him."

The constable flushed. "We're a bit busy. If you have any information, I'll take it."

"I'll give any information I have to the lieutenant."

"I'll see what I can do, but we already know who the victim is."

This gave Akitada some hope. The police were unlikely to have seen the princess closely enough to recognize her. And there would surely be more excitement in that case.

"She's a local girl then?"

The constable nodded. "Seems like our girls are forever running away and getting into trouble."

At that moment, the door of the station opened and a wild-eyed Mrs. Inabe rushed in. "Where is she?" she cried. "Are you sure it's Keiko? Where did you find her? Amida, please make them be wrong!"

The constable took one look at her, said, "One moment, Mrs. Inabe," and left the room.

In shocked surprise, Akitada said, "Mrs. Inabe, is it your daughter they found?"

She turned a tear-stained face to him. "They said it was her, but maybe they're wrong. Keiko left early yesterday."

The constable returned. "Sorry about your loss, Mrs. Inabe. The lieutenant says you can come and have a look."

The woman wailed and swayed against Akitada, who caught her. He felt very sorry for her, but even sorrier for the pretty and cheerful girl. "What happened?" he asked the constable again, but the man merely shook his head, and walked Mrs. Inabe out of the room.

Akitada remained, thinking about the murders and the missing virgin. It seemed unlikely that these things could be unrelated. He hoped they were, but something told him that it had become important to find out about the deaths of the two young women.

So he waited.

14

Another Murder

Akitada was still trying to puzzle out the connection between the murders and the lost Virgin when the constable returned without Mrs. Inabe. His manners slightly improved, he told Akitada, "The lieutenant said you can come, too, sir."

Akitada followed him through the building and out into a graveled exercise yard. A little group of people stood in the center around something on the ground. As he got closer, Akitada saw Mrs. Inabe fall to her knees. She was sobbing loudly. The lieutenant bent to say something to her. An elderly man in a stained black gown stood beside them.

And then they parted and Akitada saw the figure on the ground.

She was still pretty, but her hair was disheveled and her head lay at an unnatural angle. The bright eyes were closed, and her lips would never smile again. They gaped in a grimace of pain.

"I'm so sorry," Akitada said, and meant it. "She greeted me the morning she left and made me feel welcome. She was both lovely and kind."

Lieutenant Matsuura nodded. "Yes. I knew Keiko before she went away to work in Mikawa. She was always laughing. What a pity."

Mrs. Inabe wailed, "Oh, I should never have told her to leave! It's my fault and all for the sake of that drunken lout. I've been a bad mother! I'll be punished in the hell of burning fires."

After a brief silence, the lieutenant said, "She was found in the woods, in some tall grass growing along the path to Oyodo. The shortcut. We think she ran into a band of prowlers."

Akitada frowned. "Didn't she leave in the morning sometime, Mrs. Inabe?"

The woman nodded. "In the morning. Oh, why didn't I believe her? She was always a good girl." She rocked back and forth in her grief. "Aiih! Who did this? What animal killed my baby?"

The Lieutenant glanced at Akitada, then said, "We don't know, Mrs. Inabe. We were hoping you could tell us."

She looked at him angrily. "Me? How would I know? She was fine when she left. I had nothing to do with this. You'd better find out who did it. Time you earned your pay. But I suppose the whores are more important than a decent girl."

"You know that isn't true," the lieutenant protested.

Akitada bent to study the dead girl's neck. It was heavily bruised and marked. You could almost make out the imprint of fingers. "She was strangled?" he asked.

The seedy man in black with an unfortunate chin beard consisting of some pitiful strands of black hair, answered, "Perhaps strangled, but she died from a broken neck, sir."

"This is our coroner," Lieutenant Matsuura said. "Kuroda. He's the pharmacist in Uji-tachi."

Akitada nodded a greeting. "Yoshimine."

The coroner-pharmacist made him a small bow. "I'm afraid she was also . . ." he glanced at Mrs. Inabe, and added softly, "interfered with."

"They raped her? Oh, the animals," she cried.

At this point, the constable appeared again, bringing with him the father of the girl.

He glowered at all of them, then took one look. "So it's true. They got our girl." He bent to put an arm around his wife. "Come, Setsuko! Come home with me. You can't do anything here."

She allowed herself to be pulled up and buried her head in his chest, weeping.

He told the lieutenant, "Find out who did this and I'll kill him personally. I'm taking my wife home. We've still got a business to run, and you've got your work to do."

They walked away together, he murmuring soothing words to her, and she nodding.

The constable left as well. Akitada, the lieutenant, and the coroner stood, watching them leave. Then the coroner sighed. "Do you want me to take a closer look?' he asked the lieutenant.

Matsuura glanced at Akitada and when he nodded, he said, "Yes, Kuroda. Just in case it will tell us what happened beyond the fact that she was attacked in the woods, raped, and strangled. It looks like the same killer as Michiko's."

The coroner cleared his throat. "Umm, in this case, cause of death is a broken neck, Lieutenant, but it may have happened when the killer was trying to strangle her. She's a dainty little thing. It wouldn't take much for a big man. However, as you know, there are other differences between this one and Mrs. Akechi's Michiko."

Akitada regarded the pharmacist-coroner with more respect. "What differences, Doctor?" he asked.

The coroner gave him a grateful smile for the courtesy title. "The girl Michiko wasn't raped, but she was beaten badly before she died."

Akitada thought back to the scene at the river. The body had been fully clothed and on its back. "Beaten?"

"Yes, sir. Her back and the backs of her legs were cut up badly."

"She had been whipped?"

"Yes. Strung up by her arms; she also had badly chafed wrists."

Akitada turned to the lieutenant. "That sounds like torture to me."

The Shrine Virgin

Matsuura looked glum. "Yes. I suppose it's possible the two aren't connected. And that just means we've got to find two killers." He nodded to the coroner. "Very well, Kuroda. Report to me when you're done." The lieutenant turned back to Akitada. "Let's go to my office, sir. I assume you didn't come here about Keiko?"

"No." Akitada's thoughts shifted again to his own problem, which seemed more insurmountable by the moment.

In Matsuura's office Akitada accepted a cup of rather sour wine and tried to find a way to get the information he wanted without revealing the true state of affairs. That seemed not only premature but dangerous. He must find some other way to learn what was going on in the district.

The lieutenant started the conversation. "I don't mind telling you, sir, I'm nervous. We've had several deaths of young women this year. All were prostitutes and all but one committed suicide. Now it looks like we've got two killers loose. I'd be very glad of any advice you might have."

"I think you have a very good coroner, Lieutenant. He insists on getting things right. It may well be significant that Keiko's neck was broken and that she was raped, while the other young woman was not but had been beaten before being killed."

"It still sounds like sexual attacks to me. It could be an angry lover. You told me yourself that Michiko had been working as a prostitute. Besides, you'd be surprised what goes on in our brothels. There are men who beat and abuse the women all the time without having sex with them. Mostly they don't kill them, and the aunties just demand more money to pay a doctor and to cover their losses while the woman can't work. I don't like this. If we have someone here who enjoys hurting women, we may never get him. Uji-tachi has a transient population."

"Yes. That means you don't have much time. But Lieutenant, consider that Keiko certainly wasn't a prostitute. And no sexually perverted male would get satisfaction from whipping his partner while she was fully dressed. I think there must be something else going on here. And there is so far no proof that the murders are connected, except that both girls were young."

The lieutenant suddenly brightened. "Wait," he said. "You may be right. Keiko was found near the road to Oyodo. It must've been those prowlers again. That puts it outside my jurisdiction. The roads are controlled by the high constable." He nodded with satisfaction. "He's in town, as it happens. I'll send a report to him immediately and ask for an investigation."

Akitada pursed his lips. "Are the roads very dangerous here? I heard about those prowlers and decided to take my sword after dark."

"Very good idea, sir. Yes, we've had nighttime attacks. They don't bother people in the daytime. There's too much traffic then, but if a visitor makes his journey homeward too late, or if he lingers too long in Oyodo or wherever, he's likely to be stripped of everything he owns and left naked and tied to a tree."

"You don't say? That must be bad for trade. How many of those prowlers are there?"

"Accounts differ. Some victims have said fifteen or more; others five or six. They're likely to exaggerate the number, being embarrassed, you see."

"Yes. Very likely." Akitada considered this information. "And the high constable," he asked, "how has he reacted to these goings on?"

"Lord Sukemichi? By doing nothing. Well, sometimes he sends some of his soldiers. They spend their time interviewing the whores." He guffawed. "They claim the prowlers collect information in the brothels."

"Well, it's possible," Akitada said judiciously. "Didn't you tell me that the high constable comes here to hunt?"

"Yes. And he brings his friends with him. But they keep to themselves, though they sometimes send for women."

"Is Lord Sukemichi a friend of Lord Minamoto, then?"

"I don't think so. I've never heard anything like that. Come to think of it, that is a little strange. Their lodges aren't far from each other and their land adjoins."

"I would think the high constable would care about the safety of the roads if he spends much time here."

Matsuura laughed. "I've heard he won't be high constable much longer. Has his eye on an appointment in the capital. I can't say I'll be sorry to see him leave."

"Oh?"

The lieutenant glanced toward the door and lowered his voice. "Just between you and me, sir, he has a bad reputation even if he is the biggest landowner in the province."

High constables were traditionally appointed from among the local gentry because they kept warriors for the protection of their own domain and could employ these for general enforcement of laws without costing the central government any money. A higher rank or a new title was all that it required. Some high constables were very capable men, but this was never certain and to Akitada's mind the temptation to use their official powers to enrich themselves was enormous. He intended keeping a close eye on his own high constable in Mikawa.

"What do you mean by 'bad reputation'?" he asked.

Matsuura looked uncomfortable. "There's no proof, mind you, but people talk. They say he's in some sort of trade that brings in a lot of gold."

"Ah!" Akitada nodded. "As it happens, I find that very interesting. I believe I mentioned to you that I had a purpose for coming here other than a shrine visit. We have been plagued by pirates along the shores of Mikawa. I thought I'd see if they might be coming from here."

Matsuura stared at this. "I can't believe it, sir. Of course we do have our troubles with prowlers, but we are inland. More than likely pirates would be on the coast."

"Yes, but someone is supplying them and collecting their loot."

"And you think the high constable might be behind it?" Matsuura looked pleased by the thought. "He's been building himself a regular palace in the provincial capital, and even the hunting lodge he keeps here is said to be large and elegant and filled with all sorts of foreign luxuries. Mind you, there's no proof. Sukemichi owns a lot of good rice land and has been lending rice to farmers. There's money to be made from that, and it's perfectly legal."

That practice tended to be usurious and might well account for the man's wealth. And his bad reputation. People were resentful when pressed to repay their debts.

Akitada said, "You may be right. I saw him pass with a very impressive retinue. Is this hunting season?"

"No. I was a little surprised. But great men will act strange. Take Lord Minamoto for example. He's been here twice, looking very agitated. The first time, he asked about prowlers, wondering if there'd been complaints lately. I told him there are always complaints, but nothing specific. Next he comes to tell me about nightly disturbances around his lodge. He wanted me to investigate. He couldn't really say what sort of disturbance, just that someone, maybe several people, had been snooping around his outer fence. Since his place is close to a road, I suggested he speak to the high constable. That made him angry and he rushed off with a curse."

"Very strange indeed. I tried to see him earlier, but he wasn't home. Frankly, he doesn't seem to have any servants there. Just an old gatekeeper who looks past his work."

Matsuura grinned. "That would be old Masaaki. He's a local man. Been with his lordship for years. His wife used to be his cook. She's dead now. One thing about Lord Minamoto, he treats his people well."

Perhaps too well, thought Akitada, recalling the gatekeeper's rudeness.

He rose with a sigh. "Thank you for the wine," he said politely. "I suppose I'll take a look around in case someone has seen him in town. Good luck with your murders, Lieutenant, and keep my secret, please."

15

The Manor on the Coast

F eeling bitter against the entire world, Tora spent the day after his quarrel with Saburo on routine matters. Not only had Saburo insulted him, but Hanae had blamed Tora and read him lecture on how one was to treat one's friends.

Friends!

Worse, his head was aching again. He was beginning to wonder if he was suffering from some sickness. He missed Seimei, who would have had some helpful potion, and Lady Tamako who was also skilled with herbs. Not only had Lady Yukiko shown no interest whatsoever in herbal remedies, but she was herself in such robust good health that Tora could not possibly go to her complaining of a headache.

And now, when he wished to show his master that he could still be useful, he was not allowed to do so.

He did not see Saburo all day. Hanae mentioned accusingly over their evening rice that Saburo had gone into town for his own meal and probably would have enjoyed Tora's company. Tora was convinced that Saburo had gone off without him on purpose and merely grunted. He went to bed before Saburo had returned.

Thus he was surprised to find a cheerful Saburo waiting outside their quarters the next morning.

"Good morning," Tora said uneasily.

"Morning, brother. How are you feeling today?"

Tora's head hurt but he said, "Great. What brings you?"

"Last night I saw someone I used to know many years ago, a fellow *sohei*."

Tora made a face. "Spare me. I've had enough of them for the rest of my life."

"Can't blame you. This character is my age and was one of their warriors. He had a bad reputation even then. He was corrupt and could be vicious on occasion. When I recognized him last night, he'd put away his monk's robe but seemed to be up to something odious anyway. I saw him in a wine shop, talking to two rascally fellows from the harbor."

Tora frowned. "Why are you telling me this? Why should I care about this former colleague of yours? Has he committed a crime here? Maybe you'd better tell

Mori in that case." He started to walk past Saburo who snatched his arm.

"Listen, Tora. I'm not done. I followed him. His next stop was at the inn where your merchant stays. They threw him out, but he must have managed to leave a message, because a short while later a fat fellow in a fine silk robe came out and went up to him. He gave him something that looked like a bag of coins and then went back inside."

Saburo had Tora's attention. "You think that was the merchant from Owari?"

"I thought it possible, but wait, there's more. I followed this Hozo on his way out of town on the coast highway. Just about where I lost him because it was getting too dark there's some large estate. I think that's where he went. The manor house is close to the bay. I thought we might find out who lives there and what business they have with boat people."

Tora stared at him. "That man at the inn, describe him."

"Not young, short, with a round face and belly, small mustache, and sleepy eyes. His robe was dark blue or green. Hard to tell in the lantern light."

"That's him. That's Takanami. Who exactly is this friend of yours?"

Saburo made a face. "Not my friend! His name used to be Hozo when he was a monk. He's originally from the capital but we trained together on Mount Koya. He's older now, of course, but still quite strong, I think. I had a hard time keeping up with him"

"Could he have become a pirate?"

"I think he would do anything that involves money and violence. He's scum."

"When do you want to go?"

Saburo, noting that all had been forgiven and he was back in Tora's good graces, smiled. "After work this evening if it suits you?"

"Fine. I'll have another talk with Mori before then."

∞

Lieutenant Mori received Tora with stiff correctness, saluting promptly but avoiding any friendly

greeting or a smile.

Tora returned the salute. He delved right into the subject of his visit. "Some additional information has been received," he said in a businesslike tone. "The accusation concerning a pirate attack made by merchant Takanami has been leveled at the province of Mikawa and its administration. We both serve the emperor here. Therefore, it is expected that we both investigate the truth of these allegations. I have asked questions in the harbor area and taken a look at the boatmen of Takanami's boat. From the looks of it, the merchant as well as his boatmen may have been lying. I think you must delay the issuing of any papers to Takanami until we know what happened."

The lieutenant scowled. "It's not our custom here to suspect important men with good reputations of lying. It will give us a very bad name with traders and shipping all up and down the coast. Besides, you're too late. I have duly issued Takanami's documents."

Tora muttered a curse, and Mori raised his eyebrows.

"He'll pack up and leave now and we have no way of stopping him," Tora said angrily." There's every reason to expect that he will be indemnified for his losses and collect his fees from the government while he's selling the goods privately. And we get blamed for not making our coasts safe for shipping."

Mori sneered. "He's entitled to his fees and you have no proof against him. We all know there are pirates here, but that's not my business. It's yours and your governor's. Now is there anything else you wanted?"

Tora seethed. It was becoming obvious that the lieutenant was hostile to the new administration of Mikawa. It would make their work much harder. The head of a provincial police force was appointed by the central government and reported separately to the capital. Mori could damage a new governor's reputation. With an effort, he contained his rage.

"There is another matter," he said. "What can you tell me about a place on the coast a few miles south of Komachi? There's a walled estate there."

"It's private and belongs to a Fujiwara. I know nothing about him. He has a *betto* who manages his interests. The estate is not under our jurisdiction."

"You have a name for the *betto*?"

"He is called Kitagawa and is a very respectable man."

Another "respectable" man, thought Tora. He gave Mori a cold nod and sketched a salute before leaving the station.

I. J. PARKER

The news that the suspicious estate belonged to a member of the Fujiwara family was troubling. As a rule, they were far too powerful to tangle with. Even if one forgot that the master was married to one of them.

Of course there was no proof that any of this was connected with the pirates, the boat in the harbor, or the merchant at the inn. Saburo's former colleague might well be a villain of the first water, but he could be staying at a different house or had some harmless business with one of the servants.

As it was still early, Tora decided to have a look himself. He returned to the tribunal for his horse and took the southern highway out of town. The sky was blue, the sea gulls swooped and dove above him, uttering their raucous cries, and the sun glistened on the surface of the bay. They had been blessed with fine weather ever since their departure from the capital. People said this coast was subject to terrifying storms this time of year, but so far autumn had seemed more like an extended summer than a time of turmoil and destruction. And yet there were signs of past devastations along the coast. Many trees still lay about splintered and broken. When they did not interfere with traffic or the growing of rice, people had simply left them where they lay.

He soon saw the estate, and here, too, there was some evidence of storm damage. The wood was still new on some buildings and fences. It testified to the fact that the estate was well managed. The same could be seen in the rice growing in the fields, a second crop almost ready for harvest. Here and there, men and women worked among other crops, vegetables for Komachi's markets.

He stopped near some men who were repairing an irrigation canal and shouted a greeting to them. They answered in a dialect that Tora recognized.

"You're from the North Country?"

They nodded, grinning.

They were *emishi,* prisoners of war or their descendants.

"You belong to Lord Fujiwara?" he asked.

That got a blank stare. "In town they told me this land belongs to a Lord Fujiwara."

One of the men shook his head. "We work for Kitagawa. All *emishi* work for Kitagawa. Planting, building, fishing, training horses."

"Ah." Kitagawa was the *betto.* The land belonged to an absentee landlord who probably never showed his face here. There were many high-ranking nobles in the capital who owned estates in distant provinces. He gave the men a nod and rode on, turning past the manor house toward the sea. This road was also well-maintained and descended in easy curves to a tiny fishing village. A new-looking dock had been built out into the water. It all looked very practical and self-sustaining.

Since it was daytime, there were no boats pulled up on the sandy beach. Seagulls had been feasting on discarded fish parts and rose into the air with angry noise. A couple of women emerged from the houses to stare at him, and children suddenly appeared and ran toward him.

The children were poorly dressed but looked well-fed. They surrounded his horse and looked up at him with wide eyes. His uniform clearly impressed them. Tora smiled and reached into his sash for his string of coppers, then carefully counted out one copper for each of them. They came shyly, holding out their small hands.

Before he could say anything to them, one of the women arrived, out of breath. "Go back!" she screamed. "Now! Or you'll get a beating."

It took Tora a moment to realize she was speaking to the children. "They are no trouble," he called out to her. "I like children."

She shot him a frightened and hostile look and drove the children away.

Tora sighed. Perhaps these *emishi* from the North Country had come here recently and still distrusted people. He looked around one more time, and then went back to Komachi.

16

The Betto Kitagawa

Tora waited impatiently until Saburo dismissed his clerks and joined him.

Saburo shook his head when Tora told him about Mori. "It will be very unpleasant working with the local police," he said.

"I can't abide the bastard. We'll just have to handle the complicated cases ourselves. Speaking of which, I've had a look at your manor. It belongs to some Fujiwara lord. The *betto* is called Kitagawa. Shall we pay him a visit and see what they're about?"

"Fujiwara?" Saburo frowned. "Have you mentioned it to her ladyship?"

"No. I have no idea which Fujiwara it is, and Mori wouldn't tell me. There are *emishi* there working the land and doing the fishing. That could mean the place belongs to the northern clan."

"Fishermen live on the estate? That's very interesting."

"Well, they've got some houses near the water, but I thought so, too. It's close to the manor and a very good road runs from the manor to the shore where they have a sturdy landing stage."

Saburo raised his brows. "Very well, we'd better see what this Kitagawa has to say."

"We'll ride. Make it look like an official call. I'd like to scare him a bit."

Saburo was not fond of riding, but he accepted Tora's reasoning. Tora looked splendid in his armor and helmet, and Saburo switched his plain blue sash for one of green brocade and wore his hat. Otherwise he could do little to improve his appearance. His heavily scarred face was somewhat obscured by a beard and mustache, both trimmed neatly, and he customarily wore a plain black robe and trousers, though these days they were new and made of ramie.

They were trotting along the coast road, with the bay to their left and fields of ripening rice to their right. The bay was a deep blue under a lighter blue sky, cloudless and hazy, fading into the distance. The rice fields were golden and passed gradually into the dark green of forests climbing the hills and turning a purplish hue.

Tora pointed toward the north. "If it were very clear, you might see Fujiyama."

The Shrine Virgin

Saburo was looking the other way. "Yes. And beyond the bay in the west, you can imagine the Western Paradise. It is very beautiful here. Truly the land of the gods."

A reverent silence fell. They both loved their country but duties too often got in the way of remembering its beauty.

After a while, Tora asked, "What will you do if you meet this Hozo?" He eyed Saburo's appearance. "I doubt he'd recognize you."

Saburo smiled a little. "Let's leave it to the circumstances. On the whole it's better if he doesn't know who I am. We didn't get along."

"But your name. Won't he recognize that?"

"You forget that I had a different name as a monk. For that matter, I doubt he calls himself Hozo these days."

It was early evening of another hot day. The sun was still shining, though at a slant, and on horseback they covered the distance to the manor quickly. The gates stood invitingly open because peasants and laborers were passing in and out.

They rode in and stopped in the forecourt. A servant came running. He bowed deeply and asked their business.

"Lieutenant Sashima, provincial guard, and Senior Secretary Kuruda. We want to see *Betto* Kitagawa."

The servant ran toward the house, and they rode up to the stairs and dismounted. As they stood waiting, they looked around. The property was sizable and looked very prosperous. A large granary, roomy stables, and many other outbuildings surrounded the main house. There was even a treasure house, a small building raised on stilts and built of stone and plaster to protect it against floods and fire. Only very wealthy families owned such buildings.

Tora wished he could look inside and mentioned this to Saburo, who nodded but was busy scanning the people in the courtyard for Hozo. There was no sign of him.

The servant returned and led them into the main house.

Kitagawa received them in his office, a room that contained estate documents and a heavy, metal-reinforced money chest. He rose from behind a low desk covered with papers, writing utensils, and an abacus or two.

The *betto* was a tall, muscular man with a red face and bristling brows over sharp black eyes. He did not smile but looked at both Tora and Saburo with great attention as if he were trying to memorize their appearance.

"Welcome, gentlemen," he said in a booming voice. "This is an unexpected honor. I regret my absence from Mikawa the day his Excellency and his staff arrived. It means that I have not had the pleasure of making your acquaintance. I hope you find Mikawa to your liking."

Tora looked around the office. "Thank you. It seems a pleasant enough assignment so far. Lieutenant Mori mentioned this estate and we decided to have a look at it."

"Ah, yes. Lieutenant Mori. A very fine police officer."

Saburo cleared his throat. "It's just a friendly visit, *Betto*," he said with a smile.

Kitagawa gave him a second look that lingered on Saburo's face. He nodded. "As I said, it's an honor to welcome you here. Won't you be seated? And how about some wine?"

They accepted. Tora eyed the papers on the desk. "I see you're kept busy taking care of this place. It seems to be a large and prosperous estate. Who owns it, if I may ask?"

"Oh, Lord Shigeie. Of the northern branch of the Fujiwara clan. He resides in Mutsu."

"Really? That explains it," Tora said with great satisfaction.

Kitagawa looked puzzled. "Explains what?"

"The people who live on his land. I've served in the North Country and recognized their dialect. They're *emishi*. I suppose they are slaves of this Lord Shigeie?"

Kitagawa bristled. "Not at all. We don't have slaves these days. They are all free. You are thinking of the bad old days when we were making war against them. These people are their descendants. They are now loyal subjects of the lords of Hiraizumi."

Tora raised his brows. "Surely you mean they are loyal subjects of the emperor. Or are you implying that the northern Fujiwara occupy their own nation?"

Kitagawa colored. "You misunderstood, Lieutenant. Of course, they are loyal subjects to his Majesty. As are we all. I only meant that their origin gives them ties to the northern clan of the Fujiwara. Really, you mustn't think that we are in any way different from any other privately owned manor in this country. We work and grow rice to pay our taxes to the emperor like anyone else."

Saburo said, "I don't recall seeing either your name or that of Lord Fujiwara on our tax rolls."

"That's because this is a private estate. Our taxes go directly to the capital."

Saburo pursed his lips. "You maintain your own roads then?"

"Yes." Kitagawa was becoming irritated —or perhaps nervous.

"What about using the main highways? Do you furnish labor to maintain those?"

The *betto* looked from Saburo to Tora, who had gone to inspect a map on one of the walls. "Lord Shigeie has dispensations. It's all legal. I can show you the documents."

But Saburo implied that he had lost interest. "Thanks. Maybe another time. Tora, wasn't there something you wished to ask?"

"Ah, yes." Tora turned from the map to look at Kitagawa. "We've had reports of pirates attacking shipping along this coast. Do you know anything about that?"

Kitagawa's eyes moved from one to the other of his visitors and back again. He made an impatient gesture. "Pirates? I know nothing about pirates. What's this all about? Why all these questions? Has someone accused me of not paying my taxes? Or something worse?" He paused. "Or are you just trying to insult me and my master?"

Tora chuckled. "Now why would we want to do that? We're just getting information about conditions in Mikawa and meeting its more important inhabitants. So you aren't aware of any pirate activity? Do you have any visiting ships or boats tying up at your dock? They might have mentioned something."

"The dock is for our own boats." Kitagawa bit his lips. "I mean it's for the fishermen who live on our land."

"Oh. I see. Well, I think that's all," Tora said, smiling more widely. "Thanks for the wine. Remarkably good stuff."

Saburo got to his feet. "Yes. Excellent wine," he murmured. "Better than what we had in the capital."

Kitagawa jumped up. "Allow me to send some to the tribunal," he said. "As a welcome gift for the governor and his staff."

"Very kind," remarked Tora, "but we are not allowed to accept bribes." He turned to Saburo. "What a pleasant excursion we've had coming here, Kuruda. It's just the sort of outing one needs after a day inside. We must do this again."

Kitagawa said nothing, but he was visibly agitated. He bowed, and they walked out, Tora chuckling softly.

Outside, they got back on their horses and trotted through the open gate and back onto the highway.

Tora laughed out loud. "Did you see his face? We put the fear of the gods into the bastard," he said. "Take my word for it, he's a crook. Did you see how red he got when you talked about taxes and conscript labor?"

Saburo smiled. "And he did not like you studying that map at all."

"But when you praised the wine, he relaxed. He thought we were extorting gifts."

"And you made sure he understood what we thought of him by threatening him with other visits."

They both laughed. Then Saburo said more soberly, "Somehow I don't think the master would have approved of that."

17

A Shocking Tale

Akitada returned to his inn. The bereaved inn-keeper was at the counter, staring into space. When Akitada asked him if he could get a bath, the man seemed to be confused for a moment.

"A bath?" he asked. Then he brushed his bushy hair back and said, "Oh, a bath. Yes, I think the water should be hot. I made a fire earlier. Sorry, sir. It's been a terrible day."

Akitada, feeling slightly guilty for disliking the man, told him again that he was very sorry for his loss, then went to take an early bath. He had no change of cloth-ing except for one undershirt, so he put this on and his black robe over it. At least he would keep himself as clean as possible. The used shirt he carried back to the entrance where he asked his host to have someone wash it for him, paying for the service with a handful of coppers.

Then he set out, stopping only for a bowl of noodles from a vendor before returning to the stable to rent another horse. The sun was setting as Akitada rode back to Minamoto's lodge, hoping to catch its elusive owner in.

He was in luck. Lord Minamoto had just returned.

As Akitada rode through the open gate, he was just getting out of the saddle. Both man and beast looked exhausted. The old gatekeeper had the bridle in his hand to lead the horse to the stable. When he saw Akitada he cried, "Not you again! Close that gate behind you and tie up your horse." Then he shuffled off in the direction of the small stable.

The young lord had turned and now stood there, looking pale and apparently not caring about much, least of all his servant's bad manners. His clothes were sadly disheveled, dirty, and torn in places.

Akitada dismounted, tied up his horse as instructed, and then shut the gate. When he turned, Minamoto still stood in the same place.

"We have to talk," Akitada told him, his anger building again. "Inside!"

Minamoto said nothing but walked ahead and into the lodge.

The big room looked the same. Apparently completely exhausted, its owner collapsed on one of the cushions, gesturing vaguely toward the other. He said tonelessly, "I'm too tired to move. There's wine over there." His hand gestured again.

Akitada saw a stoneware jar and some cups. He filled two from the heavy jar and brought one to Minamoto. "Drink and then talk!" he said sternly.

The young man looked at him dully and emptied the cup.

"Where is the princess?"

"I don't know. I've looked everywhere. I cannot find her." He stared down at his clenched hands. "I must have been cursed at birth! They should have killed me then." Covering his face, he rocked back and forth, moaning.

Akitada sat down and sipped from his cup. The wine was excellent, but it did nothing for the anticipation of disaster that had seized him. He said, "I know you had a hand in Her Imperial Highness's disappearance. What possessed you to seduce a consecrated priestess?"

There was no answer.

"I think you brought her here. What happened to her?"

Another moan, and then a muttered, "I told you, I don't know."

Akitada's anger was suddenly too much for him. He was not sure whether it was his frustration with not getting answers or the fact that the boy he had once loved like his own son had so bitterly disappointed him as a man.

He snapped, "Straighten up, man. You're no longer a child who can hide behind his tears. What have you done to her?"

The hands fell from the face. Lord Minamoto was very pale, but he looked back at Akitada with dry eyes and said in a reasonably firm voice, "You are right. She was here, but she left. I thought she'd gone back to the Bamboo Palace until Lady Tamba sent for me. She wasn't there. Since then, I've been searching everywhere. At first I thought she got lost in the forest, but it's been too long. Something must have happened to her."

Akitada said coldly, "It would seem the Tamba woman also bears some responsibility for this unpardonable incident, but ultimately whatever happened is your fault."

"Don't you think I know that?" Minamoto jumped to his feet. Akitada might have envied him such agility if he had not been so furious with him. The young man looked about him wildly. "I'll find her, whatever it takes. I'll go out again to search the forest. I swear I won't eat or sleep until she's safe."

Something did not sound quite right. Akitada stared up at him. Even he could see that the boy he had taught so many years ago had grown into the kind of man who turned women's heads. Minamoto's handsome face was pale, but the large eyes shone with passion, a passion that was not romantic in the least. While he had indeed won the love of the Ise Virgin, his own emotions did not seem those of a lover. He behaved more like someone who had failed in an important duty. Even if she had been here with him, if there had been a torrid and utterly reprehensible affair between these two, he had not been in love with her. True, he was very upset now, but that seemed more due to guilt for not having safeguarded her person than the grief of a man in love.

This realization did not endear the young man to Akitada. Rather, it made him seem callow and unfeeling. He bit his lip and said, "Sit down again! You'd better tell me the whole shameful tale."

Minamoto flushed and then paled again. He raised his hands helplessly and opened his mouth to say something, then nodded and sat.

He spoke without looking at Akitada. "Princess Takahime is a distant cousin of mine," he began. "As children, we were frequently together. I liked her. Then she became the Ise Virgin and her brother our emperor. She was proud of her appointment." He paused and glanced at Akitada. "She was only eight. Since then she has passed sixteen years here and has become lonely and very unhappy. Other young women her age are married and have families of their own, but she knows that will never happen for her. She started to write to me of her despair about a year ago. I wrote back, trying to reassure her." He paused and hung his head again. "Such correspondence is improper, but we are cousins and childhood friends, and I felt concern for her."

The young man seemed to be pleading for understanding and forgiveness, but Akitada said, "You're quite right. You should never have written. And you should certainly never have tried to see her. I assume that is what you did do eventually?"

Minamoto sighed. "One cannot put away one's feelings of pity so easily. Yes. I had purchased some land and this hunting lodge and came here from time to time. She wrote that it made her feel better to know she had a friend nearby. But we did not meet face to face until this year, and then it was because Lady Tamba asked me to come."

Again that cursed female.

"That woman is evil," Akitada snapped, adopting the chief priest's word.

The young nobleman looked a little surprised at Akitada's language. "She is a romantic," he said. "She thought our story, or at least the story Takahime told her, was heartbreaking. She wept for the princess when I first arrived there and begged me to see her because she feared she would do herself some harm." He broke off and shuddered. "I think I made things worse," he said with a catch in his voice. "I think she may have killed herself after all. I'll never forgive myself."

A long silence fell.

Akitada considered. He was inclined to give the young fool some benefit of doubt. It sounded as if he had somehow become trapped into the relationship. He thought how to ask his next question and decided bluntness would serve him best. "Did you become lovers?"

At first there was no answer, just another shudder, then Sadamu said very quietly, "Yes."

Whatever the outcome of this, the damage was done. Princess Takahime, the consecrated Ise Virgin, had been defiled. And Akitada did not have the faintest idea what could be done about it. Her lover, of course, would be condemned, perhaps to death, but more likely to exile because of his imperial blood. The princess would be replaced by some other imperial daughter. The next one was not likely to be as young as Takahime had been, and that would present problems to those who would make the selection. She would have to be a proven virgin. Possibly Takahime's brother would be blamed and coerced to abdicate and become a monk. Akitada did not know the young emperor, but he thought such a political move would be altogether unfair and bad for the nation.

Not that there was any fairness in making an eight-year-old child Ise Virgin for her foreseeable future, for Takahime was expected to serve until her brother died or abdicated.

If she was still alive.

He looked at the white-faced young man sitting across from him. His fate, too, would be unfair, even though he had acted rashly and without consideration for Takahime or the goddess she served. The two young people had stumbled into a tragic affair, she out of loneliness and despair, and he out of pity.

In a gentler tone, he asked, "Do you love the princess?"

Sadamu turned troubled eyes to him. "Yes. Yes, of course. Why else would I have done what I did?"

Good question. Akitada almost smiled. Instead he sighed. "What exactly happened? Describe the events up until the last time you saw her?"

"Lady Tamba sent me a note." He shook his head at the memory. "She said she'd found a way for us to be together. The next day Takahime arrived here. She was alone and in plain clothing, without her usual make-up, and with her hair twisted up at her neck. She looked like one of the young girls in the village. I almost didn't recognize her. She said she'd traded places with some-one, and wasn't it the most wonderful adventure?"

He stopped and looked helplessly around the room. "I didn't know what to do. This is no place for the em-peror's sister. When I said I would take her back, she started crying. She said, she had nothing to live for now that I had rejected her love. I . . . I tried to calm her, told her I cared for her . . . and one thing led to anoth-er." He sighed.

Akitada could picture it perfectly. Did it excuse his behavior? No, of course not. But he could understand it. The thing had happened not out of romantic passion but out of pity and affection.

"How long was she here?"

"The rest of that day and the night. And the early part of the next day. I went out to buy some food for her and a comb. She left while I was gone."

Akitada raised his brows. "Why did she leave?"

Lord Minamoto shook his head miserably. "We'd quarreled. I'd woken to the realization of what I had done. We talked about it. She wanted to live with me as my wife, but I said she must go back." He glanced at Akitada. "She was the Virgin, after all. I couldn't marry her."

Yes, that was impossible. The rejection would certainly send the young woman running. But had she gone to kill herself?

Minamoto had the same thought. "When I found her gone, I was so afraid. I thought she might have drowned herself in the river." He shuddered again. "I went to Uji-tachi several times to see if she'd been found. And today there was a body, but it was someone else's, and they said she'd been killed by prowlers, and I got frantic all over again. Dear Heaven, what can I do?"

Akitada said nothing. In truth, he had no idea what they could do. "Does your servant know that she was here and spent the night?" he asked instead.

Minamoto frowned. "What does that matter? He didn't know who she was. He thought I'd brought home a woman from the town."

"Lieutenant Matsuura says you complained about someone trying to get into your lodge at night."

"That was nothing. I was just trying to find out if anybody had been seen nearby."

Akitada sighed. "Go to bed now. You can do nothing in your present state. I'll see what I can find out."

The young man looked almost grateful. "I can't sleep," he protested, but Akitada saw that his eyes had glazed over with tiredness.

"I'll return in the morning," he said, and left.

18

A Deadly Assignation

It was fully dark when Akitada approached the Tanoe shrine. He left his horse in town, told Junichiro he did not have time to share his evening rice with him, and then set out on foot for the Tanoe shrine. This was one of the small shrines that clustered about the big Ise shrines and was close to the Bamboo Palace.

He did not know what to expect from Lady Ayako and was nervous about a young gentlewoman wandering about these woods. It was clearly not safe to do so for pretty girls. At least it was still early enough for a few late shrine visitors to wander about with their lanterns. Akitada carried one also, having borrowed it from the

inn, where Keiko's mother was again dealing with guests. Of her husband there was no sign.

Once he left the shrine of the goddess behind, he was soon alone on the path, but this was well marked. With his lantern he could read directions and eventually reached a small wooden building, as simple as the main shrine and also half hidden behind fencing.

Nobody was either on the path or inside the fence. Akitada walked all around the building, then decided to wait. He sat down on the stone basin at the entrance.

For a while all remained quiet. A forest at night has a special kind of silence, a waiting stillness that accounted for people's fear of it. He listened. When he heard the first slight rustle and skittering sounds, he tensed. It became quiet again. Just some small animal, he thought. The next sound came from another direction, deeper in the forest and made by something larger. As it was not the direction of the princess's palace, he tensed again and extinguished his light.

He regretted it instantly. The darkness surrounding him was total. He got to his feet and listened. Yes, there it was again, and it seemed closer. Then he heard voices, male voices, but also a cry that might have been a woman's.

Drawing his sword, he plunged toward the cry into the darkness. "Who's there?" he shouted. "Stand back and drop your weapons."

It was feeble attempt meant to scare off whoever had caught Lady Ayako and was doomed to failure. He collided with branches and shrubs in the darkness, fell twice, knew there were people close to him, and then fell a third time.

And this time he passed out.

∞

He came round with a sore head. Opening his eyes was strangely painful, though the light was dim. He was in some sort of hut. Off in one corner, an oil lamp flickered beyond the backs and heads of four men. There was no sign of Lady Ayako.

He was lying on his side and he was bound hand and foot. A rope passed around his ankles and then around his wrists behind his back. He lay in this curled position, becoming aware that it was quite painful to be tied up this way.

His sword was gone. Or rather, it now lay beside one of the men.

No matter. It would not do him much good at the moment.

One of the men drank from an earthenware flask and belched. "How long do you think?" he asked in a rough voice.

Akitada could smell the sharp odor of wine. They were drinking.

"An hour maybe. Wonder what was in that letter. Bet the boss gets rid of him."

A third man growled, "Should've done it right away. Why bring him here and let him live?"

Good point! Alas, it was not a cheerful prospect to wait an hour or so to find out if the "boss" was more tender-hearted than his henchmen. Akitada peered at the room through half-closed lids. He had no intention of cutting his precious hour of life short by letting them see he was conscious.

What was so important about this place that it was dangerous for him to have seen it? Well, if it was a hangout for these men, who were surely the much feared prowlers, he supposed they would prefer the police or the high constable's unreliable soldiers did not find out about it. But perhaps there was something else. He studied the part of the place that he could see from where he was lying.

The wood structure had a rather flimsy roof, the kind you see on storage places for firewood or farm equipment. There was no firewood that he could see, and while he did not know how far they had carried him, he guessed they were still somewhere in the Ise forest. But there were goods stacked against one wall. Alas, they were wrapped in grass mats so that he could not tell what they contained. A bench stood nearby and some sort of chain hung over one of the beams. On the bench lay a whip. It was the kind carters used on their oxen, but this one had an unusual number of knots, and its business end was stained dark.

A memory stirred and Akitada's eyes went to the dirt floor. Yes, there was a large dark stain over there. This must be the place where the girl Michiko had been tortured and then killed.

And these men were surely her killers.

They would certainly not leave him alive to lead the police to this place.

Akitada wondered who their "boss" was.

One of the prowlers got to his feet and came over to check on Akitada. Akitada kept his eyes closed and took shallow breaths.

"Out cold," the man said. "I'm going for a pee."

The others merely grunted. One of them stretched out on the dirt floor. "Might as well get some sleep while we wait. Make sure to hide the wine."

The other two made themselves comfortable. The man who had gone out to relieve himself came back in. "You're not going to sleep? How's that going to look if the boss comes?"

The first man to lie down said drowsily, "That's why you're going to stand watch."

The other prowler greeted that with a curse and sat down again.

Nothing else happened for a long time except that one or two of the villains started to snore. Akitada kept a wary eye on the last man. His head sank to his chest and his eyes closed. Very carefully, Akitada tested his bonds. They held firm. Nevertheless he persisted in moving his wrists, trying to stretch the rope, hoping to loosen his bonds eventually and get a hand free.

To his startled surprise, the rope suddenly parted. Afraid that he had made too much noise, he remained still and in the same position, eyeing the dozing guard. When nothing happened, he tried to loosen the bonds on his ankles by moving his feet. They, too, parted easily. It seemed inexplicable that he should have been so carelessly tied, but you did not question a miracle. He moved his hands and feet, trying to get the circulation back. His eyes gauged the distance to his sword.

Four against one, and the sword was close to them. By the time he got hold of it, they would have killed him. Still, he could not think of any other move.

Before he could make up his mind, a shout came from outside the hut. The dozing guard jumped up and grabbed the sword. Akitada cursed his luck. In just another moment, he would at least have had his sword and could have a chance to fight his way out. Now he would be killed. He sent a fleeting thought to his children and to Yukiko, who would be a very young widow.

But the guard changed his mind. He dropped Akitada's sword and took his own, a shorter one. Then he started kicking his companions awake. Another shout came from outside, and two of the prowlers ran out. The other two got to their feet and took up their weapons. One said "Is it the boss?"

They both looked over at Akitada and then turned back to the door.

It was his chance, his only chance. He had no idea how many people were coming and what point there was in it, but Akitada scrambled to his feet, feet that disobeyed and made him fall again when he reached his sword.

The two men at the door were fortunately slow to grasp the situation. They were still half asleep and probably not very bright at the best of times. Thus, Akitada managed to get to his feet again, a little unsteadily, but with his sword in his hand. He lunged at the one to his right.

They both cried out and simultaneously tried to get out the narrow door. Predictably they got stuck. Akitada sliced through the thigh of the man on the right and delivered a fatal slash to the neck of the other. This man simply collapsed, half blocking the doorway, while the other managed to stumble into the open. He was bleeding badly.

Akitada gave a quick thanks to the Sugawara blade, which was as sharp as ever. The sword was old and heavy but had been made by a master sword smith. He would have grieved its loss.

But there was little time to think about what might have happened because the danger was not over. The two men outside were wide awake, armed, and forewarned. And someone else was coming.

Akitada stepped over the dead man in the doorway. In a delayed reaction, his body rebelled against the sudden exertion after having been stretched into an unnatural position for hours. As he took a couple of steps to meet the attack from the other two villains, his legs gave way and he nearly fell flat. Only a superhuman effort made him catch his balance to stand and raise his sword to deflect the blade of the first man. After that, he found the strength to parry the next strike and slash off the man's head. It rolled a few feet, and the headless body fell. Slightly dazed by his quick success, he turned to look for the first man.

He lay a few feet away.

And on him sat the goblin.

"Junichiro?" Akitada gasped. "What are you doing here? Get away from him. He'll kill you."

"No, he won't," the dwarf said with great satisfaction and held up a rather large and bloody knife. "Did you get the others, master?"

"Yes. But I don't understand." Akitada checked the man Junichiro was sitting on. He was dead, stabbed in the belly and his throat slashed. "You did this?"

The dwarf grinned. "I may be small, but I'm quick and strong, and I always carry a knife in the woods."

"But what are you doing here?"

"You wouldn't tell me what you were up to, so I followed you." This he said accusingly.

Akitada could not very well complain about the dwarf's nosiness when he had just killed a man for him. On second thought: those ropes had come off very easily. He turned on his heel and went back to the hut, checking the two bodies at the door. Both robbers were dead.

Inside, he picked up the pieces of the rope and found that they had been cut. Shaking his head, he looked at the wall. A couple of boards were missing at the bottom, leaving an opening just large enough for a child to get through.

Junichiro had followed him and stood beside him. "This hut is old and badly built. Not like mine. There's a knot hole over there." He pointed. "I looked in and saw you tied up. Those missing boards behind you made it easy."

"I probably owe you my life," Akitada said in a tone of awe.

The dwarf chuckled. "It was nothing, but you really shouldn't wander around the woods alone after dark.

Next time you do that, you've got to take me along. What were you doing anyway?"

"Not now," Akitada said. "We have to leave. They sent someone to their boss. We may have company any moment."

Junichiro ran to the door. Akitada was about to follow when he remembered the bundles of goods. Using his sword, he slit one open and found it filled with short swords and long knives. There was also a keg and several rice bales. Weapons and provisions. He cast one more look around and hurried after Junichiro.

The darkness seemed impenetrable after the dimly lit hut. Junichiro, who appeared to have owl eyes, called to him, and he followed. They moved along quickly, Akitada with his sword in his hand and absolutely no idea where they were or in what direction they were headed. Junichiro was surprisingly fast for his short legs, but he could hear his labored breathing.

"Slow down," he called out.

Junichiro stopped. "Sshh!"

He heard it, too. Horses. They must be near a road. Junichiro touched his arm and pulled him a few steps toward the side. He saw lights beyond the trees, torches. They shone on several armed men and their horses. In a moment they passed quite closely, and then they were gone, swallowed up by the night.

Akitada said, "Those were warriors. The police lieutenant told me they would call in the high constable's men to secure the area. Come on, the road should be safe enough now."

"No," said the dwarf. "You can't trust anyone when it comes to the prowlers. We'll follow the road home, but we'll stay in the trees in case someone else shows up."

Akitada thought of the goods and weapons stashed in the hut and decided in favor of caution. But they slowed down their pace, and after a while Junichiro spied a rock outcropping and said, "Let's rest a bit. I've walked a far distance tonight."

Akitada felt guilty. With his short legs, the little man had taken far more steps than he had. They perched on the rock. "Is it far?" Akitada asked. "You could get on my shoulders, you know."

"Don't insult me," snapped the dwarf.

"Sorry. Just trying to help."

Junichiro snorted. Neither spoke for a while. Akitada checked the seam of his robe and found the letter from the imperial secretary gone. In whose hands was it now, and what would that person make of it? He had failed. His identity was known, and so was the emperor's concern for the princess. Meanwhile, the princess remained lost.

It struck him now that he could have run into an ambush at the Tanoe shrine, and that meant he had either walked into a trap or he had been followed all along. If Junichiro could follow him, so could others. Had Lady Ayako set him up? Perhaps on orders from the senior lady-in-waiting? Or had those who knew his purpose in Ise done this. The only ones who knew were Minamoto, Lady Tamba, and the chief priest. And

Lieutenant Matsuura knew his identity, though not his real assignment.

Akitada shook his head. It was an impossible situation. He was completely out of his depth. His head still hurt quite badly where the prowlers, or whatever they had been, had knocked him out. He must think, but first he must get some rest.

Junichiro had come to same conclusion, for he jumped down and said, "Come, it isn't far now. Time for bed for little people."

19

A Storm is Brewing

Tora and Saburo sat up late that night, going over the recent events.

"He was shaken, brother," Tora said with satisfaction. "That means he's in it up to his neck."

Saburo pursed his lips. "I agree that Kitagawa's behavior suggested unease. I noticed that his eyes went everywhere and he got angry. It is possible to interpret this as a guilty conscience, but what exactly do you mean by 'in it up to his neck'?"

"In with the pirates, of course. Think of that landing stage. Fishermen don't need landing stages. That was built for larger boats and easier unloading. And then

173

there was the treasure house. You see them in the mansions of the great nobles in the capital, but he runs basically a farm. Why does a *betto* need a treasure house? And that woman at the shore who came to get the children so they wouldn't talk to me was very hostile. I bet Kitagawa is a pirate boss."

"You forget Hozo. If he went with a payoff from the merchant Takanami to Kitagawa, how does that fit in with a pirate attack?"

Tora scratched his head. "I haven't quite worked that out yet. To tell you the truth, I need some sleep. I can't think straight at this hour. Let's plan the next step tomorrow."

∞

But the next morning, Tora was sent for by Lady Yukiko. As it turned out, the gardeners had disappeared as soon as Tora had turned his back, and there was also the matter of certain other improvements Lady Yukiko had thought of in the meantime.

"My husband has no *koi* pond," she informed Tora. "He misses that, I'm sure. He told me that he liked playing his flute sitting on his veranda and watching the fish. I think we should get some men to dig a small pond quickly so it can be finished by the time he returns." She paused. "And that reminds me. Has there been a letter from him?"

"No, my lady. I would have brought it to you immediately. It may come later today."

"I was thinking that he might only have written to you or Saburo." She looked rather forlorn as she said this.

Tora reassured her. "He would never do that, my lady. It's more likely that he'd write only to you."

She blushed and smiled gratefully. "I miss him so," she murmured.

Embarrassed, Tora cleared his throat. "I'll go see about those lazy gardeners and get someone to dig that pond. You want one about the same size as the one at home?"

"Yes. Thank you, Tora. "And could you check in town if they sell *koi*?"

Tora promised, bowed, and went to tell Saburo that the pirates would have to wait while he was busy with domestic duties. He was a little resentful, but Lady Yukiko had a way with her, and somehow he always found himself eager and willing to serve her in every whim.

Having set the gardeners to gardening with assorted threats and put three men to work digging the pond, Tora went to town to check on the availability of *koi*.

He wore his ordinary clothes for this errand, having decided that he might pay another visit to the harbor and perhaps engage some boatmen in conversation. *Koi* were for sale at the market and he made a deal with one of the sellers to deliver a dozen of the fancy ones as soon as the pond was dug. The man shook his head dubiously.

"You can't just fill a hole with water," he warned. "That just makes mud. These fish will die."

"What do you care? You'd just sell more then."

The fish seller was taken aback. After a moment, he said, "Can I send you some plain ones instead?"

Tora burst into laughter. "I was just joking. Can you come and tell us how to do it? It's for the new governor."

The man brightened. "I'll come tomorrow."

"Good. Ask for Tora."

This encounter had cheered Tora, and he now walked to the harbor. There a surprise awaited him. The merchant's boat was gone. In fact, the harbor looked thin of boats even to his eyes. He went to see the harbor master.

Having passed a greeting and a few pleasantries, Tora asked, "Where are all the boats?"

"Oh, haven't you heard? There's a storm coming. The bigger boats go out to the open water or home where they can pull their boats on land. If they stay in the harbor, they'll be smashed to pieces."

Tora stared at him. "A storm? The weather looks great. Not a cloud in the sky."

"Not here, but out at sea the storm clouds are building up. There'll be a storm. The sailors know about such things."

Tora pointed to the remaining boats. "What about them?"

"They're local. They'll leave when the time comes."

"I wanted to talk to the men who claimed they'd been attacked by pirates."

The harbor master's brows shot up. "You mean they were lying?"

Tora bit his lip. He was not sure about anything at the moment except that people seemed to have a lot to hide here in Komachi. He said, "What if they were? Would you be surprised?"

The harbor master laughed. "Not at all. I didn't like them or their master."

Tora smiled. "See? I got the same feeling. I'd like to know what's going on. Are there pirates or not? If not, why were they all lying?"

"I wish I could help you. Yes, there are reports of pirates from time to time, though this one puzzled me. But I can't help you. I will say the owner's claims seemed astonishing."

Tora sighed. "That's what made me suspicious in the first place. These pirates, are they local men? Are they operating out of Mikawa?"

"I have no idea. It's possible."

Tora thanked the harbor master and went back to the tribunal, where Saburo received him with the news of a visit by Lieutenant Mori.

"A complaint has been filed against us," he said.

Tora looked at him. "You're joking. About what?"

"About harassing people and interfering with their work."

Tora laughed. "Mori behaves like the moron he is."

Saburo cleared his throat. "Actually there are two complaints. The first one was by the merchant. The second involves both of us and our visit to Kitagawa."

"Oh, come. That's ridiculous. What can they do? We're merely doing our duty investigating piracy."

"I know, but somehow you have managed to irritate Mori to the point where he could file these charges with the authorities in the capital."

Tora sat down and cursed. "That bastard! How dare he do such a thing? And how does he plan to go on? We're here for the next four years. He's got to work with us."

"I know, Tora. I pointed all that out to him, but he insisted that his own appointment depended on keeping the capital informed." Saburo cleared his throat. "I suspect that someone in the capital has given him special instructions to report anything and everything that might be taken as malfeasance by this governor."

"Dear heaven! I thought we were finally sailing smoothly with Lord Fujiwara protecting the master."

Saburo nodded. "Yes. It comes as surprise to me also. I bet the master doesn't know. It makes me wonder if this assignment he's on might be some sort of trap. His enemies clearly haven't gone away."

Tora threw up his hands. "Now you believe me? Didn't you tell me that messenger only brought some dull instructions and the master was only visiting the shrine for his own benefit?"

Saburo looked guilty. "Well . . . you did make a very good case that something else was going on, so I considered it."

Tora gave a snort. "Sometimes you can be a pain in the ass, Saburo."

"I'm going to make up for it. I'll have a look at the Kitagawa place tonight while you sleep in the soft arms of your wife."

Tora frowned. "Hanae's been moody lately, so I doubt I'll be sleeping soft tonight. What are we going to do about the complaint and that bastard Mori?"

"Nothing. We'll try to prove that your merchant and Kitagawa were up to no good."

Tora sighed. "The merchant is gone, and so is his boat. The harbor master says there will be a storm and most of the bigger boats and ships are going out to sea to ride it out."

"Really? Maybe you'd better check the roof of the residence."

Tora nodded glumly.

20

Silk for a Princess

Somehow Akitada reached his inn and stumbled into his room. His bedding had been spread out, and he fell on it and slept instantly.

The sun was already high when he woke. His body ached and he looked in surprise at his swollen wrists. Memory returned quickly and caused him to sit up. That was when his head began to hurt again. He felt it gingerly and decided the swelling behind his ear was not serious. Neither were his other injuries. His sword lay beside him, still covered with dark stains from the blood he had spilled.

He owed the dwarf his life and must do something for him. Perhaps he would not be averse to joining the

181

Sugawara household. Akitada was in the habit of pick-
ing up stray human beings here and there, and none
had ever disappointed him. He smiled a little at the
thought of his family's faces when he arrived with a
dwarf with spiky red hair.

But the events of the night had brought serious
problems while not telling him anything about the
whereabouts of the princess. For one thing, the imperial
secretary's letter had fallen into the hands of a crime
boss. The heavens above knew what use that unknown
individual would make of it. And then there was the
likelihood that he had walked into a trap that had been
set after he started asking uncomfortable questions. He
would have to see Lady Tamba and Lady Ayako as
soon as possible.

But first things first. He got up and looked at his
sword. Shaking his head, he called for service by sticking his head out the door and shouting down the corridor.

He expected his hostess, but instead a middle-aged,
broad-faced woman with a bulky figure and a sullen
expression responded. It seemed she was the maid. He
asked her to bring him hot water and his morning gruel.

Before eating and even before washing, he used
some of the water to clean his sword. In his luggage was
a small polishing cloth, and he used some lamp oil to
return the blade to its original dull gleam.

He had killed before. Sometimes it had been the
slaughter of war, but always he had been sickened by it.
Now he was unable to eat his rice gruel and left it untouched.

Still, sword polishing was a quiet time, good for re-flection. He had been slow and awkward with his sword last night. Fortunately, the robbers had been a good deal worse than he or he would be dead now. For that matter, a dwarf had to take on one of the men. Junichi-ro was no bigger than a child and handicapped by the odd deformity of his body. He had used only a knife to kill a full-grown man.

Sometimes we survive for no good reason at all.

And for what?

Was he alive today to raise his family? To save the princess and perhaps spare his country the upheavals that the offense of the two foolish young people brought on it? To give an unfortunate creature a home? He felt capable only of the first and the last, but it was the prin-cess who needed help most urgently. He could hardly bear thinking about what had happened to her after she left Minamoto's lodge.

For that matter, she might have ended her life after all, though Akitada had begun to suspect that Princess Takahime was the sort of strong-willed female who would not kill herself over a man.

When he was done, he washed, brushed the dust off his black robe, and pushed the sword through his sash. There was no sign of Junichiro when he left the inn. Perhaps he, too, had overslept. Akitada got on a horse again and rode to the Bamboo Palace.

All was quiet here. The same dice game seemed in progress, and the guards were no more alert than they had been last time. The same servant was called and led him to the same pavilion. He did not see Lady Ayako and felt another twinge of unease over her fate. Perhaps she had really tried to meet him and had been intercepted. Too much of a coincidence, he decided and rejected the idea. He would have an explanation from her.

He had interrupted another morning meal, and Lady Tamba looked at him reproachfully. Her mother said, "Ah, there you are! And what did you learn?"

He seated himself uninvited. "Something, but not nearly enough, Lady Tachibana"

The old lady snorted. "It never is with you officials. Busybodies, all of you. What does the Minamoto youngster have to say?"

Akitada hesitated. He decided he would not mention the fact the young people had become lovers. Let them think what they wanted. He said, "He convinced Her Highness to return to her duty, and left briefly to make arrangements to take her home. When he got back, she was gone."

"Gone!" cried Lady Tamba in a tragic tone.

"Hush. He doesn't mean she was dead. Or do you, Sugawara?"

"No. She had left his hunting lodge. He searched everywhere but could not find her."

"Oh," cried Lady Tamba, "then she's been abducted by criminals." Her face was a mask of horror. "Think of what they'll do to her! You must find her at once."

Her mother snorted. "It's been two days. They most likely have already done it."

Her daughter covered her face. "She's ruined! We're all ruined. His Majesty's anger will fall on us all."

Akitada cleared his throat. "I'd like to speak to Lady Ayako."

Lady Tamba ignored him, but her mother turned a sharp eye on him. "Ayako tried to get out last night. I thought she was meeting one of the young scamps from the guard. Was she meeting you?"

"Yes. I wondered why she didn't show up."

She tsked and shook her head. "Loose morals all around. You're too old to be seducing well-born young palace women. Can't imagine what she sees in you. Best get your women in town."

Akitada flushed with anger. "Send for her," he snapped.

They complied, and after some moments, Lady Ayako joined them. She blushed when she saw Akitada and sent him a beseeching glance.

He ignored it. "When I was here last time, you made an appointment to meet me at the Tanoe shrine after dark because you had some information about the princess. Will you confirm this?"

The two senior ladies-in-waiting stared at her in surprise. Lady Ayako spread her hands helplessly. "I was just trying to help," she told them. "I thought he might find the princess."

"But what could you tell him?" Lady Tamba asked. "We already told him all that happened."

"I was going to tell him how she left. You know. About the woman with the silks?"

Akitada sat up. "What woman with silks?" Perhaps Lady Ayako was not, after all, a part of the plot to abduct the princess. He had slowly come around to thinking that nothing that happened was an accident, but perhaps some events had innocent reasons.

Old Lady Tachibana said, "Mrs. Akechi has a shop in town. She brought some special silks for Her Highness to choose from." She paused and glanced at her daughter. "You might as well tell him. It doesn't change what happened."

There she was wrong. It changed everything.

The story, as told reluctantly by her daughter, was that Mrs. Akechi's periodic visits had given Princess Takahime an idea how she might visit her lover without anyone noticing.

Her mother added, "It was a very stupid thing to do. They didn't tell me until after she was gone. It seems they got the idea from the chief priest's daughter taking Takahime's place for the big ceremony last month. The princess insisted that they try to find her a substitute who could play her part here while she was with Minamoto."

The selection had fallen on Mrs. Akechi's assistant who had played her part until she got tired of waiting. She had then left to go home. The next day, Lord Minamoto had arrived to ask if the princess had returned. Consternation had ensued.

The shop assistant, Akitada knew, had been Michiko, the girl who had been found murdered the day he arrived.

He left the Bamboo Palace, his mind in such turmoil that he barely knew what he told the women. He
got on his horse and rode to Lord Minamoto's lodge.

This time the gate stood wide open.

Akitada rode in and shouted, "Gatekeeper?"

There was no answer.

He dismounted and tied up his horse. Then he
walked up the steps to the door of the lodge and threw
it wide. The room was empty. Bedding and some clothing still lay tangled on the floor. There was no sign of
the owner, and the old servant seemed to have disappeared also.

He looked around the room but could make nothing of it other than that it had been a sudden departure.
He thought of the silk shop girl's gruesome death and
his own capture the night before and began to feel uneasy. If they—and he did not have the slightest idea who
they might be—were bent on doing away with anyone
who knew of Princess Takahime's disappearance, then
they might have seized Lord Minamoto and his servant.
But surely they would not have troubled taking an aged
servant.

Leaving the lodge building, Akitada began to search
for the old man's body.

When he approached a small kitchen building, he
was surprised to hear singing. The voice was cracked
and the words slurred, but at least he was spared the
gory sight of another slashed throat.

He ducked in under the curtain and found the old
gatekeeper reclining against a rice cooker with his arm

around a *sake* jar. He was drunk and was singing to himself with his eyes closed.

Akitada walked over and shook his shoulder.

The old man's eyes popped open; he stared a moment, then said, "Go 'way! Nobody home." He immediately closed his eyes again and opened his mouth to sing.

Irate, Akitada pulled him up and shook him hard enough to hear his teeth rattling together. "Get up, you stinking drunk! Where's your master?"

"Ouch! Don't! Can't get up. Weak." He demonstrated by collapsing instantly.

Akitada muttered a curse and lifted him off the ground, half carrying and half dragging him to the well outside. There he dropped him on the ground while he pulled up some water in the wooden bucket. He had to empty two buckets of water over the old man before his eyes focused and he started to get to his feet.

"Wha . . .," he spluttered. "What d'you want?"

"Your master, you lousy piece of useless garbage."

"Now wait! There's no call for that. It's my holiday. A man deserves a little holiday after working day in and out for sixty years." He burped and wiped water from his face with a shaking hand.

Akitada bit his lip. "Where is Lord Minamoto?"

"Gone home! I told you. I'm on holiday. There's nobody here."

"Home where?"

"To Taka city. Where his big house is. He only comes here for the hunting."

If only!

The Shrine Virgin

Akitada sank down on the well rim. So Minamoto had fled his responsibilities in the disaster he was partially responsible for. How very wrong he had been about the boy Sadamu! He had grown into another selfish, overbearing, and cowardly aristocrat.

Leaving the old man to his drunken holiday, he got back on his horse and returned to Uji-tachi. The story told by Lady Ayako had given him a sudden interest in Mrs. Akechi and her silk business.

21

Three Young Women

It was already his fourth day in Ise. No doubt they were beginning to worry at home. He must find a way to send a reassuring letter, though there was little to be reassured about except the fact that he was alive.

Two young women had been found murdered and there was no trace of the Virgin. It seemed more and more likely that she, too, was dead and simply had not been found yet.

But one fact argued against this: everything he had been told so far suggested that someone, a shadowy figure in the background, had been manipulating things. And if this was the case, the capture of the Virgin was part of a more complex plan. Alas, Akitada had no idea what this plan might be or who was behind it.

He was inclined to absolve the women of the Bamboo Palace from anything more serious than foolish dreams about young love. The atmosphere in highborn women's closed quarters tended to overexcite females. They became bored and thought of nothing but men and romantic encounters. Even older married women like Lady Tamba were not proof against such nonsense. He blamed the popularity of books like Lady Murasaki's *Genji* for this.

Lord Minamoto was another matter. Akitada might have believed his tale of merely submitting to the princess's passion, if he had not then run from his responsibility like a coward. Akitada had counted on his help and his resources in tracing the princess. Now there was little hope of finding her quickly, and the more time passed the more unlikely it was that he would do so.

The matter of his own capture surely meant that whoever was behind the grand scheme had found out why he had come and decided to remove him. Again, he considered Lieutenant Matsuura, the chief priest, and Lord Minamoto as possible players in such a plot.

What did he really know about Matsuura? He could not even recall meeting the man in the capital. Matsuura's flattery had blinded him to any possible lies. But if Matsuura had not been a police officer in the capital, then someone else had asked him to make contact with Akitada as soon as he arrived and to keep an eye on him afterward. If this was the case, Akitada had stupidly worked into their hands by promising to report to Matsuura.

The chief priest was in the best position to be the mastermind in the plot. He had known all along why Akitada was here. But if he had abducted the princess, his purpose in doing so was not clear. Surely he would not have gone this far simply to expose Lady Tamba's incompetence.

In the end, Akitada decided that there was only one person whom he could trust, and that was Junichiro. Alas, the little man was not much use when what Akitada needed were soldiers to scour the area and all its buildings for the princess.

When he reached Uji-tachi, he returned his horse to the stable and walked to the police station.

Lieutenant Matsuura greeted him eagerly. "My lord, I'd hoped to see you yesterday. Your sage advice would have been most welcome."

They were alone in Matsuura's office and the door was closed, but Akitada snapped, "No titles!" The man's carelessness suggested that he could have revealed Akitada's identity accidentally. He asked, "Have you said anything about me to anyone? A constable, perhaps, or your wife? Anyone at all?"

Matsuura's smile faded. "No. Never! I would not do such a thing, sir. I've been most careful."

"Hmm." No doubt his three visits here and the fact that they discussed their business behind closed doors had aroused the curiosity of the constables. Akitada glanced at the door and the walls. "I ask because last night someone set a trap for me in the forest. It was a miracle that I managed to escape."

Matsuura's eyes grew round. "A trap? In the forest? But why?"

Akitada did not answer that. Instead he walked over to the map of the Ise district and peered at it.

"Here's the Tanoe shrine," he said, pointing. "That's where several villains jumped me, knocked me unconscious, and carried me off."

Matsuura was still gaping at him. "Carried you off? Why?"

Akitada turned and looked at him. "I have no idea. They did search me and took an old letter and a little money. I wasn't carrying much."

"But . . . that's not like the prowlers. Or maybe it was them, but when they didn't find much to steal, they would have left you in peace."

"Hardly. I was tied up. Luckily, I managed to get loose. When they tried to stop me, I had to kill them."

"You killed them? How many did you kill?"

"Four men."

"You killed four armed robbers?"

"They weren't very good, Lieutenant." Akitada's conscience objected to this tale, but he wanted to keep Junichiro out of it at all costs.

The lieutenant regarded him with such admiration that Akitada continued quickly, "I came to in a wooden building somewhere in the woods. They had been drinking. Because they thought I was unconscious, they went to sleep. I saw later that the hut was being used to store certain goods that might have been meant for the prowlers, as you call them, or pirates. I happen to know that pirates have been busy in Ise Bay."

"But that's extraordinary, sir." Matsuura rubbed his hands. "Such a discovery should give the high constable ample reason to clean up the entire area. I shall report to him immediately. What good luck that he happens to be here at the moment."

Akitada snapped, "You'll do nothing of the sort, Lieutenant. You said yourself that the high constable has not done his job in the past. Meanwhile, you have two local murder cases on your hands, and one of the young women was found in the woods. It seems to me you have the authority as well as the duty to investigate the prowlers yourself."

Matsuura nodded slowly. "Yes, I do, don't I? He cannot complain this time. Yes, quite right. What do you suggest we'd better do?"

Akitada did not really wish to be drawn into local police work, but he wanted to know about the two dead women. He was particularly curious why the first girl, Michiko, had been beaten.

"I think you should tell me everything you know about your victims and the prowlers."

"Oh! You think there's a connection? That the prowlers killed these girls? They've never done so before."

"I don't know if they killed them, Matsuura. I don't have enough facts. What have you discovered about the first victim, Michiko?"

"Not much. We knew right away who she was. She worked in Mrs. Akechi's silk shop. Mrs. Akechi had no complaints about her and was very upset when she found out. She said she'd worked the day before as usual but didn't show up the next morning."

"How old was she and was she from here?"

"She was twenty-five, a farmer's daughter from Yamada, north of here."

"Hmm. Not very helpful. What about gossip? Junichiro thought she'd started working for one of the brothels at night."

"I checked. It's true, but she'd only just started. Still, there was quite a bit of money in her room. Two gold pieces and some silver. I think she was supposed to marry a farmer's son at home and was saving up for that."

Akitada sighed. He assumed that Michiko's willing-ness to play the princess had been partly due to extra pay. Most likely it had led to her death. But how and why? He said, "I'll speak to Mrs. Akechi. Perhaps she has remembered something else in the meantime. Now, what about the Inabe daughter? Keiko, was it?"

"She left home about a year ago to work for a family in Mikawa." Matsuura paused. "That's your province isn't it?"

"Yes, but I don't know everybody there," Akitada said with a smile.

Matsuura chuckled. "No, of course not, sir. I didn't mean that. Anyway, she'd come for a visit. Her mother said she was only there a day and a night."

"Short visit for such a long trip."

"I wondered about that, but her mother said she was needed by the family she works for. That reminds me."

He got up and went to a bamboo stand laden with papers and files. On top rested a hollowed-out gourd. This he brought back with him. "Mrs. Inabe kept asking about an amulet her daughter had worn. It wasn't on the body, but I went back to the place where she was found and there were these beads. Looks like they're from a string of prayer beads that broke. No idea if they were hers, but I meant to ask her. No amulet though."

Akitada looked at the beads. A few still had a piece of broken thread holding them. He agreed with Matsuura that they looked like prayer beads. Most were made of wood and lacquered red or black, but a few were of golden amber. The beads looked finely made and had probably cost a good deal of money at one time. Would a girl like Keiko have owned such prayer beads?

He returned the gourd bowl to Matsuura. "They might have belonged to someone else," he said. "They are very good quality. Will you take them to the mother to ask?"

Matsuura frowned. "They were very close to the place where her body was lying, though I had a hard time finding them. They were spread here and there in the grass. They may not all be from the same set of prayer beads. They don't match."

"I doubt that several sets of beads would have broken in the same place," Akitada commented. "And such rosaries sometimes use different beads to mark sections."

Matsuura nodded. "That's true. But I don't see what it proves one way or another. If she wore them around her neck, it's not surprising that they should have broken."

He was right, of course; Akitada had no better ideas. In fact, he had rarely ever felt so utterly at a loss in any case. And here, he was faced with three cases, each involving a young woman. He knew Michiko was connected with the princess, but her masquerade did not seem to call for her torture and murder.

Akitada said vaguely, "It's never wrong to pursue as many clues as possible. Maybe the beads mean nothing, but her mother may tell you something else after she identifies them." He paused. "And that reminds me. "Have you spoken with Mrs. Akechi and Michiko's friends about her activities before the murder?"

"Anybody who saw her that last day says she was just as usual, maybe even more cheerful. Mrs. Akechi is a very busy woman. She said she didn't pay much attention but didn't notice anything unusual."

That last was a lie. Mrs. Akechi knew very well how Michiko had spent her last day. She had impersonated the princess, so the princess could escape the palace as Mrs. Akechi's assistant. Akitada thought he'd better take his own advice and confront Mrs. Akechi with what he knew. She was probably not responsible for the abduction, but she might know something that would help him identify the person who was.

"Give me the beads," he said after a moment. "I'll talk to Mrs. Inabe. That should give you time to take some men to collect the dead prowlers and confiscate the goods in the hut."

Matsuura's face fell. He glanced at the map. "We'll have to find it first. You don't remember anything about the location."

"I'm a stranger here but it must be somewhere near Tanoe shrine and the road." Junichiro would know, but Akitada was determined to keep him out of it. If the prowlers' boss discovered what he had done, the dwarf would be killed. And that was another thing he needed to do as soon as possible: warn Junichiro.

Akitada collected the gourd bowl, promised to return with any new information and left for the River Palace.

22

The Silk Dealer

When Akitada entered the River Palace, he found Mrs. Inabe back in charge. Her eyes were red-rimmed and she looked older, he thought. For the first time he wondered about her strange marriage. Surely she was older than her husband. He would have guessed her to be past forty-five, while he looked to be in his thirties. Such things were not uncommon, of course, but having overheard them quarreling, he wondered.

She tried to greet him with a smile. Her bow was as courteous as always, another great difference between her and her husband who seemed to reserve his bows and smiles only for the wealthier guests like Mr. Murata.

Akitada hated to bring up the subject of their daughter, but she had asked about Keiko's amulet. He placed the gourd bowl on the ledge next to the guestbook and said as gently as he could, "Lieutenant Matsuura asked me to show you these in case they might have belonged to Keiko."

She stood on tiptoe, peered inside the gourd, and gave a little gasp. "They are the beads, but where's the amulet?" She looked at him anxiously.

"The beads are all they found and they may not all be there. We think the string broke when she was attacked and the beads flew everywhere."

"Oh," she said. "If the lieutenant would just tell me where they found my girl, I could go search myself. The amulet was a fine one. We gave her the beads and the amulet when she was five. They were to protect her." Her voice broke, and started crying again. "Forgive me, sir. It's been very hard. I loved my daughter and sent her to her death, you see. How can a mother live with such a thing?"

"You mustn't blame yourself. Blame the brute who killed her. She left in the daytime. You didn't know that those prowlers don't always just roam about after dark."

She nodded. "But it is strange. Still the police have done nothing about those prowlers. That's why they are getting so bold." She heaved a deep breath. "But it's still my fault for making her leave when she'd only just arrived. You see, we quarreled, and I was angry and told her to go back."

"Ah!" This explained the very short stay. And of course it would make the daughter's death much harder to bear. Akitada knew about a parent's guilt for a child's death and said gently, "You couldn't know what would happen."

She said nothing. Stirring the beads around in the bowl with her finger, she wept silently.

To break the heavy silence, Akitada said, "I take it the amulet was attached to the string of prayer beads. It could be hiding somewhere in the grass unless someone picked it up."

She nodded. "If someone found it, it's gone. It's valuable."

It should not have surprised Akitada, given the quality of the beads. "Can you describe it?"

"It was green jade and about this big," She made a small circle with her fingers. "Two dragons were carved into it. My husband said they stood for wealth and safety. It had been in his family for generations, and was much too fine for a small girl. But he doted on Keiko, and when she reached her fifth year, he went to a curio shop in the capital and bought the best string of prayer beads they had and had them attach the amulet. I told him she was only a girl, but he wanted her to have it."

Akitada pondered this generosity and fatherly love in view of what he knew of the loutish Mr. Inabe. It was evidently still easy for him to misjudge men.

Then she said, "He died two years later. Keiko loved him and she took very good care of the amulet, always wearing it under her clothes, so it wouldn't get lost." She paused to look at him. "The animal who attacked her must have found it and ripped it off. But if he wanted the amulet, why did he have to kill her?" She started to sob again.

Akitada was glad that Mrs. Inabe's current husband was not, after all, the pretty Keiko's father. He put his hand on her mother's arm. "Don't think about it. Think about her the way she was. She loved you, too."

It was the wrong thing to say, for now she burst into a storm of tears, moaning under her breath, her shoulders shaking.

Upset by such grief, Akitada said, "Please be calm. I'll have a look around for the amulet and also tell Lieutenant Matsuura to check the local curio dealers in case someone found it and sold it there."

She nodded, and he left her to her tears.

∞

His next visit was to Mrs. Akechi's silk shop. Here all was business as usual. The shop was full, two customers being waited on and a third peering at the bolts of many-colored silks resting on the shelves. Two sales women and a shop boy were occupied with them. Mrs. Akechi could be seen in the back, working over her accounts.

Akitada caught the eye of the shop boy and told him he wished to see Mrs. Akechi privately. He waited and saw the boy deliver the message and his employer looking up and at him. He thought she had seemed startled, but she relaxed when she recognized him.

The boy returned and took him to the backroom where Mrs. Akechi now stood and made him a deep bow.

The Shrine Virgin

"You honor my shop again," she said with a smile. "I'm grateful and will do my very best to serve you. I trust the silks you bought were satisfactory?"

"Yes. Please sit down again, Mrs. Akechi." Akitada cast a glance toward the shop and decided they were private enough, given the distance and the preoccupation of the customers and staff. He sat down himself. "The silks are fine. I'm here on another matter."

She looked mildly surprised and made him another small bow. "Please go on."

"It concerns your sales girl Michiko and her activities before she was murdered."

She stiffened a little at this. "May I ask why the gentleman takes an interest in the crime?"

"A friend has asked me to help him find out what happened."

"Surely that is for the police to do?"

Akitada could see that this woman was not easily manipulated. She was a businesswoman after all and used to protecting herself and her affairs. But it struck him that there was a big difference between Mrs. Akechi and Mrs. Inabe. The latter had not asked questions and simply accepted his interest. She, too, owned a business, but she had inherited it after her first husband died. Instead of remaining single, she had married again, while Mrs. Akechi, a much handsomer female, had remained single. The two women's personalities seemed almost diametrically opposed.

"The police are aware that I'm taking an interest. I may be able to help them. I assume you want Michiko's killer found?"

I. J. PARKER

"Of course. But I must tell you that I know nothing about her murder. She worked here that day and left at the usual time. The next morning she did not arrive for work. That's all I can tell you."

Akitada pursed his lips. "I think you took her along to make a delivery that day. Am I right?"

She looked startled. "You are well informed. Yes. That happens from time to time. When highborn ladies wish for silk, we go to them. The shop is mostly for or-dinary visitors. And like yourself, they are usually men."

"This delivery was intended for the Ise Virgin her-self, I think."

Now she compressed her lips. "We made a delivery to the palace. I cannot tell you who the silk was for. We are not admitted to the inner apartments."

"Come, Mrs. Akechi, you know very well why you and Michiko were there that day. In fact, you left the Bamboo Palace without Michiko, didn't you?"

Now she had grown pale. She was glancing around, and he saw that her hands shook inside her full sleeves. "I don't know what you mean? It was a perfectly ordi-nary delivery and we both returned."

"I have Lady Tamba's confession, Mrs. Akechi."

"Who are you? I've done nothing. I've had nothing to do with Michiko's death. I did as I was told. You cannot blame me." She sounded panicked.

"Ssh!" Akitada glanced over his shoulder. One of the salesgirls had heard and was looking toward them.

Mrs. Akechi controlled herself with an effort. "What do you want?" she asked more quietly. Her voice still shook a little.

The Shrine Virgin

Akitada considered her reaction. If she and Michiko had only acted on instructions from Lady Tamba, then she should have nothing to fear. But there was fear in her behavior. He did not answer her question and let the silence between them stretch. She reacted with more nervous movements and then repeated her question, "What do you want? If you know that Michiko stayed behind, then you know as much as I do. I never saw her again."

"I see. Where did you take the young woman who took her place?"

"She walked out with me through the front gate and a short distance along the road. Then she took a path leading up the hill and into the forest. I don't know where she was going. She didn't talk to me." She ran a hand over her neat hair. "I think she was one of the palace ladies, going to meet a man. It was very careless of her. So many girls have disappeared, and now there are murders. It's terrible. The police are useless." She took a deep breath and went on. "Michiko was a hard worker and a great help to me. Now I'm short of staff and have to do more work myself. I was only doing a favor for Lady Tamba, and look what it's got me."

She had talked herself into a calmer mood by suggesting that she was another injured party. Akitada said nothing.

She shot him a brief glance and plucked at her gown. "If you ask me, all those young noblemen who are supposed to guard the palace carry on with the young ladies there. That's what I thought was going on when one of them borrowed Michiko's clothes to slip out."

Apparently Mrs. Akechi had not known who her companion had really been and where she was going. But she could also be a good actress and know more about the affair than she was letting on. In any case, that still left the murder of Michiko. Who had killed her and why?

"What exactly was Michiko's part in this?"

"Lady Tamba took Michiko to another room. When she came back, she told me Michiko had agreed to let one of the young ladies take her place for an hour or so. The young lady would leave with me, and Michiko would come home by herself later."

"And you did not think this very strange and improper?"

"Strange, yes. Improper, no? What is improper for the good people? They do as they wish. Who was I to question Lady Tamba? Besides, I need the palace business. I thought it was some sort of silly game. They get bored and think up entertainments. Only poor Michiko didn't come back. I thought they'd kept her at the palace overnight, but then they found her body the next day. If she left after dark, the prowlers probably got her."

She fell silent and looked at him. Now that she had told her story, she was quite calm again. Perhaps she had merely panicked earlier because he had surprised her and she was afraid Michiko's murder would be laid at her door. It was impossible to tell how much of her tale was true.

He rose and said, "If you or her co-workers should recall anything else about Michiko's role in this or about her plans for the rest of that day and night, be sure to report it to Lieutenant Matsuura."

She got up and bowed, murmuring, "You have my word, sir."

23

An Ally

When Akitada emerged from Mrs. Akechi's shop, he saw that the sun was already high. As if to confirm the time, his stomach growled. He had not eaten all day, and he had also not seen Junichiro. The latter was disturbing. He owed the dwarf his life. The night before, he had been too tired to thank him properly. Now he began to worry. It was unlikely that Junichiro had been seen last night, but if he had, his life was in danger.

Junichiro was by nature curious, and this curiosity could lead the little fellow into serious trouble. He had followed Akitada even though he had not been invited to accompany him. On the other hand, it made him

211

extraordinarily useful to Akitada. Not only had he been there to help him the night before, but most likely he knew a lot of the secrets of the people of Uji-tachi. Even if he did not realize what he knew, he might help Akitada find the killers of the two girls.

Given the fact that he owed Junichiro his life and could not trust anyone else in this place, Akitada made up his mind to tell him something about his mission.

But first he must be found. He started the search by walking out of town to check Junichiro's shed. Not finding him there, Akitada turned back to pass slowly between the houses and businesses of the town, looking from side to side, hoping to see him peddling his pictures or offering his services to out-of-towners.

Again nothing.

Hunger eventually asserted itself. He decided to return to the place that served the good fish soup. As he passed his own inn, he heard shouting and saw that a small crowd had gathered before its entrance. Raised voices suggested an argument. Akitada was about to pass without looking—he hated gawkers—when he recognized one of the raised voices.

Junichiro!

Then he heard the dwarf howling with pain and pushed through the crowd. Elbowing the last watchers out of the way, he saw what had caused Junichiro's outcry. Before the entrance to the inn stood his host, the burly Inabe. He had Junichiro by the scruff of his neck and was shaking him like a dog while shouting insults at him.

The Shrine Virgin

"I'll kill you next time you come near my place, you piece of dung" he shouted. "I told you to stay away, you repulsive cripple. You're driving my customers away and getting me in trouble by stealing from my guests." Junichiro protested, but Inabe shook him harder. "Do you hear me, or do I have to cut off your ears, you god-damned freak?"

Akitada had reached them. "Put him down this instant!" he barked.

Inabe looked up and stared at him. Reluctantly, he let the dwarf drop to the ground. Akitada balled his fist and struck Inabe squarely in the face. It hurt like the devil, but he had the satisfaction of seeing blood spurting from the man's nose and a split lip. He felt good.

Junichiro scrambled up and ran behind Akitada where he clutched his leg like a frightened child. "I was looking for you, master, and he attacked me."

Inabe touched his streaming face and looked blankly at the blood on his hand. "You hit me," he said, sounding both surprised and outraged. "You hit me over a deformed little bastard like that?"

"Certainly. You were mistreating him. As you are much bigger and stronger than he is, that makes you a brute and a coward. For the future I'll expect you remember that Junichiro is a friend of mine. If you ever lay hands on him again or insult him, I'll hurt you worse than this. You will allow him access to the inn and to my room whenever he desires it. Do you understand me?"

Inabe pressed a sleeve to his nose and blustered, "We'll see about that. I'm going to report you for hitting me. A stay in jail will teach you a lesson about attacking local businessmen. And you can leave my inn. I don't rent rooms to scum like you."

Mrs. Inabe had come out and listened. Now she ran to her husband and shook his arm. "No, Seijiro. Don't do this. The gentleman was in his rights. Apologize to him."

He flung her away so violently that she stumbled. "I'll get to you later, woman!" he told her, scowling. Turning back to the crowd, he shouted, "What are you waiting for? Call the constables! I'll see this seedy tax collector jailed if it's the last thing I do."

Nobody made a move to call the constables.

Akitada bent to Junichiro. "Are you hurt, my friend?"

The dwarf had tears in his eyes but they seemed tears of anger because he cursed Inabe at length and with some colorful names. Akitada chuckled. "I'm sorry, Junichiro. Shall we go have a bite to eat? I'm famished."

Junichiro brightened immediately. "Whatever you say, master. But what about the police?"

"They are more likely to arrest him than us. Come along."

Inabe started to shout again. "Stop them! What's the matter with you people?"

The onlookers did nothing. They grinned or shook their heads and walked away.

As they walked to the restaurant, Akitada said, "I hope Mrs. Inabe is all right. The man's a brute. I wonder what she saw in the man."

The Shrine Virgin

Junichiro snorted. "She wanted him in her bed. He just wanted her business, that's all. This is the price she pays to have a stud to pleasure her."

"Ahem!" Akitada felt he should curb such offensive remarks, but refrained from reproof. After all, he owed the little man a great deal and he had just been sorely provoked. Besides, it was quite true that Mrs. Inabe was plain and middle-aged, while her husband was at least ten years younger. It was also possible that some women might find the tall, well-muscled, and hairy individual irresistible, but Akitada much preferred the motherly types to remain widows.

Because it was late, the restaurant was nearly empty. Even so, Akitada chose to sit as far from other guests as possible. They settled down amicably to their fish soup, and Akitada expressed his gratitude properly. Junichiro waved it off. "You've been good to me, master. What are friends for if not to help each other out of a pickle?"

Akitada received this in silence. After thinking about it for a moment, he said, "I have decided to help you out, too. And as you are truly my friend, I will trust you. You see, I was sent here on a secret assignment. You must promise never to mention what I'm about to tell you."

The dwarf's eyes grew large. "I swear it! Please, tell, master," he said eagerly. "It will make it much easier to look out for you."

Akitada smiled at this. "It's a serious and dangerous matter, Junichiro. You will have to be very careful or you could get hurt. Promise?"

Junichiro nodded. "Go on, tell," he said impatiently, ignoring his second steaming bowl of soup.

Akitada looked around to make sure nobody was in earshot, then leaned forward. "I was to look into the disappearance of one of the young ladies from the Bamboo Palace."

This made Junichiro laugh. "Never! That's funny. Somebody's been telling you fibs, master. Such a thing cannot happen. Those highborn ladies live far inside that big palace with the princess, many servants, and an army of imperial guard soldiers all around them. They never come out except on high holidays, and then there are many people around them. Nobody's as well guarded as those ladies."

Akitada sighed. It would not be easy. He took up his bowl to fortify himself.

Junichiro watched him. "Is that all? That's the whole secret? That's why you were wandering around in the forest in the middle of the night? You were looking for some lady?"

Akitada set down his bowl. "No, Junichiro. And don't look at me like that. I haven't lost my mind. I was told to meet someone from the palace at the Tanoe shrine."

"And you went? That was very stupid, master. Do not go out into the forest after dark. It isn't safe." Junichiro was looking at him with a furrowed brow. "Are you feeling all right?"

Akitada snapped, "I'm feeling perfectly fine. I may have been stupid to venture there alone, but I couldn't tell anyone. In any case, the person claims she intended to come but wasn't allowed to leave."

Junichiro snorted. "You were meeting a woman? Take my word she made a fool of you . . . or worse. Is she very pretty?"

Akitada muttered something under his breath and hoped the dwarf had not understood. "She is pretty, but that's not what this was about. She knew something about the missing lady's whereabouts. I had to find out what it was. Now will you let me tell you what I know?"

Junichiro grinned. "All right, but if you want a girl, I can get you something better than one of those ladies who just lie there like dead fish."

Akitada frowned. "You know nothing about fine ladies."

The dwarf giggled. "One hears stories, master. But do tell!"

"It appears the young woman wanted to visit her cousin who lives nearby. In order to leave the palace she traded places with a girl from the town. Some of the others knew about it."

"A cousin?" Junichiro showed renewed interest. "You mean she snuck out to meet a man?"

Akitada sighed. "Yes, Junichiro. And that's why you must not tell anyone about this."

"Lord Minamoto lives nearby. I didn't know he has a cousin in the palace." The dwarf cocked his head and thought about it. "Yes, I can see that. He's very handsome."

"It is an offense against the goddess. If people found out they'd blame the princess. And the emperor."

"Not their fault," Junichiro said quickly.

"There are people who would say it was."

"But why can't she just go back? Nobody'd be the wiser."

"She cannot go back because someone abducted her when she tried to return."

"You're kidding. She's not with her cousin?"

"I'm quite serious. She left her cousin but never reached the Bamboo Palace."

The dwarf scratched his head. "Let me think," he muttered and finally started eating his soup.

Akitada waited, wondering what solution the little man would come up with.

When his bowl was empty, Junichiro belched. "We've got to find her and take her back," he said.

"Brilliant! I would never have thought of that. How will we do it?"

The dwarf chuckled. "I'm not done. Who has her?"

"I have no idea. Possibly the prowlers."

"Ah! The ones that grabbed you?"

"I don't know, but I think someone might be up to some scheme to hurt the princess."

"Oh! That's bad. Like what?"

Akitada threw up his hands in frustration. "I don't know, Junichiro. It would be easier if I did. But there is something else I've learned. Your friend Michiko was the one who traded places with the lady."

"Michiko? You're sure?"

"Yes. Michiko worked for Mrs. Akechi. Mrs. Akechi took her along when she was delivering some silks to the palace."

Junichiro flushed with anger. "I knew that Akechi woman was behind Michiko's murder." He clenched his small fists. "I'll kill the witch. I'll kill her tonight."

"No," cried Akitada. He glanced about to see if anybody had heard, but they were quite alone now. It was long past midday and there would be no more guests until night time. The waiter was at the far end of the room washing dishes. A little calmer, he said, "I've talked to Mrs. Akechi. She claims that Michiko was to follow her home later. But it may have been dark by then and she may have run into the prowlers."

Junichiro glowered. "It's still her fault. She should have looked after her better."

It was true. Akitada sighed. And Lady Tamba and the other ladies-in-waiting should have looked better after the princess. Women were liable to do the silliest things to put themselves into danger. He said as much to Junichiro, who nodded, and said, "Some men, too."

Akitada ignored this and watched his companion thinking it over. In the end, Junichiro asked, "So what shall we do, master?"

"I hardly know where to start, but we have two murdered girls and one young woman who has disappeared. I think we should find out who is behind the murders. The lady may also be dead, you, know."

Junichiro nodded.

"You knew both Michiko and Keiko, the girl from the inn, and you also know the people who live here. Will you help me find out what is going on? I will pay you for your time and work."

Junichiro brightened. "No need to pay. I'll do it for Michiko."

"I insist," said Akitada and took five pieces of silver from his sash, handing them across. "That is for yesterday and today. Is it enough?"

The dwarf snatched up the coins with a laugh and said, "I shall enjoy working for you, master."

24

The Girl Michiko

"Come," said Akitada. "We've sat here long enough. Let's take a walk in the woods and make a plan." Akitada paid what they owed, plus a generous tip for having kept the waiter past his normal hours. The waiter bowed deeply and asked them to come back soon.

"As long as your soup's good and the servings generous, I'll second that," the dwarf said with a grin.

They walked to the Uji bridge, saying little because they were among many other pilgrims. But eventually they turned down a path to one of the lesser shrines, and the forest closed in with its fragrance and birdsong. They were alone.

Akitada said, "Tell me about Michiko."

Junichiro looked melancholy and did not answer right away. "She was very good to me, master," he said eventually. "I find it hard to talk about her."

"I know and I'm sorry. But if we want to discover who killed her and why, you must speak. Let me ask you some questions."

Junichiro nodded.

"After the police pulled her from the water, you said that Michiko had died because she had started working as a prostitute. So far, no one else has suggested this. Are you certain?"

The dwarf nodded. "She told me. I wasn't to talk about it. She hadn't been doing it long and she hated it, but she needed the money. She got a letter from home that said her mother was very sick and to come home. She wanted to take some money with her to pay for medicines."

Akitada raised his brows at that. "A letter? Could she read?"

"No. She took the letter to the school master and paid him something to read it to her and to write an answer."

"What was the answer?"

"I don't know, but Michiko said she had to earn a lot of money quickly to save her mother's life. So she started working at the Peach Bower after she finished at Mrs. Akechi's. That's why I thought some man she'd been with had killed her."

"Well," said Akitada, "I talked to the coroner. She wasn't raped. She was beaten and then had her throat slashed."

Junichiro gasped. "She was beaten?"

"Yes. Whoever beat her didn't bother to take her clothes off. I'm sorry. You had to know. My point is that this doesn't strike me as something a brothel customer would do."

"Some of those bastards are mean. " He shook his head. "It doesn't make sense. Michiko was gentle and . . . and loving. Why would someone do this to her?"

Akitada's understanding of the odd relationship between Junichiro and this girl suddenly grew a little clearer. The dwarf was a young man, whatever his size." He placed a hand on his shoulder and squeezed it lightly. "I'm very sorry, Junichiro."

The dwarf blushed and shot him a glance. "I loved Michiko," he said simply. "I shall never love anyone like that again. And if I find who did this to her, I'll kill him."

Akitada believed him. "The picture you drew of her, was that the way she looked when she was working at the brothel"?

Junichiro nodded. "It wasn't for the pretty clothes that she did it. Maybe she thought it was all she was good for. The gods know I was no use to her." He looked up at Akitada. "Michiko was beautiful. She was much too good for me. Look at me! I'm a dwarf and as ugly as a goblin. I frighten children, but she was kind to me because she felt sorry for me when I told her how much I loved her. She had great kindness. No other woman in her right mind would make love to someone like me."

Akitada had taken him for a goblin the first time he had laid eyes on him. He thought of the women he had loved and who had loved him. All had been beautiful. And now he was middle-aged with the first gray strands in his hair and had won a young beauty of only twenty years. What could he possibly know about someone like Junichiro? Deeply ashamed, he squeezed Junichiro's shoulder again. "There is more to love than wanting beauty," he said helplessly.

Junichiro snorted his derision of Akitada's comforting words. "Never mind. Let's get busy. I can find out who she was with at the brothel. She could have gone straight to work there after the palace. What about you?"

"I want to know more about those prowlers. If they expected the lady and were lying in wait for her, Michiko may have run into them on her way back from the palace."

"You're only thinking of your lady," Junichiro said accusingly. "The prowlers never attacked women before. They rob travelers."

Akitada thought about it. The dwarf had a point. On the other hand, in his experience such villains were very prone to rape when a chance offered. He said as much and asked, "Any idea who the prowlers are working for?"

Junichiro pursed his lips. "I've been wondering about that for a long time now. They're not local. I've snooped around for information about them, but nobody knows what's going on. Most people think the prowlers work for themselves."

"But surely they frequent the local brothels and eating places?"

"Maybe, but not often or someone would know something."

"Where do they live?"

"Elsewhere. Oyodo maybe or maybe someplace in the forest."

"Somebody must know. How long have they been working around here?"

"About a year. Off and on. That's what makes me think they're outsiders and just come here to fleece the visitors when their boss needs some money."

Akitada shook his head in frustration. "Perhaps the police will find out something from the four bodies they've collected. I'll ask Lieutenant Matsuura."

"Don't trust him, master!"

"Why do you say that?"

"Just don't trust him. He smiles too much."

"He's just friendly. By the way, he knows who I am. He said we met when he was with the police in the capital."

Junichiro looked surprised. "In the capital? So you know him well?"

"No, I don't know him at all, but it's possible that he's seen me there. It creates a problem."

The dwarf stopped. "Are you going to tell me who you are or will I have to find out for myself?"

Akitada laughed. "Oh, sorry. Yes, of course. My name is Sugawara. At the moment I serve His Majesty as governor of Mikawa, but my home is in the capital. I used to work in the Ministry of Justice."

The dwarf's eyes grew round. "What? You're a governor? Are you sure? You don't look or act like one."

Akitada looked down at his black robe, by now creased and rather dirty, and smiled. "Thank you. I think. These aren't my regular clothes."

"Why are you pretending to be a tax collector?"

"Best I could do on short notice. I don't think people would have talked to me if I had come here as a governor."

Junichiro grinned. "Maybe. You'd be surprised what poor people will do for someone like you. Begging your pardon, your Excellency." He made Akitada an elaborate bow.

"Don't do that. It isn't useful at present. Perhaps you are right, but not everybody is poor here. There is Lord Minamoto, for example. I do know him. We met many years ago. And what about the high constable?"

"Lord Sukemichi? You talked to him?"

"No, but perhaps I should. Lieutenant Matsuura doesn't like him. He says he's not doing his duty controlling the roads."

"I saw that lieutenant bowing so low to the high constable that his nose touched the ground."

"Really?"

Junichiro kicked a stone on the path. "Might as well have. Don't trust him."

"What about Sukemichi?"

"Him either."

You recall the merchant at my inn? Murata?"

Junichiro brightened. "There's another! He's a mystery. He comes here regularly on some kind of business. And when that's done, he visits the Peach Bower, but that's no mystery. The Peach Bower has the best girls."

"Would Michiko have known him?" Akitada was careful to phrase his question so as not to add to Junichiro's pain.

"Yes. She didn't like him."

"Oh? He might have been angered by a rejection."

"I doubt it. I told you, Michiko was kind. She'd never set out to make a man feel small. But she stayed out of his way."

"Did she say what the others talked about?"

"No. I can find out, if you like."

"Yes. And I'd also like to find out what he's up to when he isn't visiting brothels."

"I'll do my best, master."

Akitada peered up at the sky between the branches of towering pines and cryptomeria trees. "It's getting late. We'd better get back and start to work." He paused to look down at the little man beside him; Junichiro looked like a strange child but there was nothing childlike about him except his size. He had great courage, intelligence, and a gentle heart. "Be careful, Junichiro," he said. "Never forget that we're dealing with killers and don't know who they are."

"I know, master. I'm worried about *you*. If I'm to work for you, I can't be following you everywhere like last night."

Akitada tousled the dwarf's hair, hoping he would not take it as an insult because of his small stature. "Thank you, Junichiro. I think I've learned my lesson.

Shall we meet for a late meal, say a couple of hours after sunset? Where should we eat this time?"

"Come to my place, master. I caught a fine carp last night. It will be delicious."

Akitada had some doubts about Junichiro's cooking skills or indeed his inadequate kitchen facilities, but he agreed.

25

The Monk

After parting from Junichiro, Akitada went to get more information about the prowlers from Lieutenant Matsuura.

"Any news of the prowlers?" he asked, walking into the lieutenant's office.

"It's only been some hours, sir. No, nothing. The men found a number of sheds in the forest, but none had bodies or contraband in them."

It was disappointing. "Ah. We must hope for the best, then."

The lieutenant's broad smile reminded him of Junichiro's warning. He found it difficult to ask his questions casually.

"Lieutenant, do you remember the year we had all those fires in the capital?"

"Of course, I do, sir. Terrible time. The Superintendant was beside himself. You were very helpful to him, as I recall."

"Yes, I happened to suggest that the beggars' guild might be involved."

Matsuura nodded. "That beggars' guild! No surprise there. Nothing but an organization of thieves and criminals. I'm sure the decent people were grateful for your help, sir."

Akitada regarded him thoughtfully. "As it happened, I was wrong, Lieutenant. The fires had been set by some young rascals on orders of a rice merchant. How could you forget that?"

The lieutenant was taken aback for a moment, then said, "I wasn't in the capital that summer. I imagine someone told me about it, but I must've gotten two separate cases mixed up."

It was plausible, but Akitada would be more suspicious in the future. For the present, he just nodded. "That would explain it. I've done the same myself. The reason I mentioned it is that the activities of the prowlers here reminded me of that time. It seems to me that they are part of an organization. I was hoping you could tell me something more about them."

Matsuura spread his hands helplessly. "What can I say? We get reports from travelers who've been robbed while on the roads between here and the coast. It's been happening for a long time now. We report all highway robbery to the high constable office in the provincial capital. Sometimes he sends down twenty-five or thirty soldiers to patrol the roads. That is, unless they visit our brothels. Only once have they actually arrested someone."

"I see. And what have you done?"

Matsuura flushed. "I just told you. And I told you last time. It's not in my jurisdiction."

"Have you complained to the governor?"

The lieutenant glowered. Clearly he could not take criticism. "No," he snapped.

"Ah!"

"What good would it do? You cannot possibly judge conditions here. This is not Mikawa."

So Akitada had managed to anger the lieutenant. For better or worse? If better, then perhaps the man had something to hide and was using bluster to avoid answering. If for worse, well, then he felt secure enough under the protection of someone else to deal with Akitada so rudely. In that case, things could get uncomfortable. Akitada was becoming very curious about the high constable.

He had just decided to calm the man down and make his departure when a constable came into the room, saluted, and announced proudly, "We've got the killer, Lieutenant."

Matsuura was out the door in a flash, and Akitada followed.

They ran into the courtyard of the police station where only a short time ago Mrs. Inabe had wept over the body of her daughter. Almost in the same place now cowered a pathetic individual.

He was a monk to judge by his threadbare black robe, but he clearly had not seen the inside of the monastery in some time. The hair on his head had grown back in patches as if he had made several ill-advised attempts to shave it off with a dull razor. The stubble on his face made him look more unkempt than he was, and he was certainly dirty. His robe had not been washed for a long time and he had clearly been sleeping rough, because dead leaves and bits of grass clung to it. His bare arms and legs were scratched, bruised, and of a uniform grayish color.

His arrest had probably earned him some additional bruises. One of his eyes seemed to be swelling alarmingly and he had a cut lip. Given his condition, Akitada was startled to hear him break into song.

The guard standing beside him kicked him in the ribs and the singing stopped with a cry of pain.

"Found him in the woods near the Bamboo Palace, Lieutenant," the constable explained. "He's the man sold the amulet all right. The merchant identified him."

"Good work, Kitamora," said his superior, eying the prisoner with a contented smile.

Akitada looked over the lieutenant's shoulder at the monk. He caught a whiff of sour wine when the monk opened his mouth to say, "Found it," and belched.

"No doubt," the lieutenant told him. "Where'd you get it?"

"Found it." The monk touched his swollen face and pointed at the constables. "They beat me. I wasn't doing anything and they beat me." He tried to get up. "Gotta go."

The Shrine Virgin

The constable pushed him back and slapped him on the swollen side of his face. The monk howled.

"Stop that!" Akitada snapped. The constable gaped at him. Akitada said in a more reasonable tone, "I have found that beating a prisoner may produce a confession but it is rarely the truth. Most of the time, the prisoner just says anything to stop the beating. Besides, this man is drunk. You're likely to get more cooperation if you let him sleep it off."

"He resisted arrest," the constable protested. "That proves he's guilty."

The lieutenant cleared his throat. "Well, we'll have the truth out of him sooner or later. Take him away."

Akitada opened his mouth to protest. He had a question he had wanted to ask the monk. But seeing Matsuura's face with its compressed lips and the frown, he decided to leave it alone. He merely asked, "He tried to sell Keiko's amulet?"

Matsuura nodded. "The curio dealer said a begging monk had brought it in, and he'd given him ten coppers for it."

"Ten coppers? Are you sure it's the right amulet. Mrs. Inabe said it was jade—."

Matsuura glared. "A jade disk with two dragons. Yes, I'm sure. We're not total dunces here."

"Forgive me, Lieutenant. I didn't mean to imply any such thing. But ten coppers is hardly enough for a valuable piece like that."

"Whatever. The monk was happy enough with the coppers and promptly bought wine with them. As you

saw. I guessed as much and sent my men out looking
for him. Now if there's nothing else . . ."

There was nothing else. Akitada left.

∞

The arrest of the monk troubled Akitada. From what
he had just observed, they would beat a confession out
of him. The man was middle-aged and looked un-
healthy. He was not the type to withstand much pain
before agreeing to whatever they asked for. But was he
innocent?

The fact that he had had the amulet was strong evidence. Keiko had been raped and strangled. Akitada
was not so naïve to think a Buddhist monk incapable of
raping a woman. In fact, this particular specimen in his
drunken and filthy condition seemed the very type to
do such a thing. No doubt he had been tossed out of
every monastery he had ever been a part of and ended
up roaming the highways of the land begging for food.
But the fact remained that he could have found the amulet. It seemed more likely than raping and strangling a
young woman near a roadway and then stealing her
amulet.

Pondering this, he decided to talk to Mrs. Inabe
again. He hoped things had calmed down at the inn and
that her husband was elsewhere.

He was lucky. Only Mrs. Inabe sat in the reception
room. She looked glum. When she raised her head at
the sound of his steps, her face became even longer.

"Oh," she said. "It's you."

This was not promising. He had taken her for a
pleasant and accommodating hostess, but now it

seemed she wanted nothing more to do with him. He said, "I trust your husband has calmed down."

"No, sir. He's very angry. He's been in a terrible mood ever since Keiko died. I think it will be best if you go to one of the other inns."

Akitada was irritated at being thrown out of a mediocre hostelry like this. "I understand the place belongs to you. Do I take it that you agree with that brute?"

She flushed and looked away. "He's my husband."

Angered further, Akitada snapped, "And was he also the reason you sent away your daughter who had come to visit you?"

To his shock, she turned absolutely white and gulped. He said quickly, "I'm sorry. I had no right to say this. But from what I have seen of your husband, he has been treating you badly. I can do nothing about that, but when he took his ill temper out on my servant Junichiro, I was in my rights to object. However, I shall, of course, remove myself and my things. Please prepare my bill."

He walked to his room where he quickly shoved the laundered shirt, some sheets of paper, and his writing box into the bag he had traveled with and returned to the inn's reception area. Mrs. Inabe was busy with another customer, the merchant Murata. Akitada had not paid enough attention to the man, and it struck him now that Murata's presence here might well have something to do with one or two of the events that had been preoccupying him.

Murata seemed to be leaving also, for he was paying his bill. When he had settled his account, he shoved a small bag toward the landlady, saying, "This is for your husband, as agreed." The bag clinked but it was impossible to see how much money it contained. From the phrase "as agreed," Akitada deduced that it wasn't a tip for running an ordinary errand.

Akitada cleared his throat, and when Murata turned, he said, pleasantly, "I see you're also leaving. I trust you've had a pleasant visit to the shrines."

Murata narrowed his eyes and said stiffly, "Yes. Quite pleasant." Then he nodded to Mrs. Inabe and walked out quickly.

Akitada filed away the man's curious manner and turned to his hostess. "I saw Lieutenant Matsuura earlier. It seems they got your daughter's amulet back."

She nodded. Her face filled with pain again. "I went to identify it. They were looking for a monk. He sold it to the curio dealer Usami. Why would a monk have my daughter's amulet? Someone must've given it to him for alms." She looked at him, perhaps hoping for some assurance that such a thing could have happened.

Akitada said, "They have arrested the monk for Keiko's murder, Mrs. Inabe."

"Oh?" To his surprise, a look of relief crossed her face for a moment, then was gone. She became sober and shook her head. "A monk? How could a monk do such things to my daughter? It's horrible." For a moment she sat, looking past Akitada to the street outside, then she sighed and reached for her account book to make out his bill.

26

The Cry of a Child

Saburo set out as soon as it got dark. He wore his black shirt and trousers under an ordinary brown robe. Among the small items he carried in his sleeves were a pair of black slippers that were both more silent and more practical for climbing roofs and balancing on beams than the sandals on his feet, a black cloth useful for covering his face and for carrying items, a very sharp knife, a set of metal hooks and thin blades that could open locks, and a length of light, but very strong silk rope.

He walked, having debated the advantages and disadvantages of a horse only briefly, and was tired when he finally reached the manor. He was older than either

Tora or the master, and his former agility and stamina had deteriorated rapidly lately. The realization that he was no longer capable of the things he had done in an earlier life was depressing. When he reached the manor, he decided to rest before making his entrance, so to speak.

The night was dark. There was a weak new moon that was made even weaker by a hazy sky.

He was sitting under a pine that grew close to the tall fence surrounding the compound and dozing a little when he heard the sounds of activity from inside. This late at night, he had not expected it. People being awake and busy would make his work more difficult and perhaps impossible. On the other hand, it was so odd that it might well reveal some criminal undertaking and thus make further efforts unnecessary. He decided to investigate.

He walked away from the area, took off his sandals, rolling them up in his brown robe and hiding the bundle in a clump of weeds. With his slippers on his feet, the scarf covering most of his face, and the other items tucked away inside the close-fitting black clothing, he climbed a section of fence, swung over a leg, and dropped softly down on the other side.

Their visit the day before had given him a general idea of the layout of the compound. The noise had come from the entrance courtyard, and he now made his way there, following the fence, walking softly, and keeping to the shadows provided by buildings, crossing open spaces at a crouched run after making sure no one was about.

He could see the flickering light from torches and heard shouts directing men to move something. Perhaps they were hiding contraband goods, he thought. It would not really be surprising after he and Tora had let Kitagawa know that he was under suspicion.

Before him was a stable building. He could smell it and hear the horses moving inside. Beyond the stables was the courtyard where people were working.

Saburo instinctively shied away from open, well-lit places. Instead he crept along the back wall of the stables until he found an open doorway. The stables appeared to be in darkness, and he slipped in. The horses knew he was there. They moved nervously as he passed. The stable gates to the courtyard were closed but small openings under the eaves let in enough of the torchlight outside to help him find his way.

He located some bales of straw piled high enough the let him climb up to one of the beams that crossed the stable under the roof. Using the beam to walk across the intervening space, Saburo reached one of the openings. There he lay down on the beam until he could bring his face close enough to peer out.

What he saw astonished him. The men in the courtyard were building an elaborate funeral bier. He wondered briefly who had died but dismissed the thought. It was irrelevant. His hopes had come to nothing. The unusual activity after dark was merely due to the urgency of funeral preparations.

He abandoned his look-out and returned the way he had come with the same care as before. But when he reached the section of the fence where he had climbed in, it occurred to him that he might as well have a look at a few other buildings. It was a good time, since the household was distracted by death.

Saburo found no access to the main house, but a large, two-story building that probably housed servants adjoined it via a covered gallery from which he could climb the roof of the residence. After that, he would have to find a way inside.

Seeing an open door to the servants' quarters, he slipped inside, hoping to find the corridor empty. It was. He moved silently toward the gallery when he heard someone weeping upstairs and paused. But he decided grief was normal when someone had died, and started forward again.

Above him, the weeping ceased, and a woman's voice pleaded with someone.

Saburo stopped again and listened.

"Please, please," the woman begged, "don't hurt her. She's just a baby." Then she started to weep again.

For a moment Saburo stood frozen. He looked up toward the upper floor, wondering how to get up there without being seen. Then he hurried on to the door to the gallery. There he swung himself quickly onto the railing and climbed one of the supports to the roof of the gallery. He paused for a moment, cast a longing glance toward the main house, then moved quickly back to the servant quarters.

Like the main house, this building had a lower roof section that wrapped around it. The roof of the gallery adjoined this, and Saburo merely stepped across from one roof to the other, then walked along until he reached a window.

He was in a hurry after what he had heard but had to move slowly and carefully because people were inside.

The room with the window was blessedly empty. He climbed inside and eased the door of the room open. The weeping woman, a crouching figure in the darkness, was in front of another door a few doors away.

He returned to the window and looked up toward the roof. The distance to the eaves was not great. Climbing onto the sill, he took out his rope, threw it over one of the eave beams and pulled himself up. From here he got onto the main roof. It was covered with boards that were held down by heavy rocks.

He found a loose board and shifted it enough to let him slip inside. He was now in a space very familiar to him. Beams crossed each other in all directions and below the beams were rooms. It was dark, but he saw a glow of light to his left. That must be the room where someone was hurting a small child.

As he started his journey along the beams toward the light, he heard the child cry out.

A man's voice spoke. It was deep and rough but the tone was soothing. It got quiet again and Saburo moved forward. Then the child cried out again, this time clearly in pain. The woman started wailing again, "Don't hurt her. Don't hurt my baby."

The man grunted, "Shut up!"

Saburo realized what must be happening and was sickened. He covered the last few steps toward the lighted room as quickly as he could.

Peering down, he saw the room was just large enough to spread some bedding. An oil lamp burned on a clothing trunk. On the bedding the back of a large man was moving rhythmically while the child whimpered.

He was too late. The child sobbed, and the man moved uncaringly, focused only on gaining his pleasure.

Nauseated by what was happening, Saburo drew his knife and dropped down behind the man and seized him by the collar, pulling him off the child.

He had only time for a brief glimpse of her. Her eyes were closed, her face wet with tears. She was half naked and very pretty. She could not be more than ten years old, but Saburo had no time to think about that, because the man in his grasp reared back with a shout of surprised fury and flung Saburo against the wall with unexpected strength. Saburo dropped his knife and slid down the wall as the man turned.

It was Hozo!

Saburo's surprise cost him a few precious moments. Rage distorted Hozo's face as he flung himself at Saburo. If he had not stumbled over the trousers that hung about his ankles, the fight would have been over. As it was, Saburo rolled away and grabbed for his knife.

Hozo cursed as he kicked off the trousers and came for Saburo again. He saw the knife in Saburo's hand and stopped. "Who the fuck are you?" he snarled, backing away.

The Shrine Virgin

Saburo tore the black cloth from his face. "Someone from your past, Hozo. We trained together until they sent me to Mount Hiei. I see you still have disgusting habits. But raping children is more than even I can stomach. You want to say a prayer first?" Saburo closed in on him, baring his teeth.

Hozo's eyes had widened when he heard his name. He backed away some more. "You! Almost didn't know you with that beard. I heard they didn't quite kill you. A pity when I'd warned them about you."

This stopped Saburo. He stared at Hozo. "You warned them? What do you mean? We were on the same side."

Hozo laughed. "You thought we were." His eyes slid to the knife.

Saburo almost missed it, but he remembered Hozo's training. Hozo was a fighter and both bigger and stronger than he. Even with a knife in his hand, he would find this an uneven contest.

When Hozo attacked, Saburo slipped aside and kicked at his enemy's thigh. Hozo stumbled, caught himself, and dove for Saburo's legs. They both slammed to the floor, kicking and struggling for the knife.

At that moment that the door opened a crack. The crack widened, and the woman crept in, stared at the struggling men, then ran over to gather up her child and lead her out of the room.

Saburo was dimly aware of the movement, but Hozo was about to break his wrist to loosen his grip on the knife and he had no time to look. Then the pain in his hand and wrist became unbearable and his fingers opened.

He was certain he was about to die.

At the hands of this animal!

The thought gave him the strength to ram his knee into Hozo's groin.

Hozo gave a shrill scream and curled up. The knife was back in Saburo's hand, and he thrust it deep into the other man's belly, twisting it to cut across. Blood poured forth, and Hozo screamed again.

The cut was the same a warrior used when committing suicide after a lost battle and much too good for Hozo, but it served.

Saburo staggered up and away from the bloody, writhing figure on the floor. The knife fell from his fingers, either because his hand was slick with Hozo's blood or because his wrist had finally given way.

The room was empty except for Saburo and the dying man. The little girl was gone. Saburo was glad. But Hozo's screams had been heard. There was shouting outside and the sound of people running.

It was not over yet.

He glanced up at the beams. They were his escape route, but it was much easier to jump down from a beam than up to it. Besides, all his strength seemed to have left him, and his right hand was throbbing and useless.

The shouts were coming closer. Saburo saw an old clothes trunk and pushed it under one of the beams. Making use again of his silk rope, he pulled himself up with his left arm. It took two tries and a final desperate effort. The running steps were on the stairs and then in the hallway by the time he managed to get his lean belly onto the beam and pulled his legs after.

The door flew open below and people pressed in, calling out in shock.

Saburo slid into the darkness, then got up to walk along the beam to the opening in the roof. There he had another unpleasant moment, but this time the distance was not great. He jumped, gripped, pulled himself up, and slid out onto the roof.

The night had become cloudy. Below, he saw people milling about with torches and decided he had wasted too much time already. Running lightly across the roof, he jumped down to the roof below. He paused a moment to see if he had been noticed, but the firelight made it unlikely that anyone would see the dark figure on the dark roof, and inside the dying Hozo held their attention. He slid down one of the gallery supports and then dropped over the railing to the ground at the back of the building.

A short time later he was outside the compound, breathing hard, cradling his damaged hand against his chest, and so exhausted that he fell into one of the irrigation ditches next to the road. He lay there without moving, letting the water seep through his clothes, welcoming its coolness, and regretting that he had not come on horseback.

27

Fireflies

Since his choice of inns was small, Akitada simply walked the short distance to the Golden Dragon and requested a room. Somewhat to his surprise, the innkeeper, a short, rotund man with a wide smile, treated him as an honored guest in spite of his disreputable attire. The room was more expensive than the one in the River Palace but it had the added attraction of being far in the back and over the river. Instead of the noise from Uji-tachi's main street, which tended to last into the morning hours, he would sleep to the soothing sounds of the water. Akitada left his baggage and went back to pay for two nights and to order a bath for later.

He had decided to abandon his pseudonym—too many people already knew his true identity—and signed the register as Sugawara, giving the capital as his home. He doubted that this innkeeper would compare notes with the Inabes.

Back in his room, he unpacked his writing utensils and wrote two brief letters home. One sheet was for Yukiko. He told her he hoped to return soon but complications had arisen. He added a brief line: "I dream of orange blossoms, recalling your sleeves about my neck." It was not very good, but he hoped she would know how much he missed her.

Then he dashed off a second note to Saburo, assuring him that all was well and to tell Tora to keep an eye on things for a few more days. These he posted at the local post station.

It was still too early to visit Junichiro's shed. He had intended to find out all he could about the prowlers, but Lieutenant Matsuura, his best source, had become unhelpful. His lack of progress depressed him. To be sure, the sense of urgency to rescue the Virgin was gone. By now she was either dead or being held somewhere. In either case, there was nothing he could do for her. His duty then was to discover what was going on and, if possible, prevent further disaster. He had spent four days here already and achieved nothing. And that reminded him that he had promised to report to the chief priest.

The Shrine Virgin

The visit presented a couple of problems. He could hardly reveal the truth about the princess's love affair with Minamoto, and he was no longer sure if he could trust Nakatomi. If the princess had been abducted, then someone was playing a dangerous game and this shadowy person's interests were not local but must lie with the court in the capital. He did not think Nakatomi was the mastermind behind this, but the priest could be an accomplice.

He shuddered at the thought that the imperial succession itself might be the object of the plot.

At the chief priest's house he was received by Lady Nakatomi, a grandmotherly sort of woman with a sweet smile. He was instantly tempted to absolve her husband of all nefarious activities because he had no wish to see this pleasant lady hurt.

"My husband is filling in for one of the other priests today," she said. "He should be back soon. Won't you come and take some refreshment?"

She did not know his name, proof that Nakatomi had kept his secret, but since there was no longer any point in the pretense, he introduced himself.

She bowed, led him into a very pleasant room that faced the garden, and placed a cushion near her own where she had evidently been sewing some piece of clothing. Clapping her hands for a maid servant, she ordered some light refreshments.

"I don't like to interrupt your work, Lady Nakatomi," Akitada said, gesturing to the sewing implements. "I could wait for your husband elsewhere."

"Not at all." She smiled at him. "If you'll allow me, I shall go on with my sewing while you refresh yourself. I think a meal is always nicer eaten in company."

"Very true. This is kind of you."

The maid returned with wine and chilled fruit juice as well as a plate of nuts and sliced fruit. He asked for the fruit juice and drank thirstily. It was delicious, as were the slices of melon and segments of oranges.

She smiled at him between stitches. "It has been a bountiful year. The gods have blessed us. Have you enjoyed your visit to Ise?"

"Very much. Thank you for your concern." No point in burdening this charming lady with his worries or the fact that he had nearly been killed. It struck him that the good people living in their mansions, palaces, and hunting lodges were probably as unaware of sinister bands of prowlers roaming about outside as they were of the hectic life in Uji-tachi with its wine houses and brothels.

She surprised him, however. "I believe you are the new governor of Mikawa across the bay. Did you find the problems with coastal piracy very troubling?"

He said cautiously, "I have not been in Mikawa long enough to be very familiar with such matters, but I shall certainly be keeping an eye on it. Is Ise province taking any action?"

"I have not heard that they have. We hear rumors now and then of ships being boarded and travelers robbed. If they were on their way here, they report to our police, but the police are ill equipped to deal with crime on the seas when they have their hands full with visitors losing their money in more usual ways."

So much for Lady Nakatomi's ignorance of the troubles outside her walls. He smiled and said, "You must wonder about the princess."

"I did not want to ask. Many men would consider it none of my business."

"Your husband told me that you assisted in the impersonation for the summer festival. It was very helpful and great credit is due to you and your family for avoiding a scandal. I'm afraid I have not yet discovered the princess's whereabouts and came to tell your husband."

"Oh," she said and dropped her sewing in her lap. "Poor child. Something must be very wrong."

"I hope not," said Akitada, though he had little faith in it.

"She is always very sweet. We have known her from the beginning. Princess Takahime is an imperial lady, but to me she was like another daughter when she came." She looked at Akitada beseechingly. "I have been so worried. You must do what you can."

This simple plea had the effect of changing Akitada's attitude toward Takahime profoundly. He had taken her to be a foolish young woman who risked the safety of the nation for selfish and prurient reasons. In fact, he had felt little beyond irritation and disgust for her. Now he saw her through the eyes of this kind lady as a young girl who was surely suffering great fear, and possibly worse. He said, "I will, Lady Nakatomi.

There were noises of arrivals outside, and a moment later, the door was pushed wide and a young woman in bright red silk trousers and a white silk jacket glided in gracefully, crying "Mother . . ." and stopping with a look of dismay on her pretty face when she saw that her mother had company. She bowed deeply. "I beg your pardon."

"My daughter Nobuko," Lady Tachibana introduced. "She has assisted her father. Nobuko, this is Lord Sugawara who has come to speak to your father."

Lady Nobuko was a shrine maiden, and as such she had impersonated the princess during the great summer ceremony. Akitada regarded her with some respect. Shrine maidens were frequently the daughters of priests and were raised in shrine duties which included not only the protocol of the ceremonies themselves, but also the performance of sacred dances. Lady Nobuko wore the traditional costume of a shrine maiden and looked charming, though clearly embarrassed at the moment.

Akitada bowed and smiled at her. "No need to apologize, Lady Nobuko. I was so thoughtless as to arrive unannounced myself."

Nakatomi, still in his white robe and trousers, arrived next, nodded to Akitada, and said to his family, "Forgive us, but we have business to discuss."

His wife hurried to gather her sewing, but Akitada said, "As both your wife and your daughter know already about the princess, perhaps they may wish to stay. I have just told your lady that I have not yet laid eyes on Princess Takahime and came to report my failure."

Nakatomi frowned, but came to sit down beside his wife. His daughter took a seat somewhat behind them.

"You have made no progress at all?" Nakatomi asked.

"Only a little and I'm afraid that little gives even greater concern. It appears that Princess Takahime has disappeared while on a stroll outside her palace. This happened two days ago. Since then there has been no sign of her."

Lady Nakatomi gave a small cry and covered her mouth. Her husband put his hand on her arm as if to calm her and asked, "Two days ago? But she's been gone for over a month."

"No, it appears that she was in her palace all along but indisposed and unable to perform her duties."

"She's really been ill?" cried his wife. "Oh, the poor girl. I wish I might have gone to look after her. What was the matter?"

"I'm not sure," Akitada lied.

"That lying female Tamba," Nakatomi exploded. "I knew she'd do anything to prevent me from speaking to Her Highness. And I take it she's still hiding the truth. But what has been done to find the princess?"

"I can only speak for myself. I have no idea what steps the palace has taken, though I suspect Lady Tamba was too afraid to turn to the local authorities."

"Well, at least she's not created a scandal, but what have *you* done?"

"I have taken an interest in certain local events in hopes of understanding who might have abducted the princess."

"Abducted?" cried the priest.

"There are only two reasonable explanations. Either the princess was injured and died, or someone took her and is hiding her."

"You think she is dead? Oh, how terrible!" moaned Lady Nakatomi. Tears had risen to her eyes.

"Forgive me, Lady Nakatomi. No body has been found, so it's unlikely that she is dead."

"Then someone has her." The priest glowered at Akitada as if he held him personally responsible for such a thing.

His daughter suddenly said, "There may be another explanation."

Her parents looked at her reprovingly, but Akitada asked, "Yes, Lady Nobuko?"

She blushed and said in a low voice, "She may have gone to someone of her own free will."

"Nobuko," scolded her mother. "What a thing to suggest!"

Her father snapped, "Impossible. She's the Ise Virgin."

Akitada suppressed a snort. He said, "Lady Nobuko is quite right. I suspect she may have set out to do just that, but she never arrived."

"Where?" cried Nakatomi? "What are you suggesting? I forbid all of you to bandy about such sacrilegious nonsense."

Akitada sighed. "Let us concentrate on finding her. It would help me if you could tell me something about all the persons in this district who may be said to be important in one way or another. For while there is a gang called the prowlers who prey on travelers on the roads, it does not seem likely that such men would dare an abduction without being ordered to do so."

Nakatomi had turned very pale. He stared at Akitada and dabbed perspiration from his forehead. "Dear heavens, what is happening to us all? Gangs on our roads? Abductions of young women? Two recent murders? Are they also part of this?"

"Perhaps. I'm trying to find out what I can. Unfortunately, the local police chief has become tired of my meddling."

Nakatomi bowed his head. "Apart from those belonging to the Bamboo Palace, I know of only two men of rank and power. They are Minamoto Sadamu and Sukemichi Yasunori. Minamoto is distantly related to the princess and above reproach. Sukemichi is the high constable of Ise province. Both men come here to hunt. I find it difficult to associate either with the scenario you have described."

Akitada had not expected great revelations but was disappointed nevertheless. He asked, "Have you had further instructions from the capital?"

The priest shrank even more into himself. "Only a request for news. Dear gods, I shall have to report this. I suppose you have already done so?"

"No. It is, of course, up to you, but I shall push on with my investigation in hopes of finding out something soon. I don't want to risk being recalled."

The priest looked at him searchingly. "You have some idea then? I shall wait a little longer if you can give me some hope."

"Just a hint of an idea," Akitada said, knowing full well that his vague ideas had no foundation is actual facts."

He left after this. The sun had set and night had fallen, and he had a long walk ahead of him. It was too early for the prowlers, but Akitada walked quickly and kept his hand on his sword hilt. The woods had become ominous to him and every small sound startled him. He wished for Tora for the first time. Tora's cheerful optimism and his raw courage would have lifted his spirits. For that matter, Saburo, the former spy, would be highly useful once he had some notion where the princess was kept.

When he saw the lights of the town ahead, he put these thoughts aside. He was not yet a helpless old man who could not handle himself without assistance. This was a chance to prove to himself that he was still young and active enough to be a fit husband for Yukiko.

Alas, his dinner invitation reminded him that he owed his life to a dwarf.

Junichiro's shed was lit festively by a number of paper lanterns. Akitada called out when he reached the door, and Junichiro shouted, "Come around back, master."

There were more lanterns here. Akitada's heart warmed to the grand effort the little man had made to give him a festive entertainment.

Junichiro was bent over a large *hibachi*, stirring the charcoal and testing the heat of the griddle with a drop of water. "Please be seated, master," he said, turning to greet him, his face almost as red as his spiky hair.

Akitada sat down on a cushion placed near the railing and at some distance from the cooking area. A chipped flask and several unmatched cups stood ready. Junichiro had also been shopping in town for pickled plums, radish, and seaweed crackers. These were displayed on large cabbage leaves.

"I hope you haven't spent all the money you earned on this feast," Akitada said, eyeing the offerings with amazement.

"Don't worry. The best part was free. Look!" He lifted up a very large, fat carp. "Still alive until a few moments ago. I kept him in a cage floating in the river. And there will be rice, too. The good kind, not the dirty brown stuff they sell me as a rule. Have some wine while I make this fish comfortable on the fire."

The wine was also good. Akitada felt both ashamed and flattered—flattered that Junichiro, though desperately poor, should have gone to such expense for him, and ashamed that his own status laid such a burden on the young man. He decided to express his appreciation by praising the food and eating with gusto.

As they waited for the fish to cook, Akitada reported on his day. The dwarf frowned when he heard about the arrest of the monk but was inclined to think that he could well be guilty of attacking Keiko. It appeared that there was no love lost between the dwarf and Buddhist priests. The visit to the shrine priest left him shaking his head.

"So everybody now knows who you are and what you're doing here?" he asked. "Don't you think that was stupid? Whoever's behind this will try to kill you again."

"I doubt it. They probably knew already. Confirmation may make them afraid to stir up a great outcry."

Junichiro looked doubtful. "As for me," he said, "when I wasn't busy with your dinner, I asked around about Murata. He always stays in the River Palace and goes out during the day, but nobody knows where. At night, he's back. He visits the brothels sometimes, usually the Peach Bower, but not so much lately. He must have a woman somewhere. I tried to find out, but the madam chased me away." Under his breath, the dwarf called her something Akitada did not understand. He refrained from asking for a translation.

As it turned out, praising dinner was easy. The carp, when presented fried along with white rice was delicious. They sat together, eating, commenting on the food, exchanging tales of fishing and watching the fireflies gradually adding their starlike points of fire to the night. Replete and warmed by the wine, they relaxed as the clear waters of the river moved darkly past on their way to the sea. Akitada could not remember a more wonderful entertainment and said so.

The dwarf looked surprised. "And you a great lord, even if you go around in poor clothes and pretend to be like everyone else?"

Akitada looked up at the sky. "At this moment I envy you, Junichiro. Your life seems perfect to me here beside the river . . . my belly filled with good wine and delicious carp . . . under the stars that dance like the fireflies." He felt pleasantly drowsy.

Junichiro chuckled. "The wine is good. Have some more, master."

Akitada did. At some point he must have dozed off. When he awoke, he was leaning against the wall of the shed and the dwarf had placed a quilt over him. Junichiro lay beside him, curled up in another quilt, small and defenseless as a child. Akitada felt a great surge of tenderness for the little man. Then he closed his eyes again and went back to sleep.

28

The Funeral

Tora was exercising his guard troops in the main courtyard of the tribunal when he noted some excitement at the gate. Since the sun had not yet risen and a vague gray light merely gave a hint of the coming day, he could not make out the cause of it.

Giving the command to stand at ease, he strode over to see what was going on. The guards were arguing with some pitiful beggar, it seemed. Then he looked more closely. The bedraggled figure in black rags with another rag tied around his head was Saburo.

"What happened?" he called out and ran to him.

The gate guards stood aside, looking blank. Saburo swayed.

"He says he's the tribunal secretary," one of the gate guards said with a guffaw. "He must be mad."

Saburo said nothing and swayed again.

Tora caught him before he fell. The gate guards stopped laughing. One of them asked uneasily, "Do you know him, Lieutenant?"

"Shut up and help me get him inside," Tora snapped.

Somehow they managed to support the wet and shivering Saburo up the stairs and into his office where one of the clerks had already arrived and stared open-mouthed.

"Get some wine!" Tora told him as they lowered Saburo onto a cushion. Tora turned to the soldiers. "Thanks. Return to your duties and tell the others that drill is over for today."

Then he had a good look at Saburo, noted that he had a swollen eye and was clutching his right arm to his chest. He peeled Saburo's fingers off gently. The right wrist and hand were badly swollen.

And covered with dried blood.

He did not see any other injury and asked, "Where are you wounded, brother?"

Saburo thought about it, shook his head, and held up his wrist again.

"There's blood. And why can't you speak?"

Saburo moved his lips, then croaked, "Parched."

The wine arrived, and Saburo drank two cups, one right after the other. Since he was normally not much of a drinker, Tora watched this with a frown. He glanced at the clerk who still stood by, goggle-eyed. "Get back to work," he said. "I'll take the secretary to his quarters."

When the clerk was gone, he asked, "Well?"

"Blood's Hozo's. Killed the animal!" Saburo covered his face with his good hand. "Too late, but I killed him."

Tora put an arm around Saburo and raised him to his feet. "Come along, brother. You need a bath and a rest."

Saburo managed a brief smile. "Thanks, Tora."

Tora busied himself helping Saburo into the bath. He was relieved to see no fresh wounds, though the torture scars Saburo bore on all parts of his body were sickening enough. He refrained from asking questions as he washed his friend's body. Not until Saburo was to his neck in the bath, did he point to the swollen wrist.

"Broken?" he asked.

Saburo grimaced and looked at it. One by one he moved his fingers. "Maybe not. But it's useless. How am I going to do my work?"

Tora chuckled. "You tell the clerks to do it. What are they for? Feel like talking about it now?"

Saburo closed his eyes. "I'm trying to forget," he muttered.

"What? If you killed this Hozo, I expect he deserved it."

"Oh, yes. He deserved that and the worst the devils in hell can dish out."

"Really?"

Saburo opened his eyes. "Think of our little lady Yasuko. When I found him he was raping a little girl her age. She was screaming, and her mother cowered outside the door pleading with the bastard."

Tora expelled a breath. "Dear gods! Weren't there enough grown women around?"

"He liked them young and weak. Liked to hear them scream."

"Well," said Tora after a moment, "I'm glad you killed him."

"I was too late. If I'd hurried more . . . Tora, I'm too old for my work. I was useless."

"You were not useless. You killed him so he couldn't do it to another child."

Saburo said nothing.

After a while, Tora asked, "Did you find out anything while you were there?"

"Not really. After I cut open Hozo's belly, he made a lot of noise and I had to run for my life."

"Can't be helped. We'll find another way to check out their storehouses. I still think Kitagawa is in the piracy business."

"Oh," said Saburo, "You'd better wait a day. "They were getting ready to bury someone. And now they have Hozo dead, too. Though I doubt they'll make such preparations for him. The other person must have been someone of importance. They were building a big bier with a decorated box and fine curtains on it."

"Maybe someone in Kitagawa's family. Never mind. You're going to spend the rest of the day in bed."

∞

With Saburo settled in his room, Tora got on his horse and took the road to Kitagawa's manor. He was a little late for the funeral procession. The bier and the mourners were already disappearing into

the forest beyond the manor.

Tora followed, suddenly suspicious, but he found soon enough that the woods had concealed a private cemetery. There the small group of people stood around some men who were digging a new grave. In front of the mourners stood Kitagawa, dressed in hemp like the rest.

It looked very much as if the *betto* was the chief mourner. Perhaps his mother or father was being laid to rest. In the country, they still buried their dead.

Tora had seen enough. He turned his horse around and returned to Komachi.

All seemed quiet in town, and even more so in the harbor. There were few boats left, though the ferry still took on passengers. Tora glanced up at the sky. It was a hazy blue, but the sun shone brightly. It was another hot day. He wished the elusive storm would come already. The heat had been constant, and it was time for it to break. He decided to spend the rest of his day inspecting the governor's residence to make sure it could withstand rain gusts and high winds. The gardens, he thought, would be improved if a few trees bit the dust.

When he returned to the tribunal, he was told that Lieutenant Mori had arrived and was speaking to Secretary Kuruda.

Irritated that Saburo's rest had been disturbed by the hateful police chief, Tora hurried to Saburo's office. He found Saburo and his visitor in the small private study beyond the large room where clerks and scribes were busy with their chores.

Tora gave Saburo a searching look. He looked a little better, but his eye was turning black and blue and he held his right hand tucked inside his robe.

"The lieutenant was kind enough to commiserate with me on my fall from the horse," Saburo said.

Mori gave Tora a crooked smile. "I'm happy to see that *you* have escaped injury, Lieutenant Sashima," he said. "I was beginning to think that Mikawa was not good for your health."

It sounded like a threat.

"What brings you, Mori?" Tora said though clenched teeth.

"Well, as I was telling Secretary Kuruda the other day, there have been certain complaints. I'm investigating them."

Tora sat down. "Do these complaints involve the tribunal?"

"Oh, you might say that. The complaints are about the tribunal. More specifically they concern you and the secretary."

Tora raised his brows to Saburo who said nothing. Tora wished he knew if this was about Saburo's exploits during the night. If it was about the man Saburo had killed, he wanted to know what Saburo had told Mori. He cleared his throat. "You'd better be more specific, Mori."

"One of our most respected citizens, the Fujiwara *Betto* Kitagawa, has charged you with harassing him and insulting Lord Shigeie. It appears that you questioned him about pirates and implied that Lord Shigeie was behind the pirate activities along the coast here and to the north."

Tora turned to Saburo. "Did we mention the coast north of here?"

"Not to my knowledge."

"There you are, Mori. Though now you mention it, it's an interesting concept. What do you think, Saburo?"

"Very interesting."

Mori exploded. "How dare you make such accusations? If this starts any rumors, we'll all be in deep trouble. Lord Shigeie is immensely wealthy and powerful, and the court will not tolerate such insults to a man of his rank and importance. You will apologize to Kitagawa." He paused and smirked. "Perhaps Secretary Kuruda can compose the letter if you find it too difficult. And you will both stay away from the property."

Tora was lunging at Mori, but Saburo caught his sleeve. "No, Tora. The lieutenant misspoke. He forgot for a moment where the authority lies in Mikawa. Lieutenant, you are addressing two officials of the Mikawa tribunal. You cannot tell us what to do. We, on the other hand, can tell you to mind your manners."

Mori was on his feet. He sputtered, "The governor isn't here. I've warned you before. You have no authority without him. You've been acting on your own and without orders. We'll see who is right. I'm reporting this matter to the capital."

Tora's hands were clenched, but Saburo held on to his sleeve. When Mori was gone, he released Tora and said, "He will make trouble, Brother."

29

Minamoto Returns

Akitada woke just before dawn. Junichiro was already up, busying himself in the half light with tidying up after their feast. Akitada had a surprisingly clear head after drinking all that wine the night before. He sat up and stretched, yawned, and said, "Good Morning."

Junichiro evidently had assumed the role of servant again, for he bowed quite deeply and answered, "Good morning, my lord."

Akitada rose. "Here, let me help you with that," he said, taking hold of the large bamboo cage that had held the carp. The dwarf was struggling to get it over the side of the railing and back into the river.

"Thanks, but it isn't your place to help me."

"I thought we'd become friends, not master and servant."

The dwarf gave him an uneasy look. "That was only for a little while last night. You honored me, master."

"Nonsense, you saved my life. I can't treat you as a servant." It occurred to him that Tora had also saved his life, and yet Tora would always serve him. But Tora had a manner, a very disrespectful manner at times, that allowed Akitada to forget the gulf that separated them. He sighed. "Will you at least allow me to treat you to your morning meal?"

This he was apparently allowed to do, and they set out for town more companionably.

"What are your plans, Junichiro?" Akitada asked.

"To go back to the brothel. This time of day they may not notice me hanging about. I'll ask about Murata and also about the prowlers."

"Excellent. I thought I'd talk to the curio dealer who bought the amulet."

They returned to the same noodle vendor they had patronized before. The dwarf sniffed the air. "Hey, Haruki! What's that in the soup today? Mrs. Osumi is missing her cat."

That got a laugh from a few people and a threatening fist from the vendor until he saw Akitada behind the dwarf. Chuckling, he cried, "For you, I saved its tail."

More laughter and they were handed two bowls of noodle soup with vegetables. They moved aside and stood under a tree, slurping down the noodles and drinking the broth, when Akitada nearly dropped his bowl.

Lord Minamoto was riding past on a handsome horse. He was wearing a fine silk robe and a court hat with the rank ribbons designating the third lower rank.

"Look!" Akitada said to Junichiro.

Junichiro looked. "Ah, so he's back. What will you do?"

Akitada was so angry he could barely speak. Eventually he snarled, "Nothing. He's a coward who wasn't worth my effort."

"Hmm. I like him. He's been good to me."

"I told you what he did. An honorable man would not have abandoned a young woman in such distress."

"Well. He's back. Maybe he's found a way to help."

"I doubt it." Akitada returned his empty bowl to the vendor. "Let's get started. We'll meet again for our evening rice. My treat this time. Where do you want to eat? Pick the best place in town. After your meal last night, it's the least I can do."

"In that case, master, I've always wanted to eat at The Kingfisher. I hear they have fried abalone that people dream about." His face fell. "But I doubt they'll let me in."

"They'll let you in, or I'll make them very sorry," Akitada growled.

They parted company, and Akitada started looking for the curio shop. This proved more difficult than he had anticipated as there were a number of these. It was the third shop that he found the man who had bought the amulet from the monk.

The shop was crammed to the rafters with shelves holding all sorts of things that travelers might wish to take home with them. All shapes and sizes of ceramic bowls, cups, pitchers, and flasks jostled wood carvings of Amaterasu and her three treasures. Small painted screens showed red *torii* among towering trees, small lacquered boxes held writing implements in case one had forgotten one's own, and everywhere there were amulets of every kind and even prayer beads.

Akitada asked his question of a small bald man who puttered among his treasures next to his money box.

"Shocking!" the shopkeeper said, eyeing Akitada hopefully. "The police got him, I hear. You'd think those priests would keep their monks under control. Instead they throw the bad ones out and let them roam the streets and highways, raping and murdering decent people. Can I show you something to take home as a memento of Ise?"

"Perhaps another time. I met the poor young girl before she died and am trying to understand how such a thing could happen here."

The shopkeeper looked at Akitada's black ramie robe, now distinctly worse for wear and both dirty and wrinkled. Evidently he decided the customer was a total loss, for he said, "I must tend to my business," and started drifting away.

Akitada wished he had his usual clothes, but the situation could not be helped. He said quickly, "The monk claims he found the amulet. Is that what he told you?"

The shopkeeper snorted. "A lie. He came here straight from that wine shop across the street. I watched him coming this way and was ready for him. I thought he planned to steal something, you see. But then he reeled in and he had this piece of jade in his hand. Well, I could see it might bring a few coppers and I wanted to get rid of him. So I paid him twenty coppers and he reeled right back to the wine shop to drink some more." He paused to glower in that direction and added, "I got robbed anyway. I'm out twenty coppers and the police got the jade piece."

The amulet had been worth many times the amount he claimed to have paid the monk, but Akitada did not enlighten him. He thanked the man and crossed the street.

It was still too early for the true drinkers to fill the establishment, but there were one or two men sitting about, staring morosely into their *sake* cups. Only a waitress was looking after the place and she came eagerly to serve another guest.

"Welcome, your honor," she intoned, bowing quite deeply. "What is your pleasure?" The question was accompanied by such a languid look that Akitada half wondered if he had erred into a brothel. She was a buxom, healthy-looking girl and no doubt had many admirers among the late night customers.

"A flask of your best," Akitada told her. "And then a few moments of your time."

She giggled and gave him a sideways look. "With pleasure, your honor," she fluted and swished away with a wiggle of her hips and the tiny steps of the courtesans.

Akitada sighed. He was a happily married man these days . . . not that he was tempted.

She returned with more wiggles and some rouge on her lips, knelt beside him and poured the wine into a cup which she offered him with both hands.

He drank. The wine was passable.

She asked, "Are you pleased?" in a seductive murmur and leaned a little closer.

"The wine is good, but I have another matter on my mind."

She blushed a little and looked over her shoulders at the two silent guests. "We aren't supposed to," she said, "but things are very quiet. My room is just down the hall in the back."

He had phrased his interest too ambiguously and said with a smile, "I'm deeply flattered, but it's too early for such pleasures. I wondered if you remembered the monk who was arrested by the police."

She forgave him with a charming little pout. "We're very busy at night," she murmured. No doubt this was his put-down for having refused her offer. "I didn't pay much attention, especially when the fight started. He came in, bought the cheapest wine we had and sat in a corner over there. I forgot all about him, but after things were quiet again, he called for more wine. I told the police about it."

Akitada thought about this and saw little useful information in it. "What was he doing during the fight?"

"I wouldn't know. They were starting to break things and I was shouting for help. My boss came and threw the worst troublemakers out. He told that awful Inabe never to come back. That one's been bothering me eve-ry time he was here."

"Inabe? You mean the man who is married to the owner of the River Palace?"

"Yes, him. If you ask me, I'd rather be married to that dwarf than to a man who sleeps with every whore in town."

"What was the fight about?"

She shook her head. "No idea. One moment they're sitting there drinking and talking, and the next, Inabe has this other guy by the neck and they're rolling around on the floor. That's when their friends got into it and started throwing stuff. It was awful. Anyway, I'm glad Inabe's gone for good."

Akitada thanked her, paid for his wine, and left.

Now that he was no longer pretending to be a low-level provincial official he felt he should get some new clothes. After a moment's consideration, he headed back to Mrs. Akechi's shop. Mrs. Akechi was not there this time. An assistant told him she had left on an er-rand.

It was as well. He preferred dealing with this pleas-ant saleswoman who showed him readily some suitable silks and promised that their experienced needlewoman could sew him a new pair of trousers, a robe, and a hunting jacket by the next day. He chose a silver gray figured fabric, paid for the silk, and left.

His next visit was to the Golden Dragon. No doubt the innkeeper had wondered why he had not slept in his room the night before. When he walked in, the man's face lit up with real pleasure so that Akitada thought for a moment that he had really been worried about his guest. But it turned out to be something else.

"Oh, sir," he cried, "I'm very glad to see you. Lord Minamoto was here a little while ago, asking for you. I didn't know what to tell him. He left a note for you. He asked for writing utensils and wrote it right here. I had to apologize for the poor quality of the paper and the brush. He said it didn't matter." He extended a folded piece of paper with both hands and a bow.

Akitada sighed and opened the paper so quickly that he tore it. The innkeeper sucked in his breath at such irreverent behavior.

Minamoto had written, "Please come to see me. I have something to tell you, but keep it to yourself." He had signed it "Sadamu."

Akitada chewed his lip. He really wanted nothing more to do with Minamoto, but with the present lack of progress he could not afford to pass up on anything, no matter how unlikely.

He thanked the innkeeper and then, on second thought, asked, "Do you happen to know a ship owner called Murata? He is a wealthy man who stays at the River Palace when he visits. I would have expected him to stay here instead."

"Mr. Murata used to stay here, but this summer he decided he preferred the competition. It's nothing we did. I thought at first they had a pretty maid, but I hear he's still visiting the Peach Bower. They say his favorite is Precious Butterfly, a remarkable beauty, but expensive. I can't account for his moving to the River Palace.

It's not like him at all." He shook his head at such odd behavior.

"Oh well, perhaps he just wanted a change of surroundings."

The innkeeper pursed his lips. "Hmm. Not unless the River Palace has changed."

30

The Ransom

Renting another horse, Akitada rode to Minamoto's lodge. He hoped to settle the matter of his former pupil once and for all. As soon as the spoiled young lord revealed what was so urgent, he would tell him in no uncertain terms that he wished to have nothing else to do with him.

The gate was opened rather more promptly this time, and the gatekeeper had sobered up, though his manner suggested that he was paying for his excesses.

He took Akitada's horse and said, "He's inside. You know the way, I expect."

Akitada knew the way and gave the door a sharp rap. Minamoto opened immediately, his face lit by a broad smile. "There you are, Sugawara. Good of you to come so promptly. Wait till you hear. But come in, come in! Some wine? Please sit down. The woman at the River Palace sent me to the Golden Dragon. I described you and the innkeeper let me write a note."

Akitada said nothing to this effusive greeting. He walked in but did not sit down. A look around showed that the room had been tidied somewhat but, given the gatekeeper's condition, its cleanliness and order left something to be desired. It was almost as if this high-ranking nobleman was the old man's subordinate.

But such considerations were pointless. Akitada stood and said coldly, "No, thank you. I shall not stay long enough. Say what is on your mind, and I'll be gone."

Lord Minamoto almost dropped the wine flask he was holding. He gaped at Akitada. "What's wrong? Has something happened?"

"You know well enough what is wrong. I have no time to waste waiting on spoiled lordlings when a young woman is in danger. Say your piece."

Minamoto set down the flask. The smile was gone and his face was flushed. He came closer and said, "She will be back safely in a short time. I could not spare her what must be a frightening experience, and for that I'm truly sorry, but I have done my best to bring her back unharmed."

It was Akitada's turn to be astonished. "What do you mean? Where is she? Who has her?"

"I don't know where she is or who has her, but I have been in communication with her abductors. They have demanded gold for her return. Tossed a rock over the fence with a note tied to it. I went home to raise the money and have now paid it. I repeat: she will be back soon. I have promised not to reveal the agreement to anyone, so I count on your discretion."

Akitada located a cushion and went to sit down. "Pour that wine, and then explain what you have been up to," he said.

Minamoto brought the flask and two cups, placing them on the floor beside Akitada and getting another cushion. Akitada inspected the cups. They looked reasonably clean, but he wiped them on his sleeve anyway. "Your gatekeeper is a drunken sot and the rudest servant I have ever encountered."

Minamoto sat down and poured the wine. "He is old and has been with my family for a long time. The service he has done in the past entitles him to such liberties. I can forgive rudeness when I owe a man a debt of gratitude."

This last was said so pointedly that Akitada reddened. "There are some acts that are unpardonable and a decent man should not tolerate them."

He saw the young man's fists clench for a moment, then relax again. "Let us keep to more important things," he said. "As I told you, I received a communication not long after you were here. It was unsigned and informed me that Princess Takahime was staying in a safe place, was well, and would be treated with all the care and courtesy due to her. She would be allowed to return to me if I paid a certain sum for her release and kept the transaction absolutely secret. I left immediately for home to raise the money and bring it back with me. It has now been paid. It was still dark when I left it in the designated spot and came back here. By midday, someone threw another rock over the fence. This was tied to it." He took a much crumpled piece of paper from inside his robe and handed it to Akitada.

Still dazed with disbelief, Akitada looked at the message. It read "Much obliged. 'To give is to receive.'" The brush strokes were firm, the characters correct, and the use of the quote spoke to a certain level of education. He turned the paper over, but found nothing else written on it. "Where did you leave the money?"

"There is a small shrine called Tanoe. People rarely visit it. I was to leave it under the water basin."

The Tanoe shrine again. Akitada recalled sitting on the rim of that basin waiting for Lady Ayako. The stone basin had been supported by some large stones underneath but they left spaces where one could easily hide a package.

He sighed. "How much money was involved?"

"It wasn't all money. That would have been too heavy to carry, not to mention that such a sum could not be raised quickly. There were one hundred pieces of gold, ten gold bars, and receipts for one hundred bales of rice."

It was an enormous sum. Akitada shook his head. "You could command such wealth so quickly?"

Minamoto grimaced. "I sold my land. That took care of the rice receipts and the gold bars. The rest I had in reserve."

"Dear heavens! You sold your land? How did you accomplish that?"

"Someone always wants good rice land. Local gentry aiming for higher things. Even that upstart Sukemichi is buying a house in the capital."

"So you returned with an enormous fortune and you left it between some stones in the forest?"

"That was what I was told to do."

Akitada shook his head again. This tale was either an example of extreme foolishness or Minamoto was lying. He felt as if he were walking on quicksand.

He got to his feet. "I'll have a look where you left the money."

Minamoto gave him an uncertain look. "No need to check. The note said they got it. She'll be returned here any moment."

"Do you have any proof that these people have the princess?

Minamoto shook his head. "But they must have her. Where else could she be?"

"If they have her, there's no guarantee they will return her. Besides, whoever has her may not be the same person who sent the demand. That may be someone else who knew what happened and decided to benefit from the knowledge."

Minamoto looked stricken. He said, "It had occurred to me that there was a risk, but I had no choice. Takahime was in trouble because of me." He covered his face. "I would give my life to bring her back."

Akitada almost forgave him at that moment. Or at least he forgave him for his initial carelessness and neglect. But he reminded himself that Minamoto had taken advantage of a naïve young girl who had fallen in love with him.

He banished the fleeting thought from his mind that he himself had succumbed to Yukiko's determined pursuit. That had been altogether different. He had fallen in love and taken Yukiko to wife. This had never been an option for Minamoto. And of course he still had grave doubts that he could trust Minamoto's words. The tale of raising such unheard wealth in a short time and disposing of it under a stone basin in the woods seemed too far-fetched even for someone with imperial blood in his veins.

"I want to see for myself where you left the ransom," he said again.

"I cannot leave in case they bring her."

"I doubt they'll bring her, but your gatekeeper seems reasonably sober again. He can make the princess welcome." Such an encounter was too ridiculous to contemplate, but Akitada was not naïve enough to believe it would happen.

"Why do you doubt it? I paid a great amount of money."

"For one thing, you probably have been watched. You asked me here to tell me this story when you were bound to secrecy. This may well have cancelled the deal."

Minamoto's eyes widened. "Surely not. Why should it? Nobody knows I told you." He added in a rush, "I couldn't let you think I'd run away when I could see how disgusted you were with me. I wanted you to know that I was not completely without honor."

Akitada grunted. "That was not my point. If someone saw you go to my inn, that someone also may have seen me come here."

"But it should not matter. Nobody knows who you are."

"I'm afraid that's no longer true. By now a number of people know my true identity, including the innkeeper of the Golden Dragon."

"Oh." The young man had paled. "I didn't know. Perhaps you'd better leave alone. I'll get a message to you when Takahime is safe."

"I'll leave in a moment, though it's probably too late. What do you plan to do when it is all over?"

Minamoto looked down at his hands. "I don't know. We cannot marry. I was hoping to convince her to return to her duties."

"I see." The princess would hardly be flattered by her lover's suggestion. Perhaps she would become so angry that she lost all interest in him.

One could always hope.

But there was still no proof she was alive.

31

The Shed in the Forest

The sun was setting when Akitada left Minamoto's hunting lodge. Time seemed to be passing much too fast for all that needed to be done. He turned the horse in the direction of the Tanoe shrine and hoped there would be enough light. At least he was becoming familiar with all the roads and paths between the shrines, the town, and the various dwellings.

At the shrine, he dismounted and checked the area of the water basin very carefully. There was nothing under it, but he thought he could make out traces of something heavy having been pulled out. There were too many footprints near the water basin to offer any-

287

thing else. He sighed. Minamoto's story seemed to be true.

After a moment's consideration, he decided to check something else. He got back on the horse and followed the path to the road. If he was not mistaken, this was the road he and Junichiro had found after escaping from the shed. The shed must be somewhere near it, and probably there was a path to it. The prowlers needed some way to move their goods in and out, and that would take a cart. He did not think there were enough members in the gang to carry the goods on their backs.

All he had to do was to find a track branching off the road and follow it to see where it led. Surely that would not take long. He glanced at the sky. The pink of the sunset was rapidly fading, but he had a horse this time. He glanced at his surroundings, trying to remember what the terrain had been like the night they had seen the high constable's soldiers passing, and then turned right.

He found the first path almost immediately, but it crossed the road. Taking the one to the left, he spurred his horse forward. The path climbed slightly, then leveled off as it entered a valley. The trees closed in, and Akitada began to question the wisdom of his undertaking. But there were cart tracks, and they were fresh. There was also evidence that horses had come this way recently. Even if the shed was not on this path, something else of interest might lie this way.

But the shed was there. It lay in an opening in the forest, and just enough light remained for Akitada to see. He dismounted, and approached. He saw that the bodies of the prowlers had been removed.

Of course, there could be any number of sheds in this forest, but he began to recognize things. The doorway was very familiar, and as he looked around, he could visualize again what he had seen from it when he had staggered out. Still, he had been very preoccupied at the time. He listened, then walked to the doorway and peered inside.

It was too dark to make out much and he entered. Yes, this was it. It was the right size, and over there was the charred dirt from the fire and on the other side were the loose boards and the opening Junichiro had used to cut his bonds. He saw neither the piles of supplies, nor the rope that had bound him.

But he did see an oil lamp with the flint beside it. He picked it up, struck a spark, and lit it. Then he began a careful inspection of the shed.

The blood stain where Michiko had been tortured and killed was gone. The entire dirt floor looked as though it had been swept. Gone also were the hook where she had been suspended and the whip they had flogged her with. But the bench was still here, though it had been moved.

Who had done all this? The police were supposed to remove the bodies and might have done so in the meantime, but would they have cleaned up the place?

He recalled the wheel tracks and the number of horses that had passed recently on this track. The police constables would have been on foot and have removed the bodies and the goods on litters. Why then the large number of horses?

Suddenly Akitada recalled the soldiers who had passed on the road that night. The chief constable's men.

But it was nearly dark by now, and he might be in considerable danger. If the prowlers returned, his position and rank would not protect him. It was time to leave.

He doused the light and was leaving the shed when he heard his horse whickering. He hurried to it.

Too late.

Hoof beats approached and metal clinked against metal: the sounds of armed men.

There were ten of them and a commanding officer. They carried torches and immediately surrounded him. They wore full armor, even helmets, and they looked threatening.

The man in command glared down at him. "Who are you and what are you doing here?" he barked.

Akitada had left his papers at the inn. Worse: his clothes were so dirty and wrinkled by now that he must look more like a vagrant than a person in a decent way of life. But there was nothing for it.

"Sugawara Akitada," he said with as much dignity as he could muster. "I was held prisoner here by some prowlers who used this as their headquarters and came to see if the police had cleaned up the place. And who are you?"

The soldiers muttered. Their commander frowned. "We serve the high constable of Ise province and are

• 290 •

clearing the local roads of highway men and other riff-raff. Did you say your name is Sugawara? Are you a slave belonging to the Sugawara family? Because you don't look like a retainer."

The situation was as funny as it was uncomfortable. This was the first time he had been called a slave. "No," he said, making an effort to regain his serious-ness. "I *am* Lord Sugawara. Not a slave or a retainer, but the head of my clan. Don't let these clothes confuse you. I had reason to wear a disguise."

"A disguise!" The commander snorted. His soldiers roared with laughter until the commander shouted, "Quiet!" The laughter ceased. "Arrest him!"

Akitada cried, "No. Wait!"

But five of the soldiers dismounted, their swords drawn, and surrounded him. They disarmed him and tied his hands behind his back.

They were not gentle, and Akitada's wrists had not healed yet. He protested. They became really rough. When he was bound, he asked the commander, "Where are you going to take me?"

The high constable's bad reputation with the police lieutenant did not encourage him to think the matter could be cleared up easily. Being carried off to the pro-vincial capital to be thrown into jail would mean that he would linger there for days, maybe weeks, before he could be properly identified and released. And by then the story would be so embarrassing that it would impact his career in the government. Arrested for vagrancy in a province that was not his own? It smacked not only of incompetence as a governor but suggested a degree of mental imbalance that would make him unsuitable for high office. His only hope was to make them believe who he was.

He tried his best to explain and was finally told to shut up and get on his horse. Getting on a horse with your hands tied behind your back was not possible. He attempted it anyway. His rented horse shied away and he fell flat on his face. The soldiers had another good laugh. The impact bruised his face and caused his nose to bleed, and the officer finally told them to give him a hand.

They took him back to the road, then followed this in a westerly direction and eventually turned off onto a secondary road that climbed the side of the mountain. Akitada had not been here before and wondered if they planned to take him through the mountains all the way to the provincial capital. But they turned off the secondary road also and soon arrived at a sizable estate with a number of halls and outbuildings. It was too dark to make out many details.

Someone must have been watching for them, because the large double gate swung wide and they rode onto a graveled courtyard. More torches lit the area.

Akitada was very much aware of the appearance he must present with his bloody face and gown, but there was nothing he could do about either. As it turned out, he was not taken to the main house but rather to one of the outbuildings. There one of the soldiers pulled him roughly off his horse. This time Akitada managed not to fall. They marched him into the building, pushed him into a small room resembling a cell, and slammed and locked the door behind him.

Before the door closed and the light went away, Akitada caught a glimpse of the place. There was some dirty straw in a corner and bucket. The place stank.

When the door slammed, he was in the dark. And they had left his hands tied.

He wondered if the wooden bucket was filled with water. He was parched, but did not dare take a chance on the contents. Besides the only way he would be able to drink was to kneel and drink like an animal. This he refused to do and sat down instead on the straw.

It was probably a salutary experience to see how prisoners were kept in jails, though Akitada hoped matters in his own province were somewhat better. He was very uncomfortable because he could not lean back against the wall with his hands tied behind him. His face hurt, especially his nose, which seemed to be swelling and was clogged with blood, forcing him to breathe through his mouth. Gradually his sense of outrage grew.

Better anger than self-pity, he thought.

Given the well-equipped soldiers, he decided he was being held by the high constable of Ise province, Sukemichi Yasunori. He knew nothing of the man except what Lieutenant Mori had said. Sukemichi was provincial gentry, clearly not a member of one of the old clans, but sufficiently wealthy and influential to have received the appointment by the court. Apparently he was more interested in his own pleasures than in any real effort to subdue criminal gangs like the prowlers.

The brief view he had had of the man confirmed such a reading of his character.

These negative impressions did, however, offer some hope if Sukemichi could be made aware of who his prisoner was. He would hardly wish to offend the governor of another province. Thus, when Akitada heard someone outside his cell door, he called out, demanding to see the high constable. This was ignored and the footsteps receded.

Nothing else happened for a long time, and Akitada contemplated crawling over to the water bucket after all. He had just managed to get to his knees and was shuffling across the floor when steps approached. The lock rattled and the door opened. Akitada managed to get to his feet.

There were two of the soldiers outside. One of them had a torch, and the other stepped in, gave him a sharp look as if he wished to remember his face, then untied his arms.

"I wish to see the high constable," Akitada demanded.

"He's not here. You can leave."

Akitada rubbed his sore wrists. Outrage returned. "What do you mean? Why was I brought here? How dare you arrest an innocent man and throw him into prison? Rest assured that I shall report the matter."

The soldier turned his back and walked out. Akitada followed. "Tell me! Who gave this order? I'll speak to the high constable about it. Where is he?"

The man did not answer this, but the second soldier said, "You were found at a notorious robber hide-out and arrested."

They were now outside and a groom stood there, holding the bridle of Akitada's horse. The soldier handed back his sword and pointed. "You can wash over there."

It was a trough for horses. Akitada went to it. The water looked clean. He saw his face reflected in the torch light and almost recoiled. His nose was swollen and blood had dried on his mouth and chin. There were also several bloody scrapes on his forehead.

He gathered some water in his cupped hands and drank thirstily. Then he gingerly washed his face. It was sore, especially his nose. He hoped it was not broken. At least he could breathe better now. Dabbing the water from his face, he went back and got on his horse.

"Follow the road that way," the first soldier said. "It's about three miles to Uji-tachi."

Akitada said nothing. There was no point in making further threats and complaints. He rode out of the gate into the night and turned in the direction of town.

32

Grave Robbers

Tora and Saburo spent the rest of the day separately, turning the matter of Mori and Kitagawa over and over in their heads. At one point, Tora returned to the tribunal office to ask Saburo if he thought they should write a letter of their own to the authorities in the capital, defending themselves and blaming Mori for his interference in tribunal affairs.

"Don't think so, brother," Saburo said. "They wouldn't believe either of us without the master's support. I wonder why there hasn't been a letter from him."

Tora sat down beside Saburo's desk. The clerks had glanced up but returned to their labors again. His visits were too frequent to arouse curiosity.

"Maybe something's wrong. I think her ladyship's getting distraught by now. And if there's really a storm coming, it may take even longer to hear from him. I think I should go to Ise to take a look. There's nothing we can do here anyway."

"Think, Tora. If there really is going to be a storm, you'll be needed here, not in Ise."

Tora nodded unhappily. "You're right, but I have a bad feeling."

"Well, go and try to cheer up her ladyship and the children. Maybe there will be mail later today.

∞

There was. Saburo received two letters from their master.

They arrived with news of the last run of the ferry, thus confirming the storm rumors. Saburo read the letter addressed to him and Tora, and then took the other letter across to the residence.

Lady Yukiko flew down the steps of her veranda when she saw Saburo waving her letter in the air. "Oh, Saburo, thank you, thank you. I've been so worried." She snatched the letter and opened it immediately. Saburo busied himself with greeting the children who had emerged behind her.

"Oh," Lady Yukiko breathed, having read, "he is the dearest man, but why must he go off by himself, causing us so much worry."

Saburo consoled her. "He has been very busy, my lady. And the post takes quite long. I understand there will not be any more ferries until after the storm. Has Tora mentioned it?"

She laughed a little. "Oh, yes. He's been climbing about on the roof. I was afraid he'd fall. And here I always thought you were the one to scramble about on roofs. What happened to your hand?"

Saburo managed a chuckle. "I managed to fall over my own feet, my lady. It's nothing. When I can use it again, I'll be happy to check the roofs if you wish it."

"No, no. I was just teasing. You've both been very kind to look after us in my husband's absence." She tucked the letter inside her sash and kept her hand on it. "I find I'm looking forward to this dreadful storm. You have no idea how boring life has been lately."

Saburo glanced up at the sky. It was clouding over rapidly and a slight wind had sprung up. A rain drop struck his face, and he said, "You'll get wet out here, my lady. If you need anything, just send for us."

"Thank you, and thank you for bringing the letter." She gave him one of her charming smiles and dashed up the stairs and inside.

Saburo walked back to look for Tora. In spite of Lady Yukiko's praise, he thought glumly that the master would be very displeased with their activities. He found Tora in the guard barracks organizing storm preparations. He gave him the master's letter. It was very short, and Tora managed to decipher it.

"He'll be furious," he muttered when he finished. "What shall we do?"

"Well, at least he's well and you've been fretting for nothing. As for the Kitagawa matter, I've had a wild notion about that funeral."

Tora frowned. "Why? I went, and it looked ordinary enough, except that they bury their dead here."

"I wonder if we can find out who died."

"What difference does that make?"

"What if nobody died?"

"Huh? You saw them getting ready for the funeral. And I watched them digging the grave."

"Yes, but we don't know for a fact that they buried a person."

Tora stared at him. His face broke into a wide smile. "The stolen goods. They buried the stolen goods, the dirty bastards. Kitagawa knew we were going to check up on him and he had to hide the stuff. Brother, you're brilliant! You have the wisdom of the sages, the courage of dragons, and the cunning of a snake."

"Thank you." Saburo smiled modestly. "We'll have to do some digging to make sure."

Tora's face fell. Digging up a cemetery was bound to disturb the ghosts of the departed. He did not like ghosts. But after a moment's thought, he nodded. "Very well. I'll do the digging; you do the watching. Let's go and get it over with."

"No, Tora. After dark. What if I'm wrong? Can you imagine what would happen if we're found desecrating a cemetery?"

Tora saw the wisdom of this, though the thought of the coming night made him shudder.

They set out well after dark. In fact, according to the watchman outside the tribunal, it was already past the hour of the rat when they departed on horseback, both wearing ordinary dark clothes. Tora's horse was additionally burdened with a spade wrapped in a straw mat. They had no way to bring any treasure back with them but intended merely to confirm their suspicion.

To Saburo's satisfaction, the sky was covered with thick clouds. Not a star could be seen, and a light rain fell from time to time.

Tora led the way into the woods and to the cemetery. Because they were in a clearing, they could make out the individual stone markers. Tora took a deep breath. "I don't like this. Let's hurry it up and get out of here." The tombstones gathered around them like a crowd of frozen ghosts determined to protect the dead below.

Saburo said nothing. He waited for Tora to dismount and look about him.

"It's over here." Tora strode past several tomb stones and stopped before a mound of newly disturbed earth. A large stone marker had been placed on it. "Give me a hand," he called out to Saburo. "Not really a hand," Tora amended with a nervous laugh. "Just a shove to get this thing moved a little."

They both pushed and the marker toppled. Tora muttered a curse. "We'll have to set it back up when we're done. The damned thing is heavy. Did you bring the lantern?"

Saburo held it up. "Best not light it until the last moment, and then only long enough to see. I don't trust this. The woods around us seem to breathe down our necks."

"You feel it, too? Let me tell you later about the time the master and I went into a tomb that had been cut into a mountain in Echigo. When I heard a noise, I bolted, and the master got caught by soldiers. Suddenly the whole cemetery was full of them."

"Shut up, Tora. Start digging!"

Tora unwrapped the shovel and set to work. Saburo trailed off, peering into shadows and listening. After a while, Tora became resentful that Saburo had left him alone and glanced nervously at the grave markers. Like the ones in Echigo, they seemed to be moving whenever he took away his eyes. Only his hope to defend his actions to the master kept him there.

Suddenly Saburo was back beside him. Tora nearly jumped out of his skin.

"Someone's coming," Saburo hissed. "We've got to run."

Tora dropped the shovel and looked about wildly. He saw nothing.

Saburo pulled his arm. "The horses, quick! And then ride as if all the devils of hell are chasing you."

Tora still saw nothing, but he did as he was told. They ran, untied their horses, threw themselves into the saddles, and took off through the trees, branches whipping at them as they passed.

At some point they came out of the forest and into fields. The ground was muddy and the horses faltered to a walk. Tora looked back at the black mass of forest but saw no one.

"Who was coming?" he asked.

"Kitagawa, I think. With armed men. They had torches and were coming from the manor. Let's get to solid ground and head home. I don't feel safe here."

Tora was becoming suspicious. "How could you see them through the trees?"

"I walked back to watch the road."

"Oh."

They maneuvered their mounts out of the mud and continued along a dam between rice paddies. When they reached a farm, they followed the farm track to a road.

"Where are we?" Tora asked. In the darkness it was impossible to recognize landmarks.

"I have no idea. I thought you came here yesterday."

"Well, let's just stay on this road. It will lead somewhere."

It did. It led right back to the woods they had come from. Saburo recognized it first and then saw the glimmer of torches through the trees. "Back!" he called out.

Tora halted and saw their danger. But already horsemen were separating from the darkness of the woods and galloping their way. They tried to make a run for it, but since they did not know the area, they were eventually caught. Bluffing their way out of it failed miserably, and Kitagawa's retainers escorted them back to the manor where Kitagawa himself awaited them in the courtyard.

He stared at them, then growled, "So. Now you disturb the rest of my ancestors and that of dead Fujiwara retainers. A very serious offense. Your service to the new governor will not protect you this time."

Tora growled, "What proof do you have for such a charge?"

"I have witnesses. I posted watchmen after your visits here. I knew you'd be back after dark."

Tora and Saburo received this in silence.

Kitagawa told his men. "Take them away and lock them up until the police get here."

33

The Debt

"How are we going to get out of this?" Tora asked. They sat side by side in a small, windowless room with a heavy door. The door was securely locked.

Saburo grunted. "We're not. You know I checked the door, walls, and ceiling, looking for a way out. There isn't one."

"I mean how are we going to explain this to the master?"

Saburo sighed. He guessed they had been in their cell for about an hour. It was still night, and silence had fallen. Kitagawa and his men had gone to catch a few hours sleep after their disturbed night. He and Tora should probably do the same. He was about to say so when he heard a scrabbling noise outside the door. Rats? No. He crept closer and listened. Someone was breathing on the other side.

"Who is it?" he asked softly.

A whisper: "It's me."

This was not helpful, but Saburo dispensed with the name and asked, "What do you want?"

"I want to pay a debt." A pause, then, "Are you the one who was here the other night? The one with the beard who came through the roof?"

Saburo smiled. "How is your daughter?"

"She'll forget, I hope." There was a brief silence, then she whispered, "They didn't send for the police."

"Maybe they're waiting till morning."

"No. They'll kill you. Nobody will know what happened to you."

"Then why did they lock us up?"

"They're waiting for a boat in the morning to take you out to sea."

Saburo swallowed. Such a plan was so fiendishly simple and effective that he knew she was telling the truth. Even if locked up by the offensive Mori, they would present a danger to Kitagawa. But if they simply disappeared, no one would be the wiser.

Tora had become aware of the whispering and asked. "Who are you talking to?"

"Ssh! A woman in the corridor. She says they plan to take us out to sea and drown us."

"Amida!" Tora came to join him. "She could be right."

"Yes."

The woman whispered again. "I don't have a key. Yoshi took it."

"Can you get it?'

"I don't know." Then more softly, "I'll be back."

"Who was she?" Tora asked. "Maybe it's a trick."

"No trick. Our only hope. I think. She's the mother of the little girl."

"Oh." Tora thought about it. "But even if she gets us out of here, we're still inside Kitagawa's compound. He's bound to have men at the gate."

"Don't complain. If we get out of this room, we have a chance. Now we have none."

"I wish I had my sword."

Saburo said nothing. They waited.

Finally, when they had decided that their helper was not going to return, they heard her soft steps. Then metal clinked against metal, a lock snapped, and the thick door creaked open a little.

"Ssh!" the woman in the corridor said. "Come. Be very quiet."

It was dark in the corridor, but Saburo closed the door again and relocked it, giving her the key. Then they followed her to another room. This room had a window, and she pointed to it.

Tora quickly went to look out, but Saburo paused. In the dim light coming from outside, he saw bedding spread on the floor and on it the little girl. She was sitting up and looked at him with wide, frightened eyes. Saburo put a finger to his lips and made her a bow. Then he turned to her mother. "Thank you," he said. "Will you and your daughter be safe?"

She glanced at the door. "I don't know. You must leave. Now. Before it's too late. It will be light soon."

"I'm Saburo. Kuruda Saburo. Ask for me at the tribunal if you need help."

She nodded. "Go now!"

Tora was already outside the window, looking impatient. "Ask her if there are any weapons handy," he whispered.

"No. Let's go. We are a danger to her and the child."

Saburo climbed out into an alleyway between two buildings. It was raining, but already the night had turned the bluish gray of pre-dawn. Saburo walked ahead, past several buildings to the section of wall he had climbed before. Tora helped him over it, then followed. Once outside, they ran for the road and kept running.

"Out of breath, Saburo gasped, "Our horses. We'll have to walk. Again!"

Tora snorted. "We got away, and you have my company this time." But he remembered Saburo's condition after his last escape and slowed down.

After a while Saburo said, "I'm worried about the woman. What if they guess she helped us?"

"Can't be helped. Maybe they won't catch on. I'm worried about what Kitagawa will do next. They have our horses. I'd like mine back. Best horse I ever had."

Saburo muttered, "Good grief!"

∞

They arrived home with the dawn, though it was not much lighter. Dense clouds hid the sun. The rain had gusted until they were soaked to the skin, and all around them trees tossed in the wind. The storm had begun.

In spite of the weather, the morning brought Lieutenant Mori again. He came, accompanied by ten constables and demanded to see Tora.

Tora and Saburo, dry again and in their ordinary clothes, greeted him together in an anteroom.

"What brings you this time, Mori?" Tora asked.

Mori looked at him closely, perhaps searching for signs of the night's adventure. "I'm here to arrest you, Lieutenant Sashima."

Tora raised his brows. "Why?"

"For desecrating the graves of the Kitagawa family and their retainers."

"Don't be silly. You can't arrest us. But you can arrest Kitagawa. We are charging him with attacking us, stealing out horses and confining us against our will. That sort of thing, when carried out against the rightful representatives of the emperor in this province, amounts to treason. I believe Kitagawa is looking at exile. And we'll make sure they don't send him back north among his friends. He'll go to Kyushu, to the mines there, if I have my will."

Mori stared at him. "You can't give any orders while the governor is absent. Where is he anyway? This absence is not a good start. Not when his underlings manage to insult decent citizens, threaten retainers of ranking noblemen, and desecrate grave sites."

"All lies by men engaged in illegal trade and piracy."

Mori drew himself up. "Are you going to come peacefully, or do I have to call my constables?"

Tora shot Saburo a glance and chuckled. "Have to give it to the policeman," he said. "He's got nerve and stubbornness."

Saburo was not smiling. He regarded Mori's wet police uniform and the wilting tufts of starched fabric on his official cap and said, "You should have worn a straw coat and hat, Lieutenant. The weather's nasty. Best hurry home before the storm gets worse."

Mori glared, hesitated, bit his lip, and said, "You'll be very sorry. Both of you." Then he turned on his heel and stalked out of the room.

The door closed. Tora shook his head. "Now he really hates us. You shouldn't have made fun of his uniform."

They both laughed.

A strong gust of wind shook the tribunal building. Tiles clattered to the ground outside.

"I have to go back to the residence," Tora said, glancing up at the ceiling. "Her ladyship has only her women with her. I hope this is the worst of it."

But the storm had only just started.

34

Mrs. Inabe

It was still before dawn when Akitada arrived at the Golden Dragon. He left his horse outside and went in. Only a sleepy boy was in the reception area. He stared at Akitada's face and clothes and said, "We're full up. Best go elsewhere."

Akitada was too worn out to explain. He snapped, "I'm Sugawara and I'm a guest here. Is the water still hot for a bath?"

The boy stammered, "Yes, sir. What happened, sir?"

"My horse stumbled. It's outside. Someone can take it back to the post station." He reached into his sash. Mildly surprised he had not been relieved of his money, he fished out some coins and handed them over. The boy bowed. He looked a little less nervous about this blood-stained guest.

In his room, Akitada saw with satisfaction that clean clothes awaited him. Not only had the inn had his other shirt washed, but Mrs. Akechi's shop had sent his new clothes. He went to the bath house, stripped, washed himself, and then slipped into the deep tub. The water was no longer really hot, but it felt wonderful nonetheless. He leaned back and closed his eyes. His face still stung and his nose throbbed, but otherwise he felt much better. His head had stopped hurting some time during the night.

As he dozed in the water, he considered all that had happened to him. He could understand why the high constable had sent his soldiers to the shed. No doubt, Lieutenant Mori had attempted once again to shift the responsibility for the prowlers onto someone else's shoulders. Sukemichi's men must have been responsible for removing the bodies of the four robbers as well as the goods that had been stored in the shed.

The soldiers who had arrested him were probably there to see if any of the dead men's colleagues had returned to their lair. He chuckled softly at the thought that his appearance had deteriorated to the point of making him look not just like a slave but like a robber.

Akitada was not a vain man, and the many years of poverty had not encouraged him to splurge on fine clothes, but he was quite conscious of proper and tasteful attire and becoming more so now that he had the funds to indulge himself. He looked forward to putting on the new silver-gray robe and trousers. And this reminded him of the package of silks he had purchased for his wife and daughter. He hoped they would be pleased. Alas, Yukiko, who should have been on his mind every day and night since he had left her, had been nearly forgotten over the affair of the missing princess. He drifted off into memory. His wife's melodious laugh, her graceful movements, her soft lips on his and her smooth limbs under his caressing hands . . .

At that point he got out of the water quickly, wrapped himself into the cotton robe provided by the inn, and padded back to his room for a short rest before sunrise.

∞

He did not wake until afternoon. By then he was ravenous. He dressed, enjoying the feel of soft silk on his skin again, and then went out for a meal. People glanced curiously at him, and at first he thought his new clothes were the reason, but he realized quickly that they were staring at his bruised face. This made him self-conscious and he hurried through a meal of fish and vegetables before making his way to the police station.

Here, his changed appearance was received in a slightly more gratifying manner. He had risen in status in the eyes of the constables. Lieutenant Matsuura, who should not have been astonished, also seemed a little more polite.

"Lieutenant," Akitada said after courteous greetings had been exchanged, "I've come about that monk you arrested. Is he still in your jail?"

Matsuura stiffened slightly. "Yes, sir. We should have a confession today. He was on the point of breaking during this morning's interrogation."

Akitada pictured the cruel flogging that would have accompanied this form of interrogation and flinched. "I think you have the wrong man, Lieutenant," he said more coldly. "I expect the monk was in the wine shop when the fight broke out and picked up the amulet there. As he was out of funds for more wine, he went across the street and sold the amulet, then returned to buy more wine. Your killer is most likely someone who was involved in the fighting and dropped the amulet during the tussle. I think you'd do well to find out who the fighters were and investigate them."

Matsuura had listened with a frown. "They were all local men. The monk is the only one who doesn't belong here."

"Not all strangers are murderers," Akitada pointed out. "Neither are all inhabitants of Uji-tachi above suspicion."

"Unless you have something more incriminating about those other men, I don't see myself approaching them with such an accusation."

Akitada sighed. An experienced police officer would have some idea how to proceed diplomatically in such a case. "I'll check with a few people and get back to you. But do not flog that man again until we are more certain of the true situation. Meanwhile, you might talk to the waitress in the wine shop. She will support my notion, and she might remember something else about the incident."

Matsuura was not pleased by this, but he nodded. He glanced at Akitada's face, hesitated and then asked, "Did you meet up with trouble, sir?"

There was no point in fobbing Matsuura off with a tale of falling off his horse. Besides it made him look foolish. Akitada said, "I found the shed where I was held prisoner. Unfortunately, the high constable's men mistook me for one of the prowlers and arrested me. I spent the night in some cell on Sukemichi's property. I wondered why they suddenly released me. Did someone contact you to ask about me?"

Matsuura had trouble keeping a grin off his face. He said, "I am shocked, sir. A most unfortunate mistake. Yes, the high constable did send someone to ask me if I could confirm that you were staying in the area. I thought it best to tell the truth."

Akitada nodded. "I must thank you, though Sukemichi made no attempt to apologize. I suppose, he cannot be blamed too much. In any case, it appears he's taken care of the dead prowlers and the stored goods. Did you receive any explanations?"

"No, sir. But I did ask for his support. He may eventually ask to speak to me."

"Hmm. Well, it's none of my business. I'll take my leave then and see what I can do about the monk."

He had hoped to avoid his next visit.

∞

The River Palace was very quiet. To his relief Mrs.Inabe's husband was not in sight. She sat behind the counter watching the street. Her eyes widened when she saw him and then she did another double-take when she realized who the gentleman in gray silk was. She rose to her feet and bowed.

"I hope you are well, Mrs. Inabe," Akitada said.

"Quite well," she murmured. She would not lift her eyes to his. "How may I serve you, sir?"

"Is you husband about?"

"I'm very sorry but he went out a while ago."

"Good, because I want to talk to you and don't want him to hear what I have to say."

Now her eyes met his. She suddenly looked frightened. "Is it about what Seijiro did to the dwarf?" she asked.

"No. It's about Keiko."

"Keiko?" Her voice trembled.

"The monk in jail did not kill her."

"Oh." She raised her hands to her mouth but said nothing else.

"Tell me, why is it that you sent your daughter away to work in another province?"

She did not answer, but the fear in her eyes told him he had guessed correctly.

"Did your husband try to seduce Keiko?"

She looked away. "No. It wasn't that way. He said Keiko lied. He said he could not live in the same house with her."

"So you sent her away."

The tears came then. "I . . . I was afraid of him," she muttered. "I was afraid of what he'd do to her. I thought it was better. Safer."

"Ah. But it wasn't safe, was it? Keiko came to visit you. She came because she missed her mother."

She sank to the floor, sobbing and rocking back and forth.

"When did you realize it was he who raped and killed her?"

She shook her head violently. "No, no. I didn't know. Not at first. Then they arrested the monk and I thought I'd been wrong."

"But you've changed your mind? Why? What happened?"

She raised her tear-stained face to him. The innkeeper was not particularly attractive at the best of times and looked both old and ugly now. He had wondered from the start what the much younger Seijiro could have seen in her. Now he knew. When Inabe found out that she owned the inn, he had courted her. He had married this plain woman who was much older than he for her property and accepted the pretty young daughter into the bargain. Only Keiko had not wanted him.

She got up and reached into a box under the counter. When her hand emerged, it held a small bead.

Akitada recognized it. "This is one of Keiko's prayer beads."

She nodded. "It was in his sleeve. I found it when I washed his jacket."

Neither said anything. Then Akitada nodded. "He had the amulet too but lost it in a fight in one of the wine shops. The monk picked it up."

"Oh." She had stopped crying and seemed resigned now.

"Lieutenant Matsuura is flogging the monk to get a confession."

She bowed her head and sighed.

Akitada said sternly, "Mrs. Inabe, you know what you must do, don't you?"

"He'll kill me, too."

"Take a neighbor with you and have a friend stay with you until he has been arrested."

"Yes," she said. She nodded as if to convince herself. "Yes. I must do that. I can see that I must do it for my poor child."

35

Precious Butterfly

When Akitada emerged from the River Palace, he found Junichiro waiting for him. The dwarf's eyes widened when he saw Akitada.

"How fine you are!" he cried, then looked anxiously at Akitada's bruised face. "What happened this time? Are you all right? I've been so worried."

The realization that he had somehow endeared himself to this little man almost overcame Akitada. Had Junichiro been normal size, he would have embraced him. As it was, he laid his hand on Junichiro's spiky red head, smiled, and said, "I'm well, my friend. And I

319

thank you for the compliment on my clothes. Would you like a new suit?"

Junichiro bristled. "Why? What's wrong with this one?" He looked down at his multi-colored child's outfit and struck a pose. "I think I'm very fine, too."

"I beg your pardon," Akitada said quickly. "Of course you are. I only wondered if you might like another. A man likes a change now and then."

"Oh, well, maybe. But first, what happened?"

Akitada looked up at the sky. The sun was high, but it was clouding up. Rain was coming. It was high time, too. The last weeks had been much too dry and hot for this time of year. Already some of the trees were losing their leaves. A good rain would be most welcome.

He said, "Come, it's almost time for the noon rice. Let's go to that place you mentioned. The Kingfisher, was it?"

"Your treat?"

"My treat."

As they walked, Akitada told him about Lord Minamoto paying a ransom for the return of the princess.

Junichiro whistled at the amount. "And is she back?" he asked.

"No. At least she wasn't last night. And I doubt she will be returned. She's either already dead or this is about more than gold."

Junichiro frowned. "That's not good. But what happened to your face."

"I decided to check on the ransom and then started looking for the shed."

"You mean you went climbing around in the forest at night again? After what happened last time?"

"I was careful," Akitada said defensively. "And I had a horse this time. In any case, I found it."

They reached the restaurant where they were greeted by the waiter who regarded Akitada's new silks as acceptable but hesitated when he saw Junichiro.

Junichiro eyed the crowded dining area and informed him, "Some abalone for me and my friend, the governor. And make sure you give us nice large ones."

The waiter capitulated, made Akitada a bow, and showed them to a place well in the back. When he was gone, Junichiro said, "He didn't look happy. I bet it's because he thinks you've been in a fight."

"You may be right. This is not the way governors normally look. I'm sorry I embarrassed you."

"Hmm. Never mind. Just tell me what happened. So you found the shed. I could have taken you there. For a governor, you can be pretty stupid sometimes."

Akitada raised his eyebrows. "Is that any way to address a governor? You weren't available. Where were you anyway?"

"Talking to people," Junichiro said vaguely. "Go on about the shed."

The abalone arrived and proved very good. Between bites, Akitada told him about the soldiers, the arrest, and the dark cell at Sukemichi's compound.

"What? Didn't you tell them who you are?"

"I did. They didn't believe me. That's why I've changed my clothes."

That got a chuckle. "How'd you get away?"

I. J. PARKER

"Sukemichi checked with Lieutenant Matsuura and let me go."

Junichiro looked pleased. "Don't tell me. He fell on his knees and knocked his head against the floor?"

"No. I didn't see him. I simply got on my horse and left."

"Incredible!" Junichiro shook his head at it. "How about another order of abalone, since you're paying."

"I'm paying."

The waiter returned with another platter of fried abalone. Junichiro fell on them as if he had not just demolished most of the previous order. Akitada watched him fondly for a while, then said, "When you catch your breath, tell me what you found out."

Junichiro chewed, eyed the platter and shoved it toward Akitada. "Eat," he commanded, then wiped his greasy mouth on his sleeve and began.

"You said to check the brothel about Michiko and her customers. She had only two because she was still in training with the top girl, Precious Butterfly. Murata favors Precious Butterfly. They say Butterfly expects him to buy her out and marry her." He paused. "Any help?"

"Hmm. Perhaps."

"I wish I knew who killed Michiko. I'd make him pay." Overcome by his anger, Junichiro reached for another abalone.

Akitada sighed. "As to Murata," he said, "I wish I knew what he's up to. Why the repeated visits here? What could he possibly be doing? If he's in shipping, he belongs on the coast."

The Shrine Virgin

Junichiro finished the abalone and wiped his mouth again. "It could be Precious Butterfly," he said. "He's been seeing her for a long time."

Akitada considered it. "I think I'd like a talk with this Butterfly. Can you arrange it?"

"Easy! You want to go now? In another couple of hours she might be working."

∞

It was late afternoon, a dreary, cloudy afternoon by the time Junichiro and Akitada walked up the narrow path that led to a small house set among trees. Junichiro explained that Precious Butterfly had bought the house when she had become popular. Owning her own place meant that she could entertain men privately. Her connection with the Peach Bower was tenuous these days. She lent her name and reputation to the brothel and occasionally received those customers who paid a large enough sum to satisfy both the brothel owner and the courtesan. Junichiro thought that she probably already had enough money to buy herself out, but that she was waiting for a marriage proposal from a rich man like Murata.

The door was opened by a neatly dressed middle-aged woman who did not seem surprised to see the odd-looking dwarf in the company of an elegant nobleman. She murmured, "You are welcome, sir. Please come in."

They followed her into a small reception room near the entrance where she invited Akitada to take a seat on one of the cushions. A small tray table held a flask and several cups, and on the wall hung a scroll of flowers and butterflies.

"How may I announce you?" the woman asked with another bow.

"Lord Sugawara," Akitada told her. Junichiro smirked proudly.

She poured Akitada some wine and left.

Junichiro eyed the wine. "You want that?"

"No. Please help yourself. It seems a very respectable sort of place."

Junichiro emptied the cup and smacked his lips. "Oh, yes. Precious Butterfly is well-born. They say she's the younger daughter of some lord in Owari."

"I think they say much the same about most of the leading courtesans. It drives up the price."

Junichiro faked surprise. "You don't mean it?" he gasped, then broke into a trill of laughter that he stifled abruptly when the maid returned.

"Precious Butterfly is honored, my lord. Allow me to show you the way." She glanced at Junichiro. "You may go to the kitchen, Junichiro."

"Hey," Junichiro protested. "I brought him."

She compressed her lips. "I won't forget. We'll talk about it later."

The room she took Akitada to was clearly the best one in the house. It was large and overlooked a small garden. Well furnished, it held several silk cushions, painted scrolls, a painted screen, lacquered trunks, and a lacquered clothes rack draped with exquisite silk robes.

The Shrine Virgin

The courtesan who awaited him was elegant rather than beautiful. She was tall for a woman and unfashionably slender, but her face was softly rounded, her eyes unusually large and liquid, and her clothes were of the best silk in the bright colors of pale yellow, black, and greenish blue. A short jacket of a deeper yellow was richly embroidered with flowers and butterflies.

A Precious Butterfly indeed.

She extended a slender hand toward one of the cushions. "Please," she murmured. "I'm deeply honored that someone of your rank should visit my humble retreat. Allow me to serve you."

She had not asked for money, but it was surely expected. Junichiro was probably negotiating his share in the kitchen at this moment. Akitada smiled a little and sat down.

"Thank you. It is kind of you to see me when you must be very busy. I'm told you, too, hold an impressive rank."

She sat down gracefully near him and reached for a pretty painted fan. Raising this, she regarded Akitada over it. She had very pretty eyes. "Not too busy for a special guest," she murmured.

Akitada sighed. He had run out of patience with the customary flirtations and was not interested in the usual services. He said, "I have come for information."

To her credit, she received this well. Her eyes stopped smiling at him, but she said quite politely, "I live a very retired life these days. I doubt I can be helpful, but I am at your service."

"Thank you. I have taken an interest in the deaths of two young women here. One murder has been solved, I think, but that still leaves the death of the girl Michiko unaccounted for."

He watched her and saw uncertainty and perhaps fear in those expressive eyes. "That was very sad," she said. "But I know nothing about it."

Clearly she did not want to discuss the murder. Akitada persisted. "I was told that Michiko had started working in the Peach Bower, that you were training her, and that a client took an interest in her just before she died."

The fan trembled slightly. "You think she was murdered by a client?" she asked.

"Perhaps. That's why I'm here. The man may be a ship owner from Owari. His name is Murata. I think you know him?"

She was very still for a long moment. Only the fan continued trembling. Then she said softly, "I knew him."

"You knew him well enough to tell people he would buy you out. You claimed he wanted to marry you, didn't you?"

She let her hand with the fan drop to her lap. Her eyes flashed with sudden anger. She was near tears. "Yes," she said. "It was true. The papers were all drawn up." She turned and reached for some documents on a small desk and handed them to Akitada. "I was telling the truth about the offer. He had the papers drawn up and brought them to me for approval. I accepted, but he did not complete the negotiations. He has not paid the small sum still owed to the Peach Bower." She paused. "It's been very hurtful. We'd been together for almost two years and he claimed he loved me."

Akitada glanced at the document and returned it. It was as she had said. He murmured, "I'm very sorry. Both for having doubted you and for your loss."

She turned her head away and blinked. "Thank you," she said softly.

"Perhaps he will still change his mind."

"I don't think so."

"Do you love Murata?"

Without looking at him, she shook her head. "He's very wealthy and I'm very poor," she said simply.

Akitada respected her for her honesty and humility, two qualities he had never associated with successful courtesans.

"What do you know about the young woman who was murdered?"

Her eyes flew to his. "I liked Michiko, but I know nothing about what happened to her. She needed to earn some money and may have gone with the wrong client."

"Did Murata ever take an interest in Michiko?"

She flushed. "Maybe. He met her here."

Akitada was astonished—not so much that Murata might have pursued Michiko, but rather that Precious Butterfly should admit to it. If it was true, it gave her a motive for the murder. "Could he have left you for Michiko?"

"No. And Michiko wouldn't have accepted. She knew about our relationship." She took up her fan again. "I don't think he left me for another woman. I think it was business and had to do with Lord Sukemichi."

Astonished, Akitada asked, "How do you know that?"

"He knew him and bragged about it. He told me he would introduce me to him. That was when he still courted me. I know he went to see Lord Sukemichi recently."

"When was this?"

She frowned and thought. "I think it was the third day of the month. I haven't seen him since." She hung her head.

Akitada thought back. It must have been just before Michiko took the princess's place. Michiko had been killed on her way home, and the princess had been abducted the following day.

Suddenly Akitada thought he saw what had happened. If either Murata or Sukemichi had found out about the substitution, then it all began to make a kind of sense. He was inclined to believe that Michiko was blameless. She had not revealed the whole truth until she was tortured.

Could Murata have arranged the abduction? Possibly, if he had employed the prowlers.

But he was not the one who would gain from such a shocking act.

Neither did he have a place to hide the princess.

Akitada sat lost in his thoughts, and Precious Butterfly made a sudden movement. She was using her fan vigorously. Akitada became aware of the stifling heat in the room and of the courtesan's impatience. Outside there was a clap of thunder.

"I beg your pardon," he said. "I was thinking about what you told me. You must have come to know Murata well in the years he courted you. What sort of man is he?"

She answered readily enough. "He is demanding, but he was generous to me. He paid for all my gowns, sending the silk dealer to me whenever I asked for a present." She gestured to the clothing rack and its gorgeous and colorful robes and embroidered trains. "I thought he loved me. There was money, too, whenever he came. I thought he came only to see me, but he said he had some business here. When I asked what business he could have in Uji-tachi, he only said it was none of my concern. I kept asking, but he got very angry." She looked at Akitada. "This happened just before he left me. Maybe it was my own fault."

Akitada sighed. "Do you think that Murata may have been involved in some criminal enterprise? It might explain why he got angry about your questions."

"Oh! There was some talk among the girls, but I thought it was just jealousy. Surely not when he was a friend of the high constable."

That fact did not cancel out the other, Akitada thought. He said, "Thank you. You have given me much to think about and I've taken up a great deal of your time." He reached into his sash for a coin and a piece of writing paper. Wrapping the gold piece carefully in the paper, he laid it before her with a small bow. "I'd like to express my gratitude to your maid."

She bowed in return. "I have enjoyed your visit, my lord. Please come back." She gave him a warm glance from behind the fan and rose with him. The scent of sandalwood escaped from her perfumed gown.

Akitada walked outside. A wind had sprung up and angry clouds covered the sky. There was no sign of Junichiro. He leaned against the gate post. A piece of gold had been a generous reward for her answers. She would keep the money, as he had intended, but Junichiro would get a small fee for bringing him here. And on second thought, perhaps it had been a small enough price to pay to have confirmation of his suspicion.

Another matter troubled him. He was low on funds, having spent lavishly on silks for his ladies and clothes for himself. There was also the bill from the Golden Dragon. He could not stay much longer. And when he left, should he take Junichiro home with him?

The dwarf materialized beside him. "Well? Did she know who killed Michiko?"

36

A Killer Confesses

A kitada looked down fondly at the eager face under its unruly crop of red hair and smiled. "Not really, Junichiro, but she has given me some ideas."

"What ideas?"

"Too soon to tell." They walked toward the center of town together. "Would you like to come with me when I leave here?" Akitada asked.

"To Mikawa?" Junichiro clapped his hands. "I've always wanted to pay a visit to another province. And I'd get to ride the ferry, too. Yes, master. I'll come."

"I meant to live with me and my family."

Junichiro stopped. He looked surprised and then angry. "You're joking. Don't joke about a thing like that."

Akitada sighed. "I'm not joking. I've come to be fond of you. I think you would serve me loyally and you would have a home and be looked after."

Junichiro said nothing. He started walking again. His face worked. Finally he muttered, "You would regret it. Nobody wants Junichiro around. You saw how they treat me. That bastard Inabe would've liked to beat me to death. He would've hurt me if you hadn't come."

"Nobody will treat you like that in my house. And I will protect you against others."

He shook his head. "They'll mock you. I wouldn't want that to happen."

"Junichiro, I'm the governor. Nobody mocks my friends." This was perhaps an exaggeration but Akitada was finding it hard to make his case.

"Thank you. I'll think about it."

It was not the reaction Akitada had expected and he felt a little hurt, but he nodded. "Good."

"So what did Precious Butterfly tell you about Michiko?"

"She says she liked Michiko, but doesn't know what happened. She thinks she went with a dangerous client."

The dwarf's eyes widened. "I don't believe it." Then he added, "He must've paid her well."

"She needed money."

"What else did you find out?"

"Murata left Precious Butterfly. This was before the princess was abducted."

"Oh!" Junichiro thought this over and clenched his fists. "He got Michiko to tell him about the princess and then he killed her."

"I'm not sure if he killed her, but Murata had some secrets he kept even from Precious Butterfly."

The dwarf nodded. "He's been careful about his business. I couldn't get any information."

"Yes. Precious Butterfly said he got very angry with her when she asked him about it. It means he had a lot to hide."

"What do you want me to do, master?"

Thunder rolled again, and both looked up at the sky.

"I'm going to the police station to see Lieutenant Matsuura. Mrs. Inabe has promised to tell him what she knows about Keiko's departure. Perhaps you could find out who Murata's friends are."

"Friends?"

"Well, someone he shared a meal with or paid a visit to."

"Oh."

They stopped in front of the police station. Junichiro did not look at Akitada. He shuffled his feet, and said shyly, "Thank you for being my friend," then scampered off.

∞

Lieutenant Matsuura received Akitada politely. It was hard to tell if this change in manner was due to

Akitada's new clothes or to revelations by Mrs. Inabe. Akitada came to the point immediately.

"Has Mrs. Inabe spoken with you?"

"Yes. But please be seated, sir. I regret we parted on less than friendly terms. I suppose I was too sure of myself and felt you were critical." He paused, blushed, then said quickly, "You see, I still have to prove myself or I'll be replaced."

"Never mind. It doesn't matter. Only the governor can ask to have you replaced. I see no reason why he would want to do so."

"Thank you. That's very kind after the way I behaved."

Akitada thought of the monk and hardened his heart. "I assume the monk did not confess?"

"No. Or rather he said he couldn't recall that morning but that he would never do such a thing."

"He was flogged?"

Matsuura sighed. "A little. I stopped it. Didn't see any use in it. He was drunk."

"Precisely. Well then, I would very much like to hear your thoughts on the case. Unless, of course, you consider that meddling in your affairs."

Matsuura was almost crimson by now. "I *am* sorry, sir. Truly sorry. I'd be grateful to have your advice in the matter."

Akitada seated himself. "Very well. Go ahead."

"First off, I appreciate you speaking to Mrs. Inabe. She wouldn't have come in otherwise."

Akitada nodded.

"She was very upset. It was difficult to get her to say what she had on her mind. I must say I was shocked by her story. She claims Inabe, her husband, had—er—been after her daughter soon after marrying her. When she found out, he blamed it on the girl, said she'd been making eyes at him and pressing up against him. The mother was angry at her daughter and sent her away to work elsewhere where she couldn't seduce him." Matsuura paused and looked at Akitada uncertainly. "I was told the mother was a widow when she became infatuated with Inabe and married him. It would explain a lot."

"Yes, most likely. Go on, Matsuura."

"Well, the girl came home to visit her mother. She got lonely for her, she said. A very filial thing to do under the circumstances, in my opinion."

"Yes, indeed."

"But it happened again. The mother caught them together."

Akitada raised his brows. "Together? How do you mean?"

"She heard noises from the daughter's room and looked in and there they were, lying together half naked. She threw her daughter out, and the girl walked away crying after accusing Inabe of trying to rape her."

Akitada nodded. "I had an idea that something like that had happened."

"Well the point of all of this is that she thinks maybe Inabe went after girl, caught up with her, and . . . and . . ." He paused, looking embarrassed.

"Raped and killed her?"

"Yes. What do you think, sir?"

Akitada regarded the policeman thoughtfully. "Unless someone saw him kill her, or at least follow her, you'll need more evidence. All you have at the moment is a motive and opportunity."

"Ah, but there is something else. You see Mrs. Inabe found one of her daughter's beads caught inside her husband's sleeve."

"Well, then," Akitada said with a smile. "There is no more to be said. You've solved the case. When are you going to arrest Inabe?"

Matsuura grinned. "Already done, sir. I was about to question him. Would you care to attend?"

"I would indeed."

∞

Inabe sat in his cell, chained hand and foot. Matsuura was taking no chances. The man, always somewhat brutish looking, was in a towering rage and practically snarled at them when the constable unlocked the cell.

He recognized Akitada, and looked startled, but his eyes went back to Matsuura.

"This is an outrage!" he shouted. "It's an insult to a decent citizen and a property owner. I shall file a complaint and have you dismissed for this, Matsuura."

Matsuura said coldly, "You killed your stepdaughter. Your wife, her mother, has laid charges against you."

"She lies. How can you believe a demented woman? She was always jealous of me and this is her punishment. I never touched the girl. She did this because I went to a brothel. My wife is old and can no longer please a husband. I have needs. And that's not against the law last time I heard."

"It is when you rape and kill your stepdaughter. There's the matter of your having one of the dead girl's beads in your clothes. How did that happen if you didn't kill her?"

"What bead? I didn't have a bead."

"You not only had the bead, you took her jade amulet away with you. Maybe you were going to sell it. Or else you wanted something to remember her by." Matsuura bared his teeth in a cold smile. "You wanted to remember how you raped her brutally in the woods beside the road to Oyodo and how you strangled her to keep her from telling her mother."

"That's a lie. I didn't touch her. I didn't take the amulet. The monk did it. The monk sold the amulet. I tried to get it back."

Akitada interrupted, "Why?"

Inabe's eyes turned to him. They rested on his new clothes. "Who are you anyway? What are you doing here? What business is it of yours what I did?"

Matsuura snapped, "On your knees. Bow to his Excellency. This is Governor Sugawara."

Inabe stared at Akitada. "What governor? He stayed at my place. Called himself Yoshimine from Owari. That's how he signed the guestbook."

Matsuura glanced at Akitada. He clearly did not quite know how to handle this.

Akitada said calmly, "Yoshimine is a name I sometimes use when I'm on an investigation. My presence in Ise has nothing to do with Keiko's murder, but your behavior raised my suspicions. I gathered that the ship owner Murata employed you. Just exactly what service did you perform for him?"

To Akitada's satisfaction, Inabe eyes wavered and he began to sweat. Murata had been very careless the day he left the River Palace and paid what he owed Inabe to his wife.

Inabe pretended ignorance. "I've never worked for Murata-san. There must be some mistake."

"Murata left your pay with your wife. I think she'll be glad to confirm this."

Inabe wiped his brow. "I may have run an errand or two. I don't pay attention to such things."

"The money purse was quite heavy. As I said, your wife will know."

Matsuura made an impatient movement. "Getting back to the murder," he said, "your wife will testify against you. You'd do well to confess or it will go hard with you."

Inabe started cursing. "That fox woman! That evil spirit! I should've known better than to marry the old hag. It's all a plot. They both were after me, she and her daughter. What's a man to do against such women? The girl seduced me so her mother would get rid of me. And it would have worked if I'd let her get away with it." He fell to his knees and looked up at Matsuura. "I went after her to beg her to go back and tell her mother it was all a mistake, but she sneered at me and called me names. I got angry. I couldn't help myself. It was an accident." He wailed and knocked his head against the stone floor of the cell.

Matsuura smirked. "Ah, a confession. That will save you some pain. Be sure you don't change your story before the judge."

Inabe sat up. "I know some things and will tell you if you go easy with me. The girl provoked me. I didn't mean to kill her."

Matsuura snapped "What things?"

"I know the prowlers work for Murata. I know who they are and what they've done. I can be a witness for you."

Matsuura raised his brows. "I don't believe you. You'd do best getting your story in order, or you'll be flogged." He turned to Akitada, "Let's go back to my office."

Akitada was not happy. He now had a clearer idea what Inabe's connection with Murata was, but when they were alone and Matsuura asked him about his interest in Murata, he said, "I've been wondering about it. Murata has been coming here regularly and until this week he always stayed at the River Palace. It occurred to me that Inabe might have been the reason for that."

Matsuura's eyes widened. "By the gods, I'll have the whole story out of Inabe. Don't you worry. He'll sing. Those bullies always do."

Akitada was inclined to agree, and this time he had no objection to the floggings that awaited Inabe.

37

Murata

Junichiro was sitting on the steps of the police station when Akitada emerged. A gust of wind raised clouds of dust from the road. It had been a dry fall, but surely now the rain would fall.

The dwarf jumped up. "I've been thinking, master."

Akitada chuckled. "Excellent! And what have you come up with?"

"I'm probably wrong but what if Murata and the high constable are in this together?"

Akitada's first thought was to laugh, but he stopped himself. It had seemed far-fetched at first, but even members of high-ranking families had been engaged in theft and murder, and Sukemichi was only provincial gentry. There was nothing to prove that he was an honorable man, except perhaps that he held an appointment from the court in the capital, and that was not always a commendation. He asked, "What made you think of him?"

Junichiro disappointed him. "I don't like him," he said, as if no more need be said.

"I cannot accuse a man of high crimes because you don't like him, imp. Have you ever seen Murata and Sukemichi together?"

"No, but I know Murata's been visiting Lord Sukemichi."

"How do you know?"

"Remember when you told me to find out something about Murata? I happened to see him rent a horse, so I followed." Junichiro made a face. "It was stupid. My legs can't keep up with a horse, but Murata can't ride. He went very slowly and held on for dear life until he got to the high constable's place. I waited outside, thinking it might be best not to be seen there. He came out again a little later and rode back to Uji-tachi. But here's the thing: the guards at the gate seemed to know him. Does this help?"

"Perhaps. I think it's time I had a talk with Murata." Akitada smiled down at the dwarf. "Yes, that helps indeed, imp. I can see that you'll make a very useful addition to my family. If I had my assistants Tora and Saburo with me, we would dare to take a closer look at Sukemichi's place. I'll have to tell you about my family when we have some time. You'll like them. Tora is an ex-soldier who is the most courageous man I know.

And Saburo was a spy until his enemies tortured him. He knows how to get into houses while their owners are asleep. He would be most useful at the moment." He tousled the dwarf's hair. "Oh well, the two of us must do the best we can. Shall we meet later?"

∞

Akitada returned to the Golden Dragon as the first rain began to fall. He had wished for rain, but now the thought of his new silk clothes made the change in weather a problem. He hesitated at the entrance, frowning at the way the large drops marked the dusty road outside, causing small mud puddles to form. The drops came more quickly now. The innkeeper joined him.

"The weather's worsening," he said. "I can provide you with a straw raincoat and hat if you need them, my lord," he offered.

Akitada gave him a grateful smile. "Thank you. I've discarded the old robe I arrived in and must purchase something simpler if the rain persists."

The innkeeper chuckled. "It will get worse. We are to have a big storm, I'm told. If you'll tell me what you need, I'll have our boy get it for you."

Akitada thanked the man again, thinking that the higher prices at the Golden Dragon did provide some welcome services. He was about to list the particulars, when another guest ducked into the inn, muttering under his breath and shaking himself like a dog.

Murata.

"Ah," Akitada said affably, "There you are, Murata. I'd been hoping to have a word with you."

Murata stopped shaking out his wet clothes and stared at him. "I don't know you," he said coldly.

"We must remedy that. I've come to know quite a lot about you. Your room or mine?"

Murata glanced toward the innkeeper. "I don't want to talk to you," he said.

"I'm sorry to say there's no way around it. There are some dubious activities to be explained."

The innkeeper tried to look busy. Murata flushed. "How dare you? You can't say such things in front of people." He kept his voice low.

Akitada compressed his lips and waited.

After a moment, Murata said, "Very well. I expect an explanation of such outlandish remarks. My room." Murata stalked off down the corridor and turned in at one of the doors, leaving it open for Akitada to follow. Akitada did so and closed the door behind him.

They were alone and Akitada suspected that he was in the presence of a killer. He was not particularly worried because he was still wearing his sword and Murata did not look dangerous. Besides, he had decided to leave Murata some false hope for his future so long as he implicated Sukemichi.

Neither man sat down. The room was impersonal as such rooms are in inns. Some chests held bedding during the day and a clothes rack was provided for the guest's robes. Two thin cushions and a small desk made up the rest of the furnishings. Oil lamps and heating braziers would be supplied as needed. Murata had added nothing to the sparse furnishings except a bundle and small trunk, securely closed and pushed into a corner.

Akitada said, "Let's not continue this pretense of your not knowing who I am. I expect you have been informed of my name, my title, my rank, and the powers given to me by the emperor." He had not been given any powers but hoped that Murata did not know this.

Murata opened his mouth to protest, but Akitada saw the fear in his eyes and glared at him. The ship owner closed his mouth again.

"Good," Akitada said. "I see that you understand. My assignment gives me the right to investigate crimes against the emperor and the nation. I'm prepared to assume that your own activities were of a more local nature. But someone else knew of your involvement with the prowlers and used you to help him carry out his own crime."

Murata had grown very pale. His eyes flew around the room and to the door behind Akitada. In his panic, his voice rose. "I don't know what you're talking about. I have nothing to do with prowlers. I don't know of any crimes. Why are you accusing me with such things? I'm an innocent businessman from Owari. You must have made a mistake. Please go away."

Akitada shook his head. "No mistake. I myself saw you pay off the man Inabe. You passed a bag stuffed with coins to the man's wife. Inabe has been arrested for an unrelated murder and Mrs. Inabe will testify against her husband."

Murata's background in shipping, his regular trips to Ise to check on a business that no one seemed to know about, his anger at Precious Butterfly's questions, and his association with criminal types all suggested that he was involved in the illegal activities here.

Murata's eyes bulged with shock. "I-Inabe's in jail?" he stuttered, then caught himself. "I was paying for my room. I stayed there just like you did. I was paying my bill."

"I watched you, Murata. You first paid your bill, and then you passed over the bag of money, telling Mrs. Inabe it was for her husband. You said it was 'as agreed.' And Mrs. Inabe saw nothing surprising in it because she had become accustomed to her husband working for you."

"So I owed Inabe some money for a few favors he did me. It means nothing."

Akitada sighed. "We are wasting time. Inabe is being interrogated at the police station at this very moment. He'll talk and he'll sell you out for a reduction in his own punishment."

Murata wilted. "Oh, that crook! I should never have trusted him. It was bad karma." Covering his face with his hands, he collapsed on the floor.

Akitada said nothing. After a moment, Murata straightened and dropped his hands. He peered up at Akitada. "Allow me to explain, Excellency."

Relief washed over Akitada. The fact that Murata had used his title meant that his bluff had worked. He could only know his rank if he had seen the papers the prowlers had taken. "Yes, you'd better make a clean breast of it or there's nothing I can do for you."

Giving him a weak smile, Murata said, "About my work here in Ise. I engaged some local men to drum up business, that's all. I offer shipping transport of lumber and other goods and earn a fee. Unfortunately, I've just become aware that my employees also engage in crimes, some of which may include robbery. I hired Inabe to investigate. That's what the money was for. He brought me information about the so-called prowlers. I'll gladly share this information if you will help me clear up any lies he may be telling the police. I know nothing about the other crime, but he's the type to blame anything else on me." He gave Akitada a plead-ing look.

It was as good a story as could be expected on such short notice. Murata was no fool.

"Hmm," said Akitada noncommittally. "Start with Inabe's reports on the prowlers."

What followed was a list of depredations, mostly in the nature of robbing pilgrims who travelled lonely roads after dark, but Inabe had supposedly also uncov-ered a supply network of pirates who worked out of Oyodo harbor. It explained the stores of goods in the shed. Of course Murata denied any connection with any of this.

When his tale came to an end with another plea for help against the infamous Inabe, Akitada asked, "What did Inabe tell you about the murder of the girl Michiko."

This was clearly a new shock. "Nothing. Nothing at all."

"Really? The girl was flogged and killed in the shed where your people stored their goods."

"That is horrible, but I know nothing about it, Excellency."

"I was told that you knew Michiko from the Peach Bower."

"Michiko? I may have seen her there. She was a prostitute."

"Tell me what were you doing at Sukemichi's place just before Michiko disappeared?"

Murata gulped. "Nothing. Just paying a friendly visit."

"I don't believe you. Remember that I can ask Sukemichi, and believe me, he will talk."

There was a silence. Akitada waited patiently. For what? Another lie probably, but even lies could contain the seeds of truth.

Finally, Murata said, "Lord Sukemichi mentioned some gossip. I like to keep myself informed about what's happening in places where I have business interests, but it was just gossip."

"What gossip?"

Murata managed another weak smile. "Some silly tale about the Ise Virgin. Someone had told him she was going to run away. Someone was to take her place so she could leave the palace for a short while."

Akitada had hoped for this confirmation, but it upset him nonetheless. With unscrupulous men like Murata and Sukemichi aware of the scandal, he would not be able to protect the reputation of the princess, or that of the young fool Minamoto, or of His Majesty. He thought for a moment, then took another gamble. "I assume the high constable decided to interfere?"

Murata hesitated but probably realized he was too deeply implicated to rescue anything. "Lord Sukemichi's a man of the world, but he thought it his duty to stop the princess."

"How was he going to manage it?"

"I don't know. I was to pass a note to my people. That was what I paid Inabe for."

Akitada did not believe that Murata did not know what was in the note or that there had even been a note, but he let it go. He said, "You will take paper and write out two confessions. One will cover your connection with Inabe and the prowlers. The other concerns your conversation with the high constable. I shall dictate them to you. Afterward, I expect you to remain here until I return. If you leave or attempt to communicate with anyone, I will see to it that you are arrested immediately. Your future depends on your cooperation."

Murata balked a few times as Akitada dictated, but eventually the two signed statements were in Akitada's hands. He said, "Remember, what I said. Stay here and don't communicate with anyone."

38

A Desperate Gamble

Akitada now knew that Murata and Sukemichi had both been involved in the abduction and the murder of Michiko, but Murata had not really confessed to anything except hiring the prowlers to drum up business and using Inabe to contact them. It did not matter. Lieutenant Mori could get the truth out of Inabe. And that truth would reveal that Michiko had died at their hands.

Murata and Sukemichi had discussed the princess's escapade and Sukemichi had taken some sort of action as a result. Although there was no proof that Sukemichi had abducted her, he was the only person with both the means and the opportunity and he was,

according to Minamoto, an ambitious man. No other
explanation was possible.

And just what had the high constable hoped to gain
from such a crime? Akitada could guess, but he had no
time left to prove it. He had to try the same bluff with
Sukemichi that he had used on Murata. And he had to
do it immediately before Murata could warn the high
constable.

Akitada borrowed the promised straw raincoat from
his host. He was convinced he knew where the princess
was, and he intended to set her free immediately.

The innkeeper cautioned him. "They say it's going
to be a bad storm, sir. Perhaps you should wait it out.
The Golden Dragon is well-built, but the rest of the
houses of Uji-tachi are not so fortunate. You could get
hit by flying debris."

Akitada peered outside. The rain was blowing at a
slant, and the street was empty. It was the worst possible
time for his endeavor, but he had no longer a choice in
the matter. He must confront Sukemichi as soon as
possible before he could be warned and take some desperate action. The biggest danger was not the weather,
but rather Sukemichi's armed guard. Akitada had no
such troops at his disposal. On the other hand, this
could not be resolved with a battle which would endan-
ger the princess. He must convince Sukemichi to release her. Any prosecution would have to come later—
or not at all. Saving the princess was more important.

The coming storm raised other fears. He hoped
Tora was making his wife and children safe. He also
wished he knew where Junichiro was. His small shed on

the river offered no protection at all and might well float away if the river rose.

He told the innkeeper, "I must go out, but shall return later tonight. If my friend Junichiro should show up, please allow him to shelter in my room."

The innkeeper promised.

After a moment's thought, Akitada added, "Murata asked me to tell you that he wants to rest. Please do not disturb him."

The innkeeper nodded again, and Akitada plunged into the storm. The water on the street was not very deep and he had his boots, but the hem of his new trousers became acquainted with Uji-tachi's mud.

He splashed his way to the police station. It was still daylight, but shops and restaurants had already lit their oil lamps. The acrid smoke from cooking fires hung low over the town and made it hard to breathe.

At the station, he found a number of wet constables peering out from under the veranda. They looked surprised to see him. He left his dripping straw coat there and went inside.

Lieutenant Matsuura was dry. Like the businesses along the street, his office was lit by oil lamps. He shot to his feet when Akitada entered. "Sir! In this weather?"

Akitada's gray silk trousers slapped wetly at his legs. He said, "We have a problem."

"Yes. The storm. We've been warned that it would be bad. Already people are coming from Oyodo to seek shelter on higher ground. Looks like it'll be even worse than our last storm. And night is coming. If houses collapse, there will be fires." He glanced at his own oil lamp. "And at night, people will be helpless. Please sit down, sir. What can I do for you?"

Perhaps Matsuura thought that mention of storm dangers would discourage Akitada from burdening him with some other, more trivial, matter. What had brought him here was anything but trivial, and Akitada did not sit down.

"I have discovered that Sukemichi is in league with the prowlers. This surely explains why he has been no help in arresting them. He has been in a partnership with the ship owner Murata who was staying at the River Palace and was running the enterprise with the help of Inabe."

Matsuura gaped at him. "You're accusing the high constable of being a highway robber? Surely that cannot be, sir. And in this weather, we cannot do anything about it anyway. Please, sir, let this matter wait. If Murata is indeed involved, we can get the whole story from him and Inabe."

Akitada took one of Murata's statements from inside his robe. His other statement, the one concerning the princess, he kept tucked away. Handing the paper to Matsuura, he said, "There is nothing for you to do, except perhaps sending one of your constables to keep an eye on Murata at the Golden Dragon. Inabe will testify against him. I'm going to have a talk with Sukemichi tonight. If I'm not back by morning, come looking for me with your constables." Akitada pointed to the statement in Matsuura's hand. "You have the whole story there! Read it!" And with that he left.

The Shrine Virgin

On the veranda, he put on his raincoat again and walked to the post stables. They balked at renting him a horse, but a piece of gold (almost his last one) convinced them. The poor beast resisted leaving the warm and dry stable, but eventually Akitada was in the saddle and trotting toward the chief priest's residence. Once he was in the forest, the trees protected him somewhat from the wind and rain.

Nakatomi received him, looking anxious. "In this weather, Sugawara? Has anything happened?"

"I have worked out that the princess must be at Sukemichi's place and am on my way to get her."

The chief priest paled. "Oh, dear. Then she's ruined. We are all ruined. And this storm that is coming is our punishment. The gods are angry because the shrine virgin has been dishonored."

Akitada did not argue the point. He said, "Look, we need to bring her back. Anything else can be settled later. I only stopped by to inform you. I'm on my way to talk to Lady Tamba now and get them to send a palanquin or a carriage. Then I'll pick up Lord Minamoto as a witness and proceed to Sukemichi's."

Nakatomi wrung his hands but nodded. He said, "Thank you, Sugawara. May the gods go with you."

∞

At the Bamboo Palace, the young guard officers for once seemed to show proper concern. All the shutters of the palace buildings were closed and secured. Uniformed guards and servants stood watch on the verandas, and building supplies of various sorts were stacked in the broad entrance courtyard. Akitada also saw buckets filled with sand, and more buckets lined up near a well in case there would be fires.

He was taken to Lady Tamba, who had her mother with her. They both stared at his wet clothing and Lady Tamba asked in a faint voice, "Is it very bad outside?"

Her mother said, "Don't ask stupid questions. Why else would he look like a drowned rat?"

Akitada was unpleasantly aware of water trickling down his neck and his robe being heavier because it was soaked. He answered Lady Tamba, "It's unpleasant and will probably get worse, my lady."

"You must dry out a little and take a bite of food and some warm wine," she said.

"Thank you, but there's no time. I'm on my way to get the princess and bring her home."

Lady Tamba gasped. "The gods be thanked! But in this weather?"

Her mother snapped, "Don't argue with the man. It took him long enough, but he has finally managed to find her. Let him do his work. And after that wild romp, she deserves a good drenching. Any other girl would get a whipping.

"Mother!"

Akitada cleared his throat. "Lady Tamba, I need the carriage, a driver, and an ox to pull it. And Lady Ayako should come along to tend to her highness."

"Ayako? She's not sufficiently senior."

Her mother gave her a push. "Fool! Ayako is the only one who knows what happened and why. Do you want the rest of the gossipy brood to find out the truth?"

"Your lady mother is right," Akitada said. "It will be best if you let it be known outside this room that the carriage is for a visiting lady who was caught by the storm and sought refuge at Lord Sukemichi's place."

Lady Tamba cried, "Lord Sukemichi's place?"

Her mother shot Akitada a sharp glance. "So that was the game."

Akitada had the uncomfortable feeling that the old lady understood far better than he what had possessed Sukemichi to abduct an imperial princess who was also a consecrated shrine virgin. He said, "The reasons are immaterial at the moment. Would you order the carriage and Lady Ayako to Lord Sukemichi's residence? I shall stop for her highness's cousin, and we'll meet your people there. And please hurry. This must be done quickly, and not just because of the storm."

She nodded. "Go then and do your best. May the goddess be with you."

∞

Akitada put on his sodden raincoat and got on his horse to head back out on the forest road to Minamoto's lodge. The wind had picked up and what he was spared by being protected from its gusts and the now much heavier rain he made up for with breaking branches and a constant barrage of smaller debris. It occurred to him that he might be putting the princess in even greater danger by sending her out in this with no more protection than the woven reed cover of the carriage.

The lodge lay in silence. Akitada rode up to the gate and shouted, "Ho! Open up!"

Nothing happened. He cursed the old gatekeeper and hammered on the gate with his fist, shouting again. The wind gusts were strong enough to push his horse against the gate.

Finally the cracked voice shouted back, "Go away!" This was followed by the slamming of a door or shutter.

Akitada shouted again, pounded again, kicked the gate and was about to attempt climbing it, when he heard Minamoto's voice. "I'm coming."

The gate opened and a windblown Minamoto looked up at him. He was pale and anxious, but not from the rain and wind. He had not shaved in a day or so. "Sugawara? Has something happened?"

Akitada dismounted, tied up his horse, and followed him inside.

A few charcoal pieces gleamed dully in a brazier and a flask of wine stood nearby. Minamoto smelled strongly of wine.

Akitada said, "I need you to accompany me to Sukemichi's place. I believe he holds the princess prisoner there."

Minamoto stared at him. "I don' believe it. Sukemichi would never dare. He's local gentry and not from a good family at that."

This was not an entirely unexpected remark from someone who had imperial blood in his veins, even if he no longer claimed imperial rank. Akitada knew the court well enough to understand its mindset. But he had dealt with criminals from diverse backgrounds and knew quite well that ambition thrived even in the humblest heart. And Sukemichi had struck him as anything but humble.

"Nonetheless. Here, read this!" He took Murata's other statement from inside his robe and held it out to Minamoto. With a searching glance at Akitada's face, Minamoto carried it over to a candle and read. He read it twice before turning around. "Who is this Murata? Do you mean to tell me that you suspect Sukemichi because this man informed him of what the shop girl said?"

"It's a little more complicated. Sukemichi has been in partnership with this man. Between them they have run the local gangs and most likely also pirates working out of Ise and Owari ports. The story Michiko told Murata and that Murata passed on to Sukemichi gave the high constable a wild idea how he could rise in the world. You said yourself he hopes for a position in the capital."

Minamoto clenched his fists. "He must be mad. He'll never get away with it."

"Well, they've already made quite a bit of money from you."

Minamoto received this news more philosophically, but he started pacing. "I cannot believe this. Even given his ambitions . . . how could such a man . . ." He stopped and turned. "Do you have any proof that he has her?"

"Very little."

"But you think Takahime is there?"

Akitada nodded.

"Then let's go." Looking grim, Lord Minamoto took his sword from its stand, pushed it through his sash, and made for the door."

"You'll need something against the rain."

"Forget it!"

On second thought, Akitada decided to abandon his own waterlogged straw cape.

They rode single file and did not speak. The world had turned into a hellish place where they had a hard time staying in their saddles. Minamoto led the way. Managing their horses took all their attention as all around them debris flew through the air and the road turned into a swamp.

When they reached Sukemichi's residence, Akitada shouted through the noise, "Ask for shelter!"

Minamoto nodded.

They pounded on the big double gates. A small window opened and a face peered out. "What do you want?"

"I'm Lord Minamoto. My friend and I were caught in the storm and need shelter."

One of the gates opened and they rode in. If the gate guards recognized Akitada, who was dressed quite differently on this occasion, they did not say so. Debris lay around the courtyard; tiles, branches, a torn flag, and assorted wooden utensils that had been blown about by the wind. They dismounted and hurried to the main house.

There a senior servant waited on the veranda. They gave their names and were taken inside and supplied with towels to dry themselves.

Sukemichi appeared in the midst of this. He hurried toward Minamoto, crying, "My lord, what happened? You are drenched. Allow me to send for dry clothes."

Akitada noted that Minamoto's birth and rank assured him of Sukemichi's respect and assistance. Minamoto on his part eyed Sukemichi much as a hungry cat eyes a goldfish. He snapped, "Later. This is Governor Sugawara. You may be aware of the purpose of his visit to this area?"

Sukemichi looked at Akitada, swallowed, and made him a bow. "I'm honored, Excellency," he managed.

Akitada did not return the bow. "My second visit to your residence, Sukemichi. The reception was less polite the last time."

"A mistake by my stupid men, Excellency. I regret it extremely. Allow me to make reparations."

Minamoto interrupted him. "Stop babbling! You know why we're here. Where is the princess?"

Akitada had not planned such an abrupt beginning and wondered how Sukemichi would react.

He did what Minamoto might have expected. He pretended ignorance. "I beg your pardon, my lord. The princess? Surely she was not out in this storm also?"

Minamoto took a step and seized the other man by the front of his robe, pulling him forward until they were face to face. "Don't lie to me. We know you have her. Your accomplice has confessed."

"I don't know what you're talking about. I have no accomplice. I don't have the princess. Please take your hands off me, sir."

Akitada said mildly, "Let him go, Sadamu."

Perhaps it was his use of his lordship's given name that made Minamoto obey. He released Sukemichi and stepped back. "I shall find her myself," he said, turned on his heel and strode toward one of the doors.

Sukemichi dashed after him, snatching at his sleeve, but Minamoto was already heading down the corridor. Akitada followed, thinking that the young man's impetuosity might serve them better than a long drawn-out discussion of the evidence against Sukemichi.

What with Sukemichi's shouting to Minamoto to stop, servants appeared from various corners but did little more than to stare and trail along behind their increasingly frantic master and his wet guests.

Minamoto made for the corridor that led to the northern apartments where the emperor's women resided in the imperial palace. The corridor led to an outside gallery, which in turn led to a separate pavilion. The gallery was roofed and enclosed by shutters, but one of the shutters had blown open and banged against the wall. The noise of the storm penetrated and large puddles of water had formed on the floor. When they reached the pavilion, Sukemichi fell back, and Minamoto knocked.

Akitada had a moment of fear that they would find themselves deeply embarrassed by an intrusion on Sukemichi's wives, but at this point he could think of no more options.

The door opened, and a pretty maid peered out. When she saw the wet and glowering Minamoto, she tried to close the door again, but Minamoto pushed it wide and strode in. "Takahime?" he shouted.

39

The Princess

Their abrupt entrance was greeted by shrieks from five women. The sixth woman was silent and pale.

Her presence astonished Akitada, but he had no time to think about it. One of the shrieking females had detached herself from the rest and flung herself on Minamoto, babbling hysterically.

Princess Takahime.

Akitada's hand shot to his sword hilt as he turned to look for Sukemichi. They were alone here with a weeping woman in the very heart of a compound belonging to Sukemichi, a place that also contained many servants and a company of trained warriors. He was not certain what Sukemichi would do now that his guilt was revealed and his life in shambles. Would he be desperate and foolish enough to have them killed in hopes that no one would find out?

Sukemichi joined them. He watched the pair of lovers with a frown but seemed otherwise calm enough.

Akitada asked, "How do you explain this, Sukemichi?"

"I beg your pardon?" Sukemichi turned to him, feigning surprise at the question. "It seems to me that it is you and Lord Minamoto who owe me an explanation for this rude intrusion into my wife's quarters."

Akitada glanced around the room. The only female present close to Sukemichi's age was Mrs. Akechi from the silk shop. "I referred to the fact that you have abducted Princess Takahime and kept her here against her will. I don't know what other crimes against the goddess and the nation you may have committed."

Sukemichi raised his chin. "Her Imperial Highness, Princess Takahime, has done me the honor of becoming my wife."

Akitada suppressed his shock. Could it be? Surely she had been forced into such a match. And what would be the outcome of such a marriage? Almost certainly *he* would be blamed for it.

He had no time to finish the thought because Minamoto abruptly released the clinging Takahime and drew his sword. New shrieks erupted. Sukemichi tried to take cover behind Akitada, and Mrs. Akechi flung herself in Minamoto's way.

"He lied," she screamed. "They're not married. Don't hurt him. It was all a foolish mistake. I tried to stop him."

This caused Minamoto to pause. "Who are you?" he asked suspiciously.

"I'm his wife," Mrs. Akechi said. "The only wife he has here. We have been together for five years, though he'll deny it because I'm not nobly born and he's ashamed of me. We have a son together."

Sukemichi snapped, "Enough, Haruko! Say no more!"

Minamoto put his sword away and turned to Princess Takahime. "What happened?"

She dabbed a sleeve at her eyes and said in a small voice, "I left after you said I had to go back. Then some soldiers came and brought me here. And that man,"— she nodded with her chin toward Sukemichi— "wouldn't take me back to the Bamboo Palace. He kept making excuses. Then the silk woman came and she also tried to make him send me back."

Akitada stepped forward, knelt, and bowed deeply. "Your Highness, my name is Sugawara Akitada. Your August brother sent me to find you. I regret that it has taken so long. May I assume that no marriage has taken place between Your Highness and this Sukemichi?"

She sniffed. "Of course not. He is an old man and a disgusting commoner. It is offensive that you should ask such a question."

Akitada bowed again. "I humbly beg your pardon, Highness. I have arranged for transport. The carriage and your escort should arrive at any moment."

Sukemichi had the nerve to protest. "But not in this storm! Her Imperial Highness cannot possibly leave. I offer my home as refuge."

Outside a loud crash underscored his words. It had sounded like a building collapsing. Akitada hesitated.

The princess had moved a little closer to Minamoto. "I'm not afraid," she said. "I want to go home."

Mrs. Akechi moved to stand beside Sukemichi and now laid a hand on his arm. "Let her go, Yasunori," she pleaded. "It's time. It was a foolish idea. I wish I'd never told you about Michiko."

Sukemichi gave her a vicious push. "It's time you left, too. In fact, nobody asked you to come. You've ruined me."

Akitada was tired of all of them. He went out to check on conditions. The wind still gusted. A second shutter had blown open in the gallery. He wondered if the carriage had reached them. He was going to see about this when a servant emerged from the main house and came running along the gallery. He called out, "There's a carriage arrived from the Bamboo Palace. Is the master inside? I can't find him anywhere."

"Your master is inside, and the lady is ready. Have them bring the carriage around."

"She's setting out in this storm?"

"Yes. Now hurry."

He ran off and Akitada went back inside. The princess still stood beside Minamoto. His arm was around her, and he was talking to her in a low voice. She was weeping. Mrs. Akechi, pale and tense, had gone to sit in a corner near the maids, and Sukemichi stood with his back to her, watching the two lovers.

Akitada said, "They are bringing the carriage around."

Mrs. Akechi got up. "Someone should go with her highness. I'll go if you like. The other women are too frightened of the storm."

"Thank you Mrs. Akechi, but one of her ladies has come for her."

Minamoto said, "I shall also accompany the princess."

Akitada nodded. "Yes. And so shall I."

He became aware of a sudden quiet outside and listened. It seemed doubtful that so violent a storm would suddenly abate so completely. There was another, rather weak gust, and then nothing, not even the sound of rain on the roof above his head.

Minamoto listened also. "Good. It's the calm," he said. "It may last until we reach the Bamboo Palace. Let's hurry."

They opened the shutters to the veranda, and there was the carriage, already backed up, with Lady Ayako peering out anxiously. Mrs. Akechi brought a silk robe and draped it over the princess's head and shoulders, and Lord Minamoto walked her out and helped her into the carriage. Akitada saw that the interior had been filled with quilts and bedding so that the two women should ride comfortably enough. The curtains were closed, the palace guard brought their horses up, and the ox driver, a sturdy man in boots and a straw cape, snapped his whip across the rump of the ox. Slowly the carriage rolled away.

Akitada wasted no more time on Sukemichi. He and Minamoto hurried to the entrance courtyard, where they got back on their horses and joined the carriage and its escort.

Above them the clouds had parted and revealed a blue sky, but the return journey shocked them with the damage the storm had left in the forest. Everywhere trees had fallen, many of them snapped like kindling halfway along their trunks. Akitada marveled at the power of this storm and how they and the carriage with its escort had managed to pass through it unharmed earlier.

He said as much to Minamoto as they rode more sedately behind the carriage.

Minamoto grunted, then said, "The storm will return and be worse than before. It's close to sunset now. When night falls, it will sound as if all of hell had opened up. Where will you stay?"

"I should go back and deal with Sukemichi. I wish I knew what to do about him. He cannot be charged with this crime, or any of his others."

"Leave him be and stay at my place. There will be another day." He bit his lip and added, "I shall hold myself responsible for seeing him punished. That I swear by the sacred gods who are all around us."

Akitada was unhappy about this outcome, but the reputation of the princess must be protected at all cost. At least he had managed to set her free. As soon as she was safely in her palace he intended to return to Uji-tachi to make sure Junichiro was safe. He said as much to Minamoto.

And then they would go home where he hoped and prayed that all was well.

They took the carriage to the women's quarters of the Bamboo Palace and backed it against the veranda as before. Doors opened and young women ran out to form two lines. The princess, followed by Lady Ayako, emerged and hurried between them into the building. Then the doors closed again, and it was over.

∞

Akitada and Minamoto paused at the intersection of the roads to Uji-tachi.

Minamoto looked as drawn and exhausted as Akitada felt, but he smiled. "She is safe," he said. "Thank you. I think I shall be in your debt forever now. If there is anything I can do for you or for someone you wish to sponsor for a position, you only have to ask."

Akitada did not return the smile. "Thank you. There is nothing. I hope you'll forgive me for some of the things I said to you."

"I deserved them and shall endeavor to be a better man in the future."

A short pause fell as they both searched for something else to say.

Then both glanced up at the sky, where the crescent of blue was shrinking rapidly. Minamoto said, "We'd better hurry. I think it's about to start again."

At that moment, one of Sukemichi's mounted warriors appeared at a full gallop. When he saw them, he brought his horse to halt so abruptly that the animal slid on the wet road and threw him.

Akitada called out, "Is anything wrong?"

The man struggled to his feet. He was covered with mud. "The high constable, sir. He's wounded. I'm going for a doctor."

Minamoto asked, "What? What happened?"

The soldier wiped at some of the mud on his armor and cast a glance at his horse, which had stopped and now stood waiting. "I'm not sure, sir. They say his woman did it. Stabbed him, I mean. They say he's bad."

Akitada glanced at the gathering clouds above. "You'll need the police also. Best hurry. The storm is about to return."

The soldier nodded, saluted, and ran to his horse.

Akitada sighed. "I'd better have a look."

Minamoto said, "I'll come with you."

∞

They reached Sukemichi's residence with the first gusts of rain. The gates stood open. Soldiers milled about in the courtyard, glanced at them, but did not stop them.

In the women's quarters, they found a scene of carnage. Sukemichi lay on the floor. Several maids hovered around him. He looked dead, but when he heard them he opened his eyes. "The doctor?" he croaked, "Hurry. It hurts. Oh, it hurts so much." He moaned.

Minamoto muttered, "Amida!"

The women made room, and Akitada knelt beside Sukemichi to check his wounds. There were at least four of them. Sukemichi's silk robe was deeply stained across his chest and his belly, and both sleeves were soaked with blood. Someone had wrapped cloth bandages around the arms, but the chest and belly wounds had been left alone. Akitada looked around and saw the bloody knife that had done the damage. It lay next to another figure. Mrs. Akechi was dead. She had been beheaded.

"What happened?" he asked Sukemichi.

"The she-fiend stabbed me. After all I've done for her and her brat." Sukemichi groaned again. "The doctor," he pleaded.

"How did you manage to abduct her highness?"

"The doctor, please."

"There will be no doctor for a while. You might as well confess while we wait."

Sukemichi was silent for a moment. He stared up at the ceiling.

"Come on," Akitada urged. How did this come to pass?"

"I spent my life serving His Majesty in this province, but there were never any thanks. All the positions at court were awarded to his relatives. I thought I'd be recognized if I had a wife with some influence. Then Haruko told me that the princess had a lover she was visiting. I thought, why not bring her here? I could court her, treat her well. It was a chance." He stopped and closed his eyes with a grimace of pain.

"Go on," said Akitada harshly. "How was Murata involved in this?"

"Murata found out where she was. His men watched Minamoto's lodge and I sent my soldiers to bring her here." He gasped with pain.

Akitada rose and got the knife. He returned to Sukemichi to cut his sash and check his wounds, but Sukemichi screamed at the sight of the knife in his hand. "Don't touch me! Get away from me . . . ahh . . ." He choked, then convulsed, screamed again, and lay still.

Minamoto came closer. "How horrible!" he said with a shudder. "Is he dead?"

Akitada checked. "Yes. Lost too much blood, I think. By the position of the chest and belly wounds it's a miracle he lived this long."

"Good! I heard what he said. Why did that woman attack him?"

They both stood and looked at the dead Mrs. Akechi. "What happened?" Akitada asked the maids.

The calmest girl was white-faced and trembled, but she answered sensibly enough. "The master and his lady quarreled. She was very angry, and he told her to get out of his house and he hoped the storm would kill her. He hit her. She left, but then she came back with the knife. She told him, 'You'll not get rid of us so easily,' and started stabbing him. The master screamed for help, and the guard posted outside ran in." She gulped. "He cut her head off."

"Thank you. You are very brave. Mrs. Akechi claimed they were married. Is this true?"

His praise made her weep. "I don't know. They were lovers. For many years. She lived in Uji-tachi but she came here to stay with him whenever he visited."

Akitada said, "There's nothing else you and the other ladies can do here. The doctor and the police will come if the storm permits it. Take the others elsewhere so you won't have to look at this."

She bowed, and they watched the women walk out. Outside, the storm had returned in full force.

40

Storm Surge

Akitada and Minamoto ended up spending the night at Sukemichi's place. Neither police nor doctor made an appearance, but it did not matter any longer. Sukemichi and Mrs. Akechi had taken their secrets with them to the lower world.

When not listening to the storm, they talked off and on. They were agreed that these deaths made the princess safer. Fewer people knew what had happened. The women of the Bamboo Palace had too much to lose themselves if word got out, and the chief priest and his family would protect the reputation of the shrine at all costs.

At one point, Minamoto expressed again his remorse over what had happened between himself and the princess.

Akitada said drily he hoped the night of passion had no unexpected results.

Minamoto had the grace to blush. "I was careful," he said.

Akitada bit his lip. So the young man had made sure that the incident would not entangle him more deeply in the affair. That tended to prove that he had never been in love with Takahime and had not seduced her. It had been the princess who had seduced him.

Sukemichi had lived long enough to tell him he had ordered Michiko's death. It did not really matter any longer who bore the responsibility. Akitada hoped that her killers had been among the four men he and Junichiro had killed.

Only Murata and Junichiro were left of those who knew of the affair. Akitada was not worried about Junichiro, but Murata was another matter. The man would realize that he could bargain with his silence. Akitada knew no way around this except to urge him to flee. It was very unsatisfactory.

Otherwise the night was frightening enough. All around them, the wind howled, trees crashed, shaking the ground, and roof tiles flew through the air and into rooms. At one point, one of the storage buildings collapsed and part of a gallery disappeared. Then the roof over the gate was lifted off and carried away. The storm deposited it in the courtyard in a pile of rubble. There was, miraculously, only one small fire.

Akitada thought of his family. Would the governor's residence withstand such forces? Would Tora stay with Yukiko and the children to make sure nothing happened to them and they were not too frightened? He knew that other worries awaited him when he got home. There would be damage everywhere. He was personally responsible for all public buildings and the temples and shrines. If the tribunal treasury could not pay for the repairs, he would have to. And the people of Mikawa would need support to help each other. He was impatient to be gone.

It was dawn before the storm abated enough for them to leave. Their own clothes, still clammy and wet, but also wrinkled and dirty by now, made them look like a pair of disreputable misfits returning from a debauch. No matter. The rain still fell sporadically. The forest around them looked devastated. Many trees were down, and others were leaning or denuded of branches. Twice they had to lead their horses around a fallen tree. Near the crossroads, they stopped to part as before, but had little to say to one another.

When Akitada reached the river, he saw that it had risen above its banks and carried large chunks of debris. He thought again of Junichiro's shed. It must be gone. No matter, as long as the little fellow had survived.

He passed shrine buildings that had collapsed, and the bridge, when he reached it, was in danger of being washed away. Shouting men were on the other side, waving to him and pointing. He looked. The debris floating down the river toward the sea, whole trees and huge branches, was caught against the bridge supports. The bridge groaned and creaked under the onslaught.

Crossing under such conditions could mean being swept away, horse and all, to certain death. But if he did not cross, he would be cut off for many days. The pull of home and his family was too strong. Spurring his horse, Akitada galloped onto the shifting timbers and made it across. The men on the other shore scattered and shook their heads as he passed.

He headed for Uji-tachi, where more devastation met him. The road was under water in places where the river had washed over the bank. Houses on both sides lay shattered like so much kindling. The River Palace leaned dangerously over the water. In one place, neighbors were carrying the dead from a collapsed building and laying them down in a row beside the street.

But the Golden Dragon had survived with only moderate damage. Akitada tied up his horse and went inside. The entry was full of weeping refugees, and the innkeeper and his staff were busy passing out food.

Akitada scanned faces, figures, bundles, looking for the colorful clothes, the red hair of Junichiro. He caught the innkeeper's eye and called across, "Junichiro? Is he here?"

The man shook his head, set down a large cauldron with rice and came to him. "Amida be praised you are safe, sir. Junichiro came right after you left. I told him what you'd said and he stayed, hanging about near the door. I think he was worried about you. People started coming and asking for shelter and I got busy, but then Murata-san came from his room with his baggage. He wanted to leave and needed a bearer. Because of the storm, no one offered to go with him. He left most of his things and went out by himself, just carrying one bag. Junichiro came to ask me where Murata-san was going in the storm, but I didn't know. The next thing I knew, Junichiro ran after him. And that's the last I've seen of either."

The shock of Murata's flight hit Akitada hard. Junichiro had followed Murata because he knew that Akitada suspected him. He had gone out into the storm late yesterday, and he had not returned.

Akitada turned and went back outside to get on his horse. He began his search along the road to the coast. This took him first to Junichiro's shed, though there was not much reason for the dwarf to have gone there. The shed was gone, washed away as if it had never been. The river was well over its banks here, and the destruction all around suggested that the water had risen five or six feet before receding again. It had left behind tree trunks, shattered boats, lumber, and parts of houses, all tangled with bits of fabric, clothes, parts of sails, and perhaps the dead.

Despairing, Akitada looked for anything red and climbed about on the piles of destruction to peer at some red remnant or other.

During his search, he came to know in his heart that Junichiro had not survived. Nobody could survive this in the open and on this road. The fact that boats, sails and lumber had washed up this far inland, meant that the sea had backed up into the river.

He tried to convince himself that Murata would not have come this way, that he would have sought refuge with Sukemichi. He was about to turn his horse around and head back when he saw it.

I. J. PARKER

Up ahead, where the road left the river and passed into the forest, there was a small patch of red.

He knew then, and a wave of nausea rose in his throat. He bit his lip until it bled, then guided his horse to the spot. The small body lay beside the road, sheltered against the storm by the low branches of a young pine. Junichiro was curled up on his side, his hands near his face, and his eyes closed. He might have been a peacefully sleeping child except for the mass of blood and brain matter that was the back of his head.

Not far from him lay a staff, its end covered with blood.

Junichiro had been murdered, and Akitada knew who the killer had been.

He knelt beside him, touching his ice-cold hands.

"Oh, Junichiro," he said. "You should have taken better care of yourself. Murata didn't matter, but you were important to me." He felt hot tears running down his face and did not care. Sitting down on the wet ground, he took the small body in his arms.

"Forgive me, little friend, he murmured. "Forgive me for drawing you into my problems. Forgive me for asking you to help me prove Murata's guilt. Dear heaven, I sent you to your death. I demanded your life after you saved mine."

He never questioned that the killer had been Murata, desperate to escape the punishment awaiting him. He had dared the storm and would not have let a mere dwarf stand in his way.

Akitada did not know how long he sat like this, but in the end, he took off his silk robe and wrapped the small body tenderly in it. Then he placed the body on his horse and mounted behind it. In this way, he rode slowly back to Uji-tachi, taking great care not to jolt his burden.

41

Homecoming

The devastation at Oyodo was much worse than in Uji-tachi. The storm surge had come from the bay and washed away most of the houses and all the boats. Nobody was leaving Ise by water.

By now Akitada was nearly frantic with worry about his own family and his new province. So soon after arriving in Mikawa, he had been absent when catastrophe struck. It was a terrible beginning.

Apart from taking care of Junichiro's funeral, he spent his time searching for any means of transport back to Mikawa. Since the overland journey would take more than a week, he needed to find someone with a boat—any kind of boat—who would take him back across the bay.

Meanwhile he paid no attention to the disposition of the bodies of Sukemichi or Mrs. Akechi. Someone else was burying them, and someone else would settle his estate.

He also felt no need to return to the Bamboo Palace or to bid farewell to the chief priest and his wife. Minamoto had offended so severely against what Akitada considered propriety that he had no wish to see him again either.

On the second day after the storm, they found Murata's body. He had drowned still clasping the satchel that held some of Minamoto's gold.

Finally, a fisherman was found who had managed to save his boat. He was willing to take Akitada home for a rich reward, promised on arrival in Komachi. It would assure him of a comfortable life for years to come.

The journey was uneventful, the sea once again calm and the sky a cloudless blue. It almost fooled Akitada into thinking that his own world was untouched by the anger of the gods.

It was a mere dream.

Komachi harbor was in shambles, and the destruction reached far inland. After initial despair, Akitada began to see signs that people were clearing the debris and that the work had been organized efficiently. They walked together to the tribunal, he and the fisherman who expected his small fortune. Akitada was unshaven and still in his muddy, stained gray silk trousers and an undergown. His robe he had left behind to comfort Junichiro's body in his cold grave.

People paused to stare at him, but no one recognized him. They did not look much better than he.

At the tribunal gate, Akitada scanned the compound and the roofs of buildings beyond anxiously. The single gate guard peered at him, then shouted, "He's back! Tell the secretary! Tell everybody! The governor's back!" He performed a little dance—shocking behavior in a well-trained guardsman— and seemed so overcome with joy that Akitada felt himself smile at him. It was his first smile in days.

Perhaps his lightened mood was also due to the fact that the roofline of his residence seemed to be intact and that such a display of joy at his arrival could only mean that his family was well.

And so they were.

Saburo came running toward him, one eye strangely discolored and one hand tucked in his robe, but he greeted him with the same joy, assured him that Yukiko and the children and everyone else were well, and that Tora was in the city, organizing the clean-up of Komachi. In fact, Saburo hardly flinched when told how much gold he was to hand over to the fisherman.

Akitada left them to it and walked quickly through the back gate to his residence, carrying under his arm the silks he had purchased from Mrs. Akechi. He was halfway up the steps to Yukiko's pavilion before he thought of his disheveled appearance. He stopped in dismay, looking down at himself, feeling the stubbles on his chin. He could not let her see this way.

But before he could turn and flee to his own quarters, he heard a shout. He looked up, and there was

Yasuko, leaning over the veranda railing, her face shining with joy.

"He's home! He's home! Father's home!" she shrieked and dashed down the steps to throw herself into his arms.

Yukiko appeared at the door, laughing and clapping her hands. "Come here, you faithless husband," she shouted, opening her arms, and then, "Your poor face!"

It was very improper. Certainly his late wife Tamako would never have done so, especially not where they could be seen, but his heart almost burst with happiness at it, and he released Yasuko, scooped up the package he had dropped, and ran up the steps two at a time to take his beautiful young wife into his arms.

They had no privacy for their meeting. The other children came, and Hanae, Tora's wife, and Yukiko's maids, and the children's tutor, and several gardeners who had begun to clear the debris from the garden. The women exclaimed over his gift of silks. Yukiko chattered about a koi pond and chrysanthemums, and Yasuko said, "You're very dirty, Father. What happened?" And then Saburo joined them to tell him that Tora was coming.

In the end, Akitada sat down as he was and tried to tell them about Ise—not everything, for the children were too young and his grief still too fresh—and he looked at Yukiko now and then and felt that he had not deserved such happiness.

∞

Much later, after a bath and a shave and in his usual, clean, and comfortable robe, Akitada went to the tribunal to hear Tora and Saburo report.

First on the agenda was the damage to Komachi. It appeared that Tora and the provincial guard had applied themselves effectively to clean up and police the streets. There had been very little looting. Fourteen people had died in the city and scores more were injured, but all in all people's spirits were amazingly high, and they offered assistance willingly to less fortunate families.

"What about the police?" Akitada asked and was astonished to see Tora and Saburo grimacing at each other. "What's going on?" he demanded.

The story of the obstructionist Lieutenant Mori came out. It angered Akitada until he began to suspect that the tale was connected with some other activities undertaken by Tora and Saburo. His question produced a confession of the muddle they had made investigating Kitagawa for piracy.

Akitada was silent for a long time as he thought the situation over. Finally he said, "What proof did you have for your accusations, Tora?"

They looked at each other again. Tora said in a small voice, "Circumstantial evidence, sir. The merchant from Owari, the payoff to Hozo, the funeral when no one had died. And the landing stage on the shore."

"Did you interrogate the merchant?"

"He denied everything and left before I could speak to him again?"

"What about this Hozo?"

Again they looked at each other. Tora said, "He is dead."

"Really? So you have nothing, and there is nothing we can do. Clearly, you acted rashly and without regard for my reputation." He turned to Saburo. "What exactly was your role in all of this? You are the tribunal secretary and shouldn't have been involved in any of it."

Saburo hung his head. "I killed Hozo, sir. I recognized him as one of the men I used to work with in my old life. Knowing him to be involved in crimes in the past, I followed him. He worked for Kitagawa. I ended up killing him." He stopped and sighed.

Akitada felt another wave of anger, much stronger this time. He should never have taken on a man with Saburo's background. Now that decision had come back to haunt him, perhaps to destroy him. He opened his mouth to express these thoughts and dismiss Saburo from his service, when Tora spoke up.

"Sir, Saburo saw the man raping a ten-year-old. He did what I or any other man would have done. The girl's mother was nearby, begging someone to help her daughter. The child is just the age of little Lady Yasuko, sir."

Akitada muttered, "Dear gods! What sort of devils inhabit our green islands?"

Saburo, slightly encouraged, offered, "The mother and child left Kitagawa's service. They came here for assistance. I've given her work as my housekeeper. They are staying in my quarters and I'm paying her out of my salary. She will testify against Kitagawa."

Akitada stared at him. "You might have mentioned that fact from the start," he said sourly. "Very well. Tora, you will go arrest Kitagawa. Have the place searched and the cemetery investigated. I doubt he has managed to move the goods again during the storm. Make it quick and return to your duties in the city."

Tora jumped to his feet. "Thank you, sir. You'll see: it will all come out now. And there will be no more piracy in Mikawa."

"Don't be ridiculous," Akitada said. "Piracy is rife in Ise Bay and along the coast to the east. Kitagawa is a small criminal. You will need to be vigilant at all times."

Tora saluted and dashed away.

Akitada looked at Saburo.

"I'm very sorry, sir. I should have thought."

"Yes. In the future I'd like you to curtail your nighttime activities unless I have approved them. Now as to Lieutenant Mori. The man clearly must be replaced. When things have settled, you will take down some letters to the capital, describing his behavior and adding my request that they send out a different man."

Saburo rose, bowed, murmured, "Thank you, sir," and walked out.

Akitada looked after him. The idea that Saburo now had a housekeeper and her child in his quarters was intriguing. Saburo would always be a very strange fellow, he thought. There was no telling what he would do next.

Then he thought of Junichiro who had been another odd character. He had failed the little man, and that grief was still an open wound that would remind him that it was more important to care for his people than for his career.

Historical Note

The time of this novel is 1031, and Sugawara Akitada is governor if Mikawa, one of Japan's eastern provinces. That year the country was generally peaceful, except that a rebel governor, Taira Tadatsune in Kazusa province, was finally subdued by Minamoto Yorinobu, governor of Kai. This year Murasaki Shikibu, the author of *Genji,* died.

Heian Japan (794-1185) took much of its culture, government, and religion from China. However, contact with China had long since been discontinued and many of the original institutions had taken on Japanese characteristics.

The central government structure had an emperor at its head and a ruling hierarchy of officials to administer the many provinces of Japan, but it was no longer a meritocracy as in China. Instead it had become a hereditary bureaucracy of the nobility, centered primarily in one branch of the Fujiwara family. Their politics had been for centuries to marry their daughters to emperors and rule through their grandsons. By the eleventh century, they furnished all the top officials and most of the empresses. They saw to it that emperors resigned young, to be replaced with another very young ruler who could be manipulated by his grandfather and uncles.

The Fujiwara ministers ran the country by appointing the governors of the provinces. These were all men of rank and members of the old aristocratic families. They functioned as administrators and tax collectors to the court. Occasionally, as in the incident mentioned above, they were also called on to raise armies and subdue rebels. Mostly, however, their tenures were peaceful and allowed them to increase their personal wealth both legitimately and by extorting excessive taxes from the inhabitants. Governorships were highly desirable, and all ranking men in the capital actively sought them whenever a position became available. Appointments changed every four years, or earlier in case of death or illness or a recall of the governor. It also happened frequently that the appointed governor remained in the capital and designated a lower-ranking man to represent him in the province while he was drawing the salary and benefits.

The duties of a governor (*zuryo*) included overseeing the Shinto institutions in his province, keeping population registers, collecting taxes, promoting agriculture, enforcing the laws, and maintaining public buildings, irrigation systems, roads and bridges. A governor was also required to stand ready to defend his province militarily. To accomplish all these tasks, he generally brought a number of trusted staff members with him, but the majority of the tribunal staff and district officials were local men. Typical of the increasing power of local landowners in a province was the appointment of high constables from among them. These gradually took over any military functions by furnishing their own troops. The militarizing of the provincial gentry eventually led to the fall of imperial rule.

The Japanese instituted early a system of law enforcement that involved police. Originally designed for the capital where it eventually took over most of the functions of the Ministry of Justice, the *kebiishicho* was soon extended to all the provinces. Each provincial senior police officer was appointed in the capital like the governor. Lieutenant Mori is such a man. Ise was a special case, and given the importance of the shrine, I have stationed a senior police officer, Lieutenant Matsuura, in the shrine district. The role of the provincial high constable, i.e. to provide armed men to keep the peace, is also mentioned in this book. Provincial nobles like Sukemichi historically proved to have ambitions to advance in the central government.

The prevalence of highway robbery and piracy during the eleventh century was a major threat to the central government because their activities disrupted trade and frequently meant lost tax shipments. The duty of stopping their depredations fell to the governors and high constables.

I. J. PARKER

And finally, the Ise shrine and the function of shrine virgins is of central importance in this novel. Shrines are part of the Shinto faith, dedicated to native Japanese deities, or *kami*, and linked to the natural world. There are many shrines in Japan, but only a few of the highest ranking shrines attract the crowds that Ise does. Ise is dedicated to Amaterasu, the goddess of the sun and the protector of the imperial line. Her shrine is the shrine of the emperor himself and only he can set foot in it. It was the repository of the sacred mirror and the sacred sword, emblems of the emperor's power and legitimacy.

Worship celebrations are performed by Shinto priests and Shinto maidens. The chief priestess of the Ise shrine was the Ise Virgin, who was always an imperial princess, chosen at the accession of a new emperor. The appointment was an honor, but life as a priestess must have been dull with its unrelieved ceremonial. *The Tales of Ise*, a poetic diary from the late tenth century describes the love affairs of the poet Narihira, one of whom was an Ise Virgin. It suggested some events in the novel.

The area around Ise Shrine, in the south-eastern part of the Kii peninsula, contains many minor shrines to different *kami*, but only the two main shrines are of real significance. *Naiku*, the inner shrine, belongs to Amaterasu, the protector of the imperial line, while *Geku,* the outer shrine, is dedicated to the agricultural *kami* who bears responsibility for the sustenance of the entire population. Between them, they are the most important shrines of the Japanese people. Already very early they were connected by a pilgrimage route that passed through an entertainment district. Throughout history, the Japanese people have combined religious worship with tourism.

A brief disclaimer on the issue of money in this novel: Japan had a rice economy; i.e. rice was used in a barter system. In fact, other valuable things, like rolls of silk or horses, could also be used to pay bills, reward people, or present as gifts. Officials were paid by being given rice farms for their livelihood, and a man's wealth was judged by how many manors and rice fields he owned. Rice could also be given as a loan against future harvests when it had to be repaid with interest. Actual money was scarce but it existed and came in the form of coins that were copper, silver, or gold. Gold and silver bars were also available. Men must have been provided with some ready cash. Japan imported coins from China, but it also pursued gold and silver mining aggressively.

The best scholarly source on these matters is Francine Herail, *Emperor and Aristocracy in Heian Japan: 10th and 11th centuries.*

About the Author

I. J. Parker was born and educated in Europe and turned to mystery writing after an academic career in the U.S. She has published her Akitada stories in *Alfred Hitchcock's Mystery Magazine,* winning the Shamus award in 2000. Several stories have also appeared in collections, such as *Fifty Years of Crime and Suspense* and *Shaken.* The award-winning "Akitada's First Case" is available as a podcast. Many of the stories have been collected in *Akitada and the Way of Justice.*

The Akitada series of crime novels features the same protagonist, an eleventh century Japanese nobleman/detective. *The Shrine Virgin* is number fourteen. The books are available on Kindle, in print and in audio format, and have been translated into twelve languages.

Books by I. J. Parker

The Akitada series in chronological order
The Dragon Scroll
Rashomon Gate
Black Arrow
Island of Exiles
The Hell Screen
The Convict's Sword
The Masuda Affair
The Fires of the Gods
Death on an Autumn River
The Emperor's Woman
Death of a Doll Maker
The Crane Pavilion
The Old Men of Omi
The Shrine Virgin

The collection of stories
Akitada and the Way of Justice

Other Historical Novels
The HOLLOW REED saga:
Dream of a Spring Night
Dust before the Wind
The Sword Master

The Left-Handed God

Please visit I.J.Parker's web site at www.ijparker.com
You may contact her via e-mail from her web site.
The novels can also be ordered in electronic versions.
Please do post Amazon reviews. They help sell books
and keep Akitada novels coming.

Thank you for your support.

26145558R00244

Printed in Poland
by Amazon Fulfillment
Poland Sp. z o.o., Wrocław